Dark Matter

Dark Matter

Kevin Laymon

Printed in the United States of America

First Printing, 2018

Edited by Danielle Fisher

Published by Ikigai Publishing ™

www.AuthorKevinLaymon.com

www.Twitter.com/Kevin_Laymon

www.Facebook.com/AuthorKevinLaymon

www.Instagram.com/Kevin_Laymon

Some kick and scream, but he feels no pain and does not listen. Most whimper and plead, but he only offers his hand in walking them down the aisle of eternity.

Table of Contents

Dear reader,

Truth is, we're all completely mad.
To deny this claim is to deny being human.
Insanity is a gift.

Dim the lights and warm some cider;
we are in for quite the evening.

Construct

A small, silver ship sailed through the vibrant pink sky of a dissonant planet. Just as the sun began to rapidly set on the western edge of the welkin, another rose to the east. The aircraft sliced through a small cloud, and as it did, something triggered an explosion onboard. One of the ship's engines bursted into flames and a trail of smoke and fire dripped from the steel comet. A white gas extinguished the flames aboard the aircraft, but the trail of fire continued to fall into the planet's atmosphere. As the flames made contact with a collection of brightly colored clouds, the sky ignited and the chain of clouds imploded into a green puff of fire.

The pilot of the spacecraft lost control of the ship, and the vessel began to sink in the sky. Cutting through another group of cyan-colored clouds, the ship vanished for a moment. It reappeared from the clouds, covered in condensation. The liquid was gooey and green and it clung to the aircraft like water to a blade of grass during an early morning dew. Beneath the liquid, the ship came back online and then continued its journey in the sky.

Within the cockpit of the small craft, the pilot, a young man with brown hair and blue eyes, struggled to see out of the now-obscured windshield. The name 'Mariotti' was etched in small red letters across the chest of his grey flight suit.

"Talk to me, Marcus," a woman's voice said from a nearby service hole in the ship's cockpit.

"We are back online, but I can't see a *fucking* thing," the pilot shouted. "We might have to bring her down for a moment so that we can clean this shit off."

"Keep engine one offline," the woman said as she climbed up from the hole. Her face was covered in axle grease and she was breathing heavily. She too was wearing a grey flight suit, and the name 'Fox' was stitched across her chest.

"Woah," the woman gasped.

Leaning in closer to the window to examine the goo, she squinted and watched the substance vibrate against the glass. "We went through a cloud?" Her thick British accent was distinct in comparison to Mariotti's rhythmic-sounding Spanish one.

"Yeah," the pilot confessed. "Cut through one when we were dead in the air."

"Have you tried the pressure skimmers?"

"Tied to the main engine," Mariotti explained. He reached over and flipped a dead switch back and forth to visually show her what he meant.

"Right. Well, at least I got us back in the air," Fox said, wiping her hands clean against a dirty, old rag.

"Was some quick thinking back there, Nat," the man complimented.

"Natalia," the woman corrected in a slightly angered tone.

The man smirked and rolled his eyes.

"Alright, bring her down," the woman instructed. "And avoid touching any more clouds. Our backup engine could blow us back into the stone age."

"It was a simpler time," the man joked as he slowly guided the ship's throttle forward and descended deeper into the planet's atmosphere.

In the distance, a flock of bird-like creatures could be seen flying in a triangle formation. Natalia watched them as they got closer. They had dark feathers and looked like birds, but there was something off about them that Natalia couldn't quite put her finger on. She swiped her hand to the right across a section of the cockpit's windshield. The transparent glass materialized a digital image of the birds as they continued their flight. Natalia then swiped again and the image was enhanced. With a close-up view, the details in the birds could be seen. Despite the flapping wings and moving heads, the birds were far from being alive. Patches of feathers and skin were missing across random spots of their bodies, and at the heart of each of their wounds was a black shard of shimmering organic matter: a spiky, tar-like substance that grew in size when the birds flew apart and shrunk as they drew near.

"That is disgusting," Marcus quavered.

"They're dead," Natalia observed out loud. "That black goo is reanimating them."

Marcus said nothing as he watched in disgust. At the heart of the flock was a bird that was far more deteriorated than the rest. It also had more of the tar in its wounds than any other bird in the sky.

"The queen is in the center," Natalia pointed. "Their formation serves as a barrier that shields her in flight."

"Are you an expert in mutated parasites now?" Marcus jokingly inquired.

"It's just common sense observation," Fox shot back before swiping her hand to the left and dismissing the image. The small section of glass returned to transparency, and Marcus continued to scan for a good spot to safely bring the ship down.

Most of the planet's landscape was wet and lush with thick, colorful bits of forestry. Oddly-shaped trees staked claim over much of the swamplands. With valleys and chasms throughout, the ecosystem was vibrant, yet necrotic.

"Over there look good?" Marcus asked as he spotted a flat plateau clearing at the edge of a stony ridge. Water flowed out from a gash along the side of the ridge, and fog rose from a shrouded depth below the far side of the mountain.

"Sure," Natalia said. She grabbed onto something and stabilized her balance in preparation for landing.

"I'm a better pilot than you give me credit for, ya' know," Marcus chuckled as the ship descended to the ground smoothly under his control.

Fox said nothing. She instead gathered tools and made way for the exit. Marcus flipped some switches in the cockpit and then unbuckled his seatbelt before standing up and following Natalia to the exit.

Fox punched a button and the ship's hydraulic doors hissed their way open. A burst of fresh air washed over the two astronauts as the light of the foreign planet slowly trickled into the aircraft. Marcus inhaled the rich-tasting oxygen with a smile on his face. Natalia also inhaled a breath of the fresh air, but her composure remained as stone. Fox led the way forward, and the two of them exited the ship in silence.

The white noise of a nearby waterfall could be heard as rocks from below the side of the plateau were baptized in a torrent of heavy rain. Its sound was mildly comforting, and Fox was reminded of home. Despite being such a strange and foreign planet, many of the things about this place appeared to be similar to Earth's topography. Blended within the tree line of a nearby forest were strange pillars of stone. They poked through the crust of the planet like the tip of a sharp needle pressed to skin. Likely created by the collision of tectonic plates shifting below the earth's crust, the structures appeared to be a naturally-occurring phenomenon. Something about the queerness of their design forced Natalia's attention. Deep cracks ran across the surface of jagged rock. Blooming with barbed edges, thin patches of black organic matter dangled from the open wounds like a veil draping the face of a decaying bride.

"I will start on this side, and you can take the other," Fox proposed. She handed Marcus a silver spray canister and a small hammer.

"This is going to take all day, Natalia," Marcus complained.

She said nothing, and Marcus left to take on cleaning his portion of the ship.

Natalia shook the canister and turned it upside down before applying the spray onto a section of the goo. It took a moment, but a small patch of the ooze began to wither as it changed to a whitish color and solidified. Natalia slid the canister into one of her jacket pockets and then gently tapped away at the hardened muck with her hammer. Thin flakes of the annealed substance chipped away and fell to the ground. Revealed beneath the unearthed layer was a second coating of the wet ooze. Alive and well, the colony of living organisms vibrated and contracted as the outer shell of their settlement flaked away.

Natalia sighed and withdrew the canister to continue.

"Hey, Natalia!" Mariotti shouted from the other side of the ship.

Assuming he was about to unleash a volley of complaints, Fox chose to ignore his call.

"Natalia, you better come take a look at this!"

Fox bit into the side of her cheek and ducked under the front end of the ship. She casually walked over to her copilot. Standing firmly in place like a deer in the headlights of an oncoming car, Mariotti just stared at Fox as she approached.

"What?" Natalia asked, but Mariotti said nothing. "Marcus!" She cried, fighting off the urge to slap him across the face.

"It's eating away at the ship," Marcus spat out.

"*What?*"

The copilot withdrew a pocket knife and pressed it into the goo. He pried up a section, but with the green tar came a thick flake of the ship's outer metal coating. Fox's eyes widened as the two pilots looked to one another for a moment before Natalia blurted out the first idea that came to mind.

"Burn 'em," she mumbled as she dropped her tools and dashed over to the rear side of the ship.

Marcus fumbled with his words. He uttered a phrase in Spanish before switching his brain back over to English. "That's crazy! They will combust!"

Natalia examined the vehicle's thrusters for a moment and then shouted back to Marcus. "They didn't get into the thrusters, so they shouldn't be anywhere near our fuel lines."

Mariotti gritted his teeth for a moment before loosening his jaw and yelping. "I don't know if her shields can absorb that kind of direct blast, Nat."

"It's the quickest way," Natalia barked back as she came forward and entered the ship. "Gonna lose her either way," she added from within. "We can let them devour it, or we blow them off and hope the ship can withstand the explosion."

Marcus stalled with a look of tremendous unease. He then hesitantly followed his copilot into the ship.

"Gather all of the extinguishers," Fox commanded as she

reached into a footlocker and withdrew a duffle bag. She unzipped the pack and flipped it upside down so that she could shake all of the contents out. A hand axe, first aid kit, MRE's, and other basic pieces of survival gear spilled out across the floor. She dug through the contents until she found a canister of lighter fluid and then bolted out the door.

"Let's go, Mariotti!" Fox barked, tearing the top of the container off and dousing the lower half of the ship in fluid. She then squirted a pool under the lowest hanging part of the ship and emptied the rest of the container into a line that led away from the puddle on the ground.

A pair of extinguishers flew out of the ship's bay door, followed by a third and a fourth. "I thought we had five!" Marcus cried from within the ship.

"Fuck it," Fox yelled, discarding the empty canister of fuel to the side and retrieving a pair of extinguishers from the ground. "Four will do!"

Marcus tripped coming through the door. Twisting his ankle in the process, he let out a yelp as he tried to catch himself. With a limp, he picked up the remaining pair of extinguishers off of the ground and followed Natalia. The two of them reached a large rock formation nearby and set the extinguishers down.

"You alright?" Natalia inquired in regards to her copilot's limp.

"Yeah, I'll be fine. How are we going to light it?"

Fox took a deep breath and then withdrew a lighter from one of her front pockets. "We've gotta be fast," she said calmly before looking Marcus in the eyes.

Marcus nodded and pulled the safety pins on the four extinguishers as Natalia stood up from behind the rock and jogged towards the line of lighter fluid. She knelt to the ground and looked at the ship before flipping the lighter open and sparking a flame. Her hand moved slowly towards the line of combustible fluid as a bead of sweat dripped from her brow. She did a double-take up towards the ship and then pressed the flame into the line of gas. In a blur of speed, Fox bolted back towards Marcus.

Once safely behind cover, the pilots shared an awkward moment of tense silence as they waited for the boom. Fox peeked her head around the boulder to see that the pool of lighter fluid had caught flame, but the fire hadn't spread to the ship or the goo that encased it. The flames were reaching up towards the belly of the aircraft like hands trying to resurface themselves after a premature burial.

"God-fucking-dammit!" Fox raged as she kicked one of her booted feet into the dirt.

Just as soon as her mind raced to find a new solution, the goo caught fire and the explosion went off. Marcus flinched as a wave of dust washed over the two pilots.

Natalia looked back to the ship. Pockets of fire blazed in spots where the goo was the thickest, but most of the ship was clear of both ooze and flame.

"Let's go," Fox commanded, reaching for a pair of extinguishers.

The two hurried towards the ship and worked to put out the remaining fires. After expending all of their retardant, Fox took off her flight jacket and began wiping it at a final pocket of flame.

With the fires out, Marcus eased his shoulders and sighed. "I can't believe that actually worked."

Natalia said nothing. She dropped her jacket and began inspecting the ship's outer shell. It was free of the goo, but there were a couple of small tears in the metal. With a sigh, she entered the ship's cockpit and booted up the computer for diagnostics.

A wall of code began processing information. The text was displayed across the transparent glass within the cockpit. Fox read through the data as it spread like lighting. Her vision drifted from the code as something rumbled in the distance. The ship rattled like a sailboat enduring the waves of a hurricane. Natalia lost her footing and was thrown into the windshield with a thump.

"Marcus?" Fox called, spitting out a mouthful of blood.

"Yeah. I don't know," Mariotti admitted. "But something is coming from the northside. Something big."

Natalia minimized the diagnostic display with a flick of the wrist and the glass was again fully transparent. A tree line in the distance swayed from side to side. The taller branches barked under the pressure of something moving within. Fox brought back up the diagnostics and read through the code as it processed.

"C'mon, ya' bloody cunt," she mumbled softly. Her pupils

compressed as her eyes caught sight of a particular line of code. "Thrusters are online," she shouted, "and fuel lines are intact!" Her facial expression shifted as red text flashed by on the screen. "But there are significant breaches to our hull…"

Natalia squirmed towards the exit. She snatched a pair of oxygen masks from a storage locker and tossed one to Marcus as she jumped out the door.

"Are we running?" Marcus questioned, his voice cracking as he frantically worked to enable the electronic mask.

"The damage will take too long to patch," Fox stated as she attached her mask to her face and then activated one of the canisters. "Channel three in case we lose each other," she added, fiddling with some buttons on the mask.

"Dios ten piedad…" Marcus said softly as he flipped a switch on his mask and withdrew a small earpiece.

The ground trembled and pebbles rattled across the ground. Natalia froze and slipped back into the ship. She grabbed the backpack that was on the floor and scooped the spilled survival gear back into the bag.

"Fox!" Marcus cried. "Come on!"

Natalia slung the bag over her shoulder as the ship continued to tremble. She jerked a lever near the exit, and a metal panel receded into the wall, revealing a pair of energy pistols within. Withdrawing the weapons, she fixed one to her belt, and after exiting the ship, handed the other to Marcus.

"I don't know what good these will do," Mariotti admitted as the nearby trees cracked under the weight of a colossal creature.

"Let's go," Fox said. She led the way down the rocky terrain and into a nearby gully.

Natalia vaulted over the ledge and watched Mariotti scale down the side of the ravine. She could hear his heavy breathing into the mic within his mask. She clung to the stone for a moment and watched as the beast ruptured through the tree line. It wasn't just one creature, but three; skinless elephants who shared similar-looking necrotic wounds. Their bodies were rotting, but their presence and strength remained colossal. The beasts surrounded the ship and began searching the ground for any signs of life. Sharp, organic bits of tar ruptured from their exposed muscle matter and squirmed across the surface of their flesh. Natalia flinched as the infected creatures screamed. Their heart-piercing cry saturated the air in all directions.

"Natalia!" Marcus cried into the mic.

Fox looked down to see that Mariotti was standing on the ground at the basin of the ravine. She glanced back towards the necrotic beasts before scaling down the rocks. Her heart raced as she pondered their existence. They were similar to the beasts of the earth, but their infection was a dark and mysterious disease not found on Earth.

"C'mon, C'mon," Marcus repeated softly into the mic as Natalia made her final drop into the ravine.

After landing, Fox lifted her eyes to the sky. An awkward silence lingered from above as a rotting pair of tusks hung over the side of the ledge. Slowly, the decrepit face of the beast wandered into view. Its eye sockets were empty, and in their place was a ball of fuzzy, black matter. It shimmered as its form shifted within the empty sockets. The living tar-like substance was watching them from above. Fox bit into her lower lip and slowly backed away as the second and third beast arrived to watch them go.

"Holy fuck," Marcus exhaled softly into his mic.

"Marcus," Natalia whispered.

The three beasts then dove off the side of the mountain and the shadows of their presence washed over the pair of pilots.

"Run!" Fox yelled and the two bolted away from the wall.

The moist sound of flesh hitting rock paired with the splitting noise of both ligament and bone sent shivers down Fox's spine. She slowed her run and turned back to face a scene of utter carnage.

The three elephants had jumped off the cliff and splattered against the ground. With their innards scattered across the dirt, the beasts were little more than the liquefied remains of muscle and brain tissue. The rot shifted as the infected matter surfaced. The organic substance twisted and shimmered as it formed a solid limb of darkness. The arm reached out towards Natalia like a flame seeking dry timber. She backed away as the living tar wiggled and wormed through the air. While maintaining its roots within its host's flesh, the infection sought new life to dominate and feast upon.

Fox raised her pistol into the air and disengaged the safety.

She then pulled the trigger twice, and a pair of laser shots severed through the stream of moving tar. The rooted half of dark matter continued to flail while the severed stream began to bubble and ooze. A hot steam squealed from the burning limb. The burn ceased and only a perfectly still puddle of dark liquid remained.

"Fuck," Marcus muttered as he arrived beside Fox to look onto the scene of carnage.

An awkward stillness mingled with the stagnant air of the rotting corpses as shadows lingered overhead.

Fox raised her eyes to find a line of wolves standing on the ledge above. The canines were missing clumps of fur and patches of skin. The black tar could be seen worming within open wounds.

Marcus followed Natalia's silent stare. He then withdrew his pistol and aimed it up towards the rotting hounds.

Natalia cocked her neck and noticed that infected birds were watching them from the limbs of leafless trees. With her weapon still in hand, she aimed at the wolves and backpedaled towards Marcus.

"We can't take them all," Marcus admitted with panic in his voice.

Fox said nothing as she continued to examine the silent observers.

The two pilots cautiously retreated as dark clouds rolled in from the western skies. The two then flinched as a flock of necrotic birds erupted from a nearby tree. With their weapons pointed towards the heart of the flock, the pilots watched in horror as the birds flew away. Natalia glanced back to the ledge, but the wolves were gone.

"Do you think it's the rain?" Marcus suggested as droplets began to plummet from the heavens above.

"I don't know," Fox admitted, "but we've got to get back to the ship."

Rivers and lakes were quick to form across the basin of the arid ravine, and the pair of pilots were forced to take a different route back towards their aircraft. As they approached a wall, Fox glanced back to Marcus and sighed.

"This is going to be the easiest way back up."

"Easiest," Marcus scoffed.

The wall of rock was wet, and mud was drooling down

sections of weakened stone. Natalia approached the wall and tried to gain traction on the slippery surface.

"I don't know, Nat," Marcus complained as he watched from the ground and slowly began to sink in a pool of mud. He struggled to pull his left leg from the muck, but as he shifted his weight over to his right leg, something below gave way and he disappeared into the ground with a sharp cry.

"Marcus!" Natalia howled as she jumped back down to the ground and rushed over to the open crater.

A colony of enormous bats screeched up out of the wound in the earth and Natalia shielded her face as the veil of living darkness encased her.

"Marcus!" She shouted through the sea of bats.

The colony dispersed into the sky and Natalia was left standing unscathed. She looked down into the hole and the noxious scent of rot wafted up with the cavern's chilly draft.

"Marcus!" She cried, her voice echoing down into the cavern.

"I landed on my leg," Marcus groaned into his mic.

"Is it broken?" Natalia fired back into her headset.

"I don't know. I can't move it, and my tac light doesn't work." The pilot's breathing was boisterous and sporadic.

"Alright," Natalia eased. "Stay calm. I'm going to find a way down to you."

The sound of Marcus vomiting could be heard through the mic.

"How did you get into the cavern," Natalia muttered under her breath as she watched the decrepit bats climb up over the horizon.

"Nat?" Marcus called over the radio. "There is ... something in here."

Natalia's heart skipped a beat. "Just stay still," she whispered into her microphone. "I'm coming."

She dashed over towards a nearby chasm and peeked over the ledge. At the basin of the twenty-foot drop was a crack that ran up across one of the stone walls.

"Bingo," Natalia whispered as she began to climb down into the crater. "I think I've got it," Fox assured as she slid to a stop in the wet soil. She then slipped into the open crevice along the stone's wall and activated a tactical light on her oxygen mask.

The corridor ahead was jagged and narrow. A noxious scent lingered in the stagnant air of the cavern and the pilot pressed on ahead with caution.

Natalia followed a winding path until the corridor opened up to reveal a ledge hanging over a great room. The pilot stepped onto the ledge to find that the room was dimly lit, and rain was falling from an open hole in the ceiling.

"I think I've found you," Natalia said as she began to descend from the dark ledge. "I'm climbing down to you now."

Natalia bit into her lower lip as she listened to the sounds of mysterious creatures moving under the cover of darkness. She descended to the ground floor and then unholstered her pistol before pressing on towards her co-pilot.

"Natalia?" Marcus called. His voice was near.

The presence of nefarious observers was camouflaged by the ambient sounds of running water and falling rain.

"Over here," Marcus said.

Natalia spun around to find her co-pilot leaning against something metallic. He had pulled himself up onto one leg, and the brunt of his weight was pressed against the strange object.

Raindrops fell from the hole above and Natalia was again baptized in the waters of the monsoon as she approached her friend.

"You're on your feet," she said optimistically.

"Sort of," Marcus huffed.

Mariotti's broken leg was twisted and mangled.

"Let's have a look," Natalia said as she knelt in the mud before her copilot. Withdrawing a dagger from her boot, she cut into the flight suit and endured the sound of her friend's wailing cry. "The scrapes aren't too bad, so we don't have to worry about you bleeding out at least... but this thing *is* broken badly."

"I'll be fine if you can bear my weight and crutch me outta here."

"Yeah..." Natalia stood back up, her attention captured by the metallic object behind her friend. "What *is* that?"

Marcus followed her gaze down towards the thing that he was leaning against. "Uh..."

The silver object was shaped like a man, and its metallic

coating was tarnished by the ailment of time. From its featureless face to the rounded tips of its arms, the statue's physical definitions were unnaturally smooth; a perfection that only modern tools could achieve.

Marcus clenched a fist and tapped his knuckles against the object.

"It's made of steel," he observed out loud, traces of agony lingered in the tone of his voice.

"Or some foreign form thereof," Fox added.

Fox leaned in a little closer and ran the tips of her fingers across small, pin-sized holes in the surface of the object. The depressions covered every square inch of the statue's frame.

"Twelve-pointed hexes," Natalia perceived out loud.

The holes shimmered under the shine of her tactical light.

"Is it robotic?" Marcus questioned, but Natalia said nothing as her mind raced for answers. "Do you think that it was alive?"

"I don't know," Fox muttered. "but *someone* ... or *something* created this."

The sound of the raindrops falling from the open wound in the cavern pelted against the ground at a sporadic pace.

"Do you know what this means?" Natalia gasped as she glanced around the cavern for any signs of a second object. Her shift in tone had grown cold, and the question came off as more of a statement than an inquiry.

Absorbing, for a moment, Natalia's sense of seriousness, Marcus remained silent.

"We always knew that extraterrestrial life existed beyond our home world," Natalia stated. "But now... now we know that something *intelligent* is out here living amongst the stars."

A brief moment of silence came to pass as the two of them stared at the construct. Marcus then choked out the word "here." His voice cracked under the strain of a sudden fright. "Something intelligent is out *here*."

Natalia slowly began to nod. Her gaze returned towards the object.

"This is far too ancient of a thing to belong to anyone living in the present," she said softly as she wicked water away from the slick surface of the ancient relic.

In total silence, the shadow of an object fell from above. Through the darkness, the body of a snake, enormous in size, twisted through the air. The great beast landed on Natalia with a thud and was quick to encase her in a wall of solid muscle.

The muffled screams of the pilot ensued as she desperately reached towards the ground for her pistol. A volley of laser fire could be heard and the snake's muscles contracted. Fox slipped her oxygen mask off and broke her head free of the serpent's grip. Gasping for air, she spotted her weapon on the ground and reached for it. Her fingers scraped and clawed against the dirt, and Marcus shouted something incoherent as he fired another cluster of shots into the snake. The serpent's grip weakened further and Fox managed to snag her weapon. She pressed the barrel of the pistol against the snake and pulled the trigger a dozen times.

Cut to pieces, the serpent's innards remained perfectly still across the ground and Natalia dropped to her knees.

"Are you okay?" Marcus cried, sliding to the ground in agony.

Winded, Natalia remained on the ground and huffed in the stagnant-tasting air. The light from her broken mask shined up towards the ceiling, where movement could be seen amongst the rocks.

"We've," Natalia gasped, still trying to regain her breath. "We've gotta ... get you out of here."

"I'm onboard with that," Marcus sighed as he gritted his teeth and tried to mitigate his pain.

A rotting assortment of blisters and wounds could be seen swirling from the serpent's skin as its lifeless corpse began to twitch across the ground.

Natalia stood up and stumbled over towards Marcus, who was leaning against the basin of the construct.

"Nat!" The co-pilot cried in terror.

Fox spun around with her pistol, aimed forward, and squeezed the trigger as fast as she could. Through the shadows, limbs of tar reached out towards her from the serpent's corpse. She managed to sever one of the noxious claws in half, and then dove to the ground to avoid being hit by the second wave of rot as it drifted through the air. Masculine screams of butchery ensued.

Natalia aimed towards the snake, where the wiggling limb

took root. She double-tapped her weapon's trigger and the living infection dropped to the ground and began hissing as it bubbled and burned.

"I... I can't see!"

"Marcus!" Fox called as she stood back up and rushed over to her friend.

"I can't see, Nat!" The co-pilot cried, his voice panicking as he reached through the darkness. Still hunched against the construct, the co-pilot's eyes were gone and red streaks poured from the open holes.

"Natalia!" Marcus cried, frightened to the core. "Natalia," he repeated, blood seeping into his open mouth.

"It's alright, Marcus. I can fix this," Fox lied as she placed a hand on her co-pilot's shoulder.

"I don't wanna die," Mariotti cried. "I don't wanna go."

Natalia cradled her sniveling friend as his mind was pulled into the eternal twilight. As the man succumbed to darkness, his legs buckled out from under him and he collapsed. Natalia held him up in place as tears began to form in her eyes. She propped the lifeless corpse back against the construct and then tried to regain control of her emotions.

The horrific sounds of creatures, dominated by the wicked infection, could be heard writhing through the darkness. Natalia sniffled as she prepared to face certain death and follow her friend's lead into the abyss.

Absorbed by the holes across the surface of its chassis, the blood of the deceased copilot leaked into the construct. Fox froze as she heard the distinct sounds of a mechanized weapon's charge. She slowly turned to watch as the construct below Marcus came to life. A blue aura began to radiate from the object's surface, and the lifeless corpse of her friend slid to the ground. A thin layer of the construct's shell effortlessly peeled back like the skin of a rabbit who had met the fate of a skilled hunter and his blade.

Standing in awe, Natalia watched as the cavern was illuminated by the glowing construct. Infected rats scurried and diseased snakes retreated back towards the walls of the room. Covered in blood, the smooth, metallic innards of the construct warped like liquid. Silver and red swirled as the surface of the ancient machine transformed into a weapon. Thin tubes ruptured from the construct's shell, and burning hot lights were projected out across the room.

Blinded by the light, Natalia raised her arms and shielded her eyes. She tried to yell and scream, but the low-frequency hum of the construct obliterated all sound. Bright lights continued to strobe and the ambient temperature of the cavern surged as rays of warmth were blasted in all directions.

At the pinnacle of intensity, a still silence loomed. The burning lights began to dim and the cavern's temperature began to drop back down.

Natalia peeked out from behind her arm. The construct was powering down, but the metal weapon still radiated with a dimming glow. Puddles of tar were scattered about the room, and the sound of the liquified infection, dripping from the ceiling, echoed across the walls of the ancient cavern.

Blood and Honor in the Wasteland of Strife

Across the orange horizon of a dry, abandoned wasteland, the dark silhouette of an enormous creature could be seen. As the twin suns set behind the beast, shadows obscured the details of both its body and face. The creature's silhouette was that of an elephant, but its legs were tall like the trees of an ancient forest. All life paled to fill even the shadow of the monster's footsteps; the contrast between the beast and its surroundings was tremendous.

"The Nag'thulia are migrating," said the feminine voice of a strange creature.

"The winds are changing. The era of ice is upon us," a second added. This one was deeper and more masculine in tone.

With thick hooves, soot-colored fur, and a crown of ebony horns, the two conversing creatures were minotaurs: muscular, bull-like humanoids. They stood on a pair of arched legs, and their towering presence reflected their natural-born strength. Both of them wore scraps of tattered leather armor. With a two-handed scimitar at his side and scars across his chest, the male was worn by both battle and time. His eyes were glazed over, and his upper lip was split in half.

"Do you think that we are ready?" The girl questioned as she turned to face the elder man. She had a pair of well-kept spears strapped to her back. Her clean fur and lack of scars was a tell to her level of innocence and immaturity.

The male said nothing as he continued to watch the giant in the distance.

Joining him in the moment of peace, the girl observed in silence as the twin suns fell into the horizon and the creature disappeared into the darkness.

As the moon and her stars came out to claim the night sky, the male minotaur decided it was time to go. The girl nodded and followed. They each picked up a knapsack of freshly cut meat, and they scaled down the side of a jagged ridge. Once in the desert valley, they pressed on through the night. They crossed through the wasteland of cracked clay and deep sands until morning arrived. As dawn approached, the younger minotaur noticed a trail of smoke in the sky.

"Is that...?" She questioned out loud, stumbling over her thoughts.

"Make haste, Sala," the elder bull ordered as he took off towards the smoke.

The two of them ran as fast as they could. Leaping over cracked earth and diving between fallen stone, the minotaurs reached the source of the smoke within minutes. Before them were the remains of a camp: their camp. Charred corpses of fallen clan members could be found smoldering among piles of ash and burning embers. The stench was unlike anything Sala had ever smelled. Her mouth hung open in utter shock as she dropped to her knees and looked down towards the defiled ground.

The elder minotaur stepped forward and the ground trembled before him. The still corpses of the dead ignored his mighty presence. The bodies were glued into the scorched earth, frozen in place under the weight of oblivion.

Sala spotted a pair of jackal-headed creatures lingering in the shadows. Their black eyes were filled with a sinister hatred as they basked in the blissful moment of conquest. Feeding off the emotions, they watched the two minotaurs from within their veil of shadows.

"Sala," the elder minotaur said calmly.

His call fell on deaf ears as the girl remained frozen in horror. Her thoughts were weighed down by the heavy thumb of sorrow and pain.

"Sala!" The bull repeated. This time his voice bellowed with a sense of urgency.

She turned to look his way with tears in her eyes. Her heartache subsided as she read her father's body language. Slowly, he repositioned one of his hands so that it hovered over the hilt of his blade. The two gazed into the depths of each other's eyes. The man's hand began to tremble as he tried to keep calm. The girl rose to her feet and - when she was standing fully - the elder man slowly blinked his eyes. It was goodbye, or at least the best she would ever get in terms of properly saying farewell.

"Run!" The minotaur shouted. He plucked his scimitar from his waist and charged towards the two jackals.

Sala took off in the direction from which they had arrived. She heard the clash of steel behind her as she ran with all of her strength. Her heart thumped through her chest and adrenaline kicked in for an extra boost of momentum. The jackals cried out. Their high-pitched shrieks raised the fine fur along Sala's neck. Her emotions churned in the depths of her belly as she pressed forward with her escape.

Sala continued to run until her legs gave out and she collapsed into the dirt. A dust cloud of debris shot up into the air as she made impact with the ground. Winded by her escape, the bulltress snorted with her chin pressed flat against the soil. Her breathing kicked up more dust as her heart thumped against the ground. Her adrenaline faded and her eyes began to water. A single tear ran down the side of her cheek. It rinsed away a line of dirt before slipping from the edge of her face. The muddy teardrop was the first of many.

After spending a moment wrestling with her emotions, Sala got up to her feet and looked back to the smoke-filled sky. She had traveled far in a short amount of time, and she felt regret for having left her father. She wiped her face and took a deep breath. Her gut begged with her heart to not return to the fallen outpost, but she ignored the nagging thoughts and set off for the besieged encampment.

Sala ventured back, but halted her travel as she came upon what she was looking for. Hanging from the branches of a tall, leafless tree was the motionless corpse of a deceased minotaur.

Sala bit into her lower lip and looked away as she silently burst into a heavy cry. As the tears continued to fall, she forced a deep breath and approached the tree. Withdrawing a spear from her back, Sala severed the rope that was tied around the basin of the tree. The shadow of the corpse above washed over her as the body fell to the ground. The sound of cracking bones could be heard as the corpse made impact and crumpled against the rocky terrain.

Sala winced as she forced herself to approach the body. She knelt to the fallen minotaur and ran the fingers of her left hand through his fur. His hide was sliced up, and his own sword was sticking from his belly.

Sala's eyes continued to water as she forced the word, "Father." Her voice was soft, but the weight of speaking was too heavy to bear.

She untied the noose from around the bull's neck and plucked the blade from his belly. After discarding the weapon, she pressed her snout against the neck of the fallen champion. The young bull cried into the hide of her deceased father until the suns set on the day of bloodshed.

Sala spent the following night dragging the body of her father to a nearby ledge that overlooked a painted canyon. She worked through the morning digging a grave and - once her father was buried - she looked out towards the chasm.

As the colors of the gorge mingled, she reflected on a time long ago when her father would bring her here to tell stories of their ancestors and how they painted the gorge with the blood of their enemies. She replayed the legend in her mind as she watched the color of the valley shift from brown to red.

Moskhar, a feral minotaur and the first of their kind, spent his entire life evading trophy hunters; that is, until the day arrived when the beast was cornered in the heart of the canyon. With no way out, Moskhar tapped into a monstrous strength. Fueled by a legendary rage, he used his bare hands to grotesquely murder his attackers. He tore their spines out from their backsides and later used the bones to craft a great axe. He carved up the bodies of his attackers and painted the gorge a collection of darkened colors.

Sala concluded the recollection of the story and looked to the fresh grave. Beside it was a leather belt sheath that now housed her father's blade. She reached for the strap and pressed her head against the hilt of the weapon. A deep breath ensued as a tear made its way down the front of her face and landed into the dry dirt below. She then reflected on the memory of another one of her father's many teachings.

Do not fear death... embrace it. In the end, it is the only thing that this world has to offer.

Sala's mind shifted to a time when she was young and her father was leading a hunting party deep into the heart of a blood god's den. The hunting party had set up camp just outside the lair. Their plan was to rest for the night and infiltrate the den come dawn. Sala and her father sat beside a campfire in private.

"They are scared," Sala's younger self pressed in reference to the clan of hunters.

"They should be," her father admitted as he read the flames of the fire like an ancient text. "Tomorrow, most of them will die," he added coldly.

Sala submerged her mind into the past. At the time, she had thought the statement was unnecessarily pessimistic, but the man she admired had never lied to her about anything in his life.

"Death is reaching out on this night. It is calling names, and those foolish enough to listen are destined to die," her father concluded as he continued to watch the heart of the fire with his stone cold eyes.

Sala shifted her train of thought to the memory of the conflict that ensued the morning after. It was a bloodbath, and her father's prophecy had come to fruition; most of the hunting party was killed in the attack. They were successful in overtaking the den, though, and after the battle was won, they had captured two of their leopard-skinned foes alive.

One of the felines was masculine with golden fur and scars across his face. His left paw was injured, and droplets of blood occasionally dripped from his sopping-wet fur. The other cat was feminine. Her unclean fur had oddly-shaped spots of various patterns and sizes. Both of the felines were ragged and greasy-looking: a common trait of their clan. Dignity and honor were not things of value in the eyes of these deviate tabbies. Down on their knees, they awaited their fate in silence as two of the hunting party's bulls stood above them with spears pressed to their backs.

Sala's father examined the two felines. The male refused to make eye contact with the bull as he stared at the ground in agony and horror. The female cat, however, glared directly into his eyes. Her face was full of hatred, and her eyes burned with a universal fire that transcended the barriers of verbal language.

"Bring her to her feet," Sala's father commanded.

The two hunters lifted their spears and raised the feline by the shoulders until she was standing on her two feet.

"Now, give her a weapon," the great minotaur instructed of his party.

One of the hunters pulled a dagger from his belt and twirled it in his hand before offering it to the feline.

"Trial by combat," the elder minotaur said as he approached the hate-fueled feline. "Go on, take it," he then suggested of the offered blade. The cat didn't understand his words but followed his eyes towards the dagger being offered. Then, with great speed, the feline lunged for a sheathed sword hanging from the belt of one of the huntsmen. She stole the weapon and transitioned into a defensive stance with her eyes bolting between the guards and Sala's father.

"Well, alright then," the lead bull said with a hearty chuckle. "Sala," he then called with a stern snort.

Surprised to hear her own name, the young heifer awkwardly stumbled forward.

"Yes, Father?"

The elder bull untied his weapon from his waist and offered the sheathed sword to his daughter. The twinkle in his stone eyes was soft.

"Do not underestimate her," her father stated. "She is fighting for her life."

The young bulltress accepted the weapon. It was heavy in her hands, but she had held it many times before in practice against scarecrows stuffed with sticks and hay.

Pulling the blade from its sheath, the young minotaur raised the weapon in the air and stared towards her foe.

The feline growled and wasted no time in pouncing forward.

Her speed was unnatural and like nothing Sala had ever before seen. After an exchange of counters and blows, Sala was thrown to the ground with a deep cut across her right shoulder.

As the feline prepared to deliver the killing blow, one of the huntsmen raised his spear and went in to intercept the attack, but the clan's leader, Sala's father, planted a firm hand on the shoulder of the huntsmen.

"Their feet are a tell of their intentions," the girl's father informed. "Watch them. Observe their posture and stance. When you take note of these things, you will never be caught off guard."

The young minotaur glanced to the feline's arched heels and watched as the cat dove forward. The bulltress rolled to the left and raised her weapon, severing one of the cat's legs clean off from the knee down. Scrambling to her feet, the minotaur then watched as the cat hissed and cried on the ground. Blood poured forth from the open shin like the glimmering waters of an oasis.

"Do not let her dwell long with the thoughts of her own demise," the girl's father instructed.

Sala regained her composure and limped towards the cat. Despite her agony, the feline glanced up to the bulltress with hate in her heart. She gritted her teeth and spat up towards her executioner before Sala plunged the tip of her father's blade into the neck of the fallen tabby.

Exhausted, the young minotaur limped over towards her father and returned the weapon. The elder bull nodded and embraced his daughter, who broke into a silent cry.

"What of the other survivor?" One of the huntsmen questioned.

Sala looked into the eyes of the lone survivor. The tabby looked pathetic, and an authentic fear lingered in his eyes as he helplessly waited for his turn to die at the hand of the hunters.

"Spare him," the leader of the clan instructed as he released his grip from around his daughter's bloody side.

The girl regained control of her emotions and listened to her father's words as he spoke directly to her.

"If all of your enemies perish, then no one is left to tell the tale of your victory in their defeat. You must always leave a survivor so that others may hear legend of our kind."

Sala's vision of the past faded, but as she returned to the present, the words spoken between her father and one of the huntsmen lingered.

"Why didn't you stop her?" One of the huntsmen asked the clan's leader, in reference to the killing blow Sala's foe was preparing to deliver.

"Because I have faith," the bull answered softly.

"Faith in the gods?"

"No," the bull rejected the sentiment. "In my daughter."

Sala's mind returned to the present. She opened her eyes and continued to stare at the ground for a moment. Taking a deep breath, she stood to her feet and tied her father's sheathed weapon around her waist. Feeling lost and confused, she silently wandered away from the grave.

As the minotaur traveled further away from the gorge, something shimmered in the distance that captured her attention. She squinted her eyes and tried to make out the details of the object. It was an obelisk and, behind it, was a city of stone standing front-and-center to an endless desert sea.

The wind howled and the overgrown vines of a nearby shrub were blown back, revealing a puddle of clear water.Sala approached the pool and glanced into the water. Her eyes were stained with the look of fear, and she quickly grew disgusted by her own reflection. She turned away and clenched her jaw as her resentment bled into anger. With tears beginning to form at the edge of her eyes, she screamed out in frustration. Her cry was drowned out by harsh winds of sand and dust.

The young minotaur turned to face the obelisk in the distance. She then gritted her teeth and snorted as she began to walk towards the structure across the desert.

After a day of travel and thought, she entered the city of servants and slaves - humans whose skin were charred red from lives spent under the blistering heat of the twin suns. Their faces were branded like cattle. Lesions and scars covered their bodies from head to toe; it was clear that they had come to know the fall of a whip. Most of the peons were huddled together in pens - their resting grounds for a cold night after a long day of forced servitude. As Sala passed by, the slaves looked to her with horror and fear in their eyes.

Gentle snowflakes drifted down from the darkened sky, and a red moon peeked through a gash in the grey clouds above. Sala was accompanied through the city by an eerie silence. Words were spoken through the eyes of the slaves, but Sala refused to gaze upon them for long. She hadn't come for them.

Magnificent stone structures lined the streets and the path forward was brightened by torches ablaze. The great obelisk towered over the city skyline, and just below it was a stone pyramid. Sala ventured towards the pyramid. An evil radiated from the entrance of the structure, but she wasted little time in entering. Once inside, the minotaur found what she was looking for. In the center of the great room was an altar, and beyond that was a staircase with a crocodile sitting atop a golden throne. A pair of jackals sat on one of the steps below the reptile, and the hounds rose to their feet as Sala entered the sacred domain. Below the stone staircase, a dozen shirtless men worshiped their lord, but the chirp of the jackals forced the men to stand and face the intruder.

The crocodile said something in a brash, foreign tongue and the jackals descended from the staircase. The men then ran towards the walls of the temple, where an assortment of weapons hung from steel hooks. Muscular and fit, these slaves were unlike the cattle in the pens outside; these men were keen warriors who were prepared to guard their master with their lives.

Once armed, the men dashed towards the minotaur.

Sala withdrew her spears from her back and twirled the weapons in her hands as she deflected the blows of her attackers. She pierced the soft flesh of the men as she exerted her delicate dance of death. One by one, the men screamed as they fell to the sand, disemboweled by the tips of the spears.

Sala maintained her fighting stance as her eyes scanned the room. An arrow slit across the surface of the minotaur's arm, and she spun around to find that a small man wielding a crossbow was standing back by the door. As the man struggled to reload the weapon, the minotaur flung one of her spears towards him. He shouted and dropped his weapon as the spear landed into the wall beside him. Dropping to the ground, the man picked his weapon up and continued to reload.

Sala slowly walked towards the man. She launched her second

spear towards him, and he screamed as the tip of the weapon disarmed him. He watched helplessly as his weapon snapped in half under the pressure of the spear's strike. The shadow of the bulltress towered over him as Sala withdrew her father's blade and proceeded to decapitate the unarmed man.

Sala glanced to the wound on her arm and then back up towards the crocodile on his throne. She approached the altar, and the two cackling jackals withdrew their blades. They circled the minotaur, and only when they were in position across from one another did they launch their attack.

Sala deflected the first strike with ease and then channeled fury into deflecting the second. She disarmed the second Jackal and kicked him in the ribs with one of her hooved feet. The sound of bones cracking was followed by a screech as the jackal was thrown to the ground. Sala then turned to face the remaining attacker. He shuffled his feet as fear took hold of his posture, and the minotaur released a volley of blows. The jackal yelped as he deflected the attacks, but the final blow split his weapon in two. He looked on in horror with the stub of his broken weapon in hand. In a desperate attempt for survival, the jackal threw the fragmented blade at the minotaur.

Sala lowered her head and dodged the imbalanced weapon as it sailed towards her. She then lifted a hand from her blade's hilt and wrapped her fingers around the throat of the jackal. The minotaur raised the hound into the air; her eyes burned with fire and fury.

The second jackal leapt onto the minotaur's back and began snipping at the backside of her neck. She discarded the jackal to the ground and began thrashing in an attempt to shake her rider off. The hound below was trampled as the minotaur continued to thrash around. She managed to throw the rider from her back, and the second jackal crashed into the stone altar with a yelp. In a single, fluid motion, Sala withdrew a dagger from her belt, spun around, and flung the blade towards the jackal. The hound yelped as the dagger landed deep into his shoulder.

Returning two hands around the hilt of her father's blade, Sala thrusted the sword down onto the first jackal below her feet. The hound rolled to the left. Sala's attack missed. She withdrew the sword from the sand and, again, plunged the blade down onto the jackal.

The dog again rolled, but this time the tip of the sword caught his right leg. He squealed in both pain and fear as he tried to crawl away, but he was pinned firmly in place.

The jackal's twin plucked the dagger from his shoulder. He stammered forward with terror in his eyes. Dropping to the ground before Sala, the creature bowed his head and offered up the blade between the palms of his hands.

Sala snorted and accepted the tribute. She then turned her eyes up towards the god who continued to watch from his throne.

The crocodile tilted his head and flared his nostrils in utter disgust over the lack of loyalty. Sala plucked her sword from the leg of the pinned jackal and stepped forward. She dragged the tip of the weapon through the ground as she approached. The ambient sound of the blade slicing through the coarse sand echoed through the chamber like waves crashing up against the rocky shores of a distant cove. The minotaur broke into a consistent stride as the badge of courage and honor shimmered in the reflection of her eyes.

The crocodile lord stood to his feet and removed a layer of his tunic. He then calmly disembarked from his throne. He slowed in his descent as he reached the bottom of the stone staircase. The weakness of fear was present in his darkened eyes.

A naked slave stepped out from the darkness and offered his king a gem-encrusted scythe, and the crocodile accepted the weapon in silence. The servant bowed his head before retreating back into the shadows.

Without breaking her stride, Sala raised her sword into the air, the tip of the blade leading way for her charge forward. She took note of the crocodile's footing, maintaining a chilling stare into the eyes of the false god.

Sala groaned with the warcry of her people. She could feel the spirits of her ancestors as they propelled her forward with unnatural speed. Just as she came within reach of the king, she pivoted her front foot and swung her body around with elegance and grace. Her charge was a trick and the crocodile foolishly took the bait. The lord swung across with his scythe, the edge of the weapon slicing through the air with a whistle. The bull channeled all of her energy and might into her swing as the power of her delicate dance was infused within her weapon and she twirled through the air. The blade screamed as it cut through the air, and the expression on the lord's face was that of shock as Sala sliced through the reptilian god with ease. The lord's intestines bled forth from his belly like water through a valley and, before the crocodile could mutter a word, the minotaur followed through with a second swing of her blade. She continued to spin and the second blow of her weapon severed the head of the crocodile clean from its corpse. The body dropped to the ground, blood spurting from its open neck stub, and the head sailed through the air before falling into the sand and tumbling to a dusty stop.

Sala exhaled softly and approached the head of the false god. She then planted her father's sword into the sand. Dropping to one knee, she withdrew a pair of daggers and planted the blades deep into the eye sockets of the decapitated head. She then approached the corpse of the crocodile and unsheathed her third and final dagger from its holster. Using the fine blade, she carved out the false god's heart. Rising to her feet and sheathing her dagger, she wrapped the organ in strips of cloth before sliding it into a small leather satchel on her hip.

Placing a single hand back around the hilt of her father's blade, Sala glanced towards the carnage before her. She soaked her soul in the waters of the moment. The ground was littered with corpses, and her weapons were stained red. The insides of a dozen or so guards were mixed in with the mangled bodies of the peasants and servants who stood against her. It was foolish for them to die for their master.

Turning back towards the entrance, the minotaur approached the injured jackals. She slid the dagger out from its holster and dropped the blood-soaked weapon to the ground. The tip of the blade sunk into the sand so that only the hilt of the weapon was visible.

"One of you dies, whilst the other lives to tell the tale of your deceased god," Sala said without emotion.

The two jackals looked at her with pleading eyes. They then turned to face one another and, immediately, their sense of helplessness turned into that of opportunity.

As Sala turned to walk away, the two Jackals lunged for the blade. The sound of their high-pitched cries ensued as they proceeded to murder one another upon the altar of their false god.

The Waves of Bermuda

In the middle of a vast, endless ocean, a small, single-engined aircraft slices through the thin clouds of a mostly clear blue sky. The seaplane is but a speck over a canvas of infinite water.

Dressed in a brown leather jacket and dark-colored cargo pants, the pilot of the vessel reads from a dashboard of moving dials. He glances out towards the ocean and observes the calm waters. He then removes a pair of bulky headphones from his head and tosses them onto the dash. The clink of the impact startles his co-pilot, and the man reaches over to comfort her with a gentle scratch behind the ears.

"Think we will find anything today, Lucille?" He says to a golden retriever who is strapped in the seat beside him. "We should be coming up on the spot shortly."

A few minutes go by as the man and his dog continue to sail over the Atlantic.

Using a lead pencil, the man makes a few marks on a paper map. The area surrounding the scratch is covered with small, overlapping triangles. Hanging beside the map is an electronic meter with a green circular display that pulses once every few seconds. A dozen blue rings make up a grid, and the image on the display is pinging something that is near. A red circle drifts across the grid and approaches the center of the image. The man then turns to face his copilot and says, "Alright, let's bring her down."

Slowly, the plane's altitude lowers until it is hovering just above the surface of the shimmering ocean.

"You're taking notes, right?"

Lucille continues to calmly sit in her upright position as she observes in silence.

The feet of the aircraft skim across the water, and the expression on the dog's face churns into one of tremendous concern. The man continues to steer with one hand, easing the dog's fright with his free hand. He rubs the fur of the canine's head and says, "You're in good hands, old girl. You know that."

Within a matter of minutes, the man and his dog are sitting idle in the middle of the Atlantic.

"Smooth as silk," the man comments as he unbuckles his seatbelt.

Taped to the corner of the windshield is a picture of a beautiful woman with long, curly red hair. Freckles cover her face, and her authentic smile radiates from the image. Inscribed on the corner of the picture are the words, *Live your life, Joel. We will meet again soon*. The man kisses a pair of fingers and then gently presses them against the surface of the image.

The man stands up, unfastens the tracking device from the dash, and straps it to a belt loop. He then reaches over and clicks in the release button of the dog's safety strap before venturing towards the back of the small plane. The dog hops out of her seat and follows.

"I've got a good feeling about this one, Lucille. I really, really do."

Joel places a hand on the hatch of the plane's door and gives it a twist. The door unlocks and opens to reveal the calm waters of a beautiful ocean. Sunlight beams into the open aircraft and the dog basks in the shine. The man inhales a breath of the cool ocean air. He smiles before working to remove his clothes. The dog stares in silence.

"It's rude to stare, you know."

The dog's ears perk up and Joel continues to undress until he is down to his skin and a pair of boxer briefs. He squeezes into a black wetsuit. When dressed, he reaches into a nearby storage locker. The man withdraws a vest, tosses it over his arms, and zips up the front. Strapped to the front of the uniform's chest are an assortment of items.

"Waterproof camera, knife, flashlight," the man double checks out loud as he pats down the items on his chest and ensures that they are secure. He then picks up his pants from off the floor and transfers the tracking device from his belt loop to the vest.

Four oxygen tanks hang on the wall directly beside Lucille. Joel pulls two of the metal tanks down and kneels with them to the floor. He fastens the tanks to a harness, and then screws a regulator system into them. Pressing a breathing apparatus to his face, he tests the unit with a quick inhalation of air before slinging the harness over his back and clicking it firmly into place.

Joel looks at a watch on his left wrist and takes note of the current time.

"Alright. You know the drill. Keep an eye on the plane, I'll be back in an hour."

Removing a pair of scuba fins from the storage locker, Joel slides them over his feet and waddles over towards the exit. He reaches over to a spool of rope that is bolted to the frame of the plane's door. Punching in a button below the spool, he drops rope from the reel. He ties one of the ends to a carabiner and clips it to his vest. He then grips the electronic display on his chest and turns a knob on the back of the meter. The image on the display enhances. The red dot is now off-center by a distance of three to four rings.

"Here we go," Joel says before taking a deep, calm breath.

He jams the apparatus into his mouth and jumps from the plane. Splashing into the cold waters, he lets himself sink freely for a moment before he takes off swimming down towards the murky depths of the ocean. As he swims deeper, the sunlight from the world above begins to fade and the temperature of the water drops.

Joel runs a finger over the flashlight that is strapped to his chest. It silently clicks on and light beams forward into the abyss.

A school of brightly-colored fish mindlessly drift by. Joel ignores them as he continues to descend for another six minutes. Air bubbles stream from Joel's mouth at a steady pace. Seasoned in the ways of deep sea diving, he is in perfect control over the rhythm of his breathing. He stops and raises the electronic meter so that he can read the display. According to the tracking device, he is swimming directly above the red dot.

The pectoral fin of a great white slices through the murky waters and Joel's spine tingles as fear manifests in the pit of his stomach. He places a hand flat against his chest and slowly wraps his fingers around the sheathed knife. An intense moment comes to pass as Joel fails to regain sight of the monstrous fish. He lets go of the knife's handle and continues his dive into darkness.

Joel comes to an abrupt stop as something tugs at his vest. The slack of rope that links him to the aircraft has run out of line. Without wasting a moment to second guess himself, Joel unfastens the carabiner that links the rope to his chest, and the lifeline drifts away with the underwater current.

A dim, flashing red light can be seen in the distance. As Joel approaches it, his eyes fixate on something greater. The light is pressed up against the side of a stone structure. With four sides and a triangular-shaped top, the structure appears to be the tip of a large obelisk. Joel activates the video camera on his vest and swims within reach of the red light. The radiating lamp belongs to an aquatic tracking drone that has a pair of pincers that are clinging to the stone. Joel reaches into one of his vest pockets and withdraws a small remote control. He clicks in a button on the remote and holds it down for three seconds. The light on the drone begins to blink, and then it switches from red to green. The pincers release their grasp and the drone begins to float up towards the surface.

Joel slips the remote back into his pocket and then looks back down towards the obelisk. He places a hand on the stone. The pillar's surface is smooth to the touch. The edge of a nearby corner is withered and rounded. Further down, markings litter the stone's surface. Joel lowers himself further and runs his fingers over the engravings, but the hieroglyphics are worn down by the torrential assault of eternity, and deciphering the code is near impossible.

As he continues to examine the obelisk, a flicker of light captures Joel's attention. He glances upwards to confirm that the drone is gone. He then looks below to where he thought he saw the flash of light. The ambient sounds of the ocean mingle with the insanity of absolute silence. The sounds obscure Joel's train of thought as he continues to scan the waters below. His flashlight illuminates the tip of a second structure, and Joel's eyes grow wide. Directly below his feet is the tip of an enormous stone pyramid.

Joel runs his light across the pyramid. Covered in barnacles and seaweed, the structure is larger than anything he has ever seen before. His sense of wonder collides with fear and excitement as his eyes confirm the greatest archeological discovery in modern-day history.

Through the depths, Joel again sees the flash of light that originally captured his attention but a moment ago. An electric current is running upwards from the basin of the pyramid. Joel watches the bizarre event unfold, and as he does, the pulse of light reveals the true size of the structure.

Joel places a hand on his mounted camera and ensures the lens is capturing the event. He then remembers he has failed to keep an eye on his oxygen levels. He glances at his watch and then holds one of his scuba valves up to his face. The indicator hand has sunken down into the red. The rhythm of Joel's heartbeat raises as he gives in to a temporary state of panic.

He glances up and immediately begins to work his way towards the surface. He tries to keep his cool and conserve his air as he swims up. His eyebrows squish together as notices that the water above is much darker than before.

Joel continues to press upwards until he breaks the surface of the water, he inhales the fresh air and lets out a tremendous sigh of relief. He looks at his gauge, which reads that he made it to the surface with some oxygen to spare. The near-death experience forces a grin on his face. His celebration is cut short as he realizes that the sun is no longer shining. He looks up to see that the clear blue sky has been slain by the dark veil of an angered god. Thunder roars in the distance, and visibility is shrouded by a wall of approaching rain. The plane is nowhere to be found through the obscured atmosphere.

"Fucking hell," Joel mutters with the apparatus still in his mouth.

The waves pick up and Joel fights off the current as he struggles to stay afloat and think. With the sun gone, his bearings are completely lost to the sea.

A wave devours the man with ease. It plunges him under and presses down upon him with the weight of a thousand stars. Joel opens his eyes as he is helplessly dragged under. The pyramid below flickers again. The discharge is slow, but the intensity is agitated. The illumination is powerful enough to brighten the ocean for as far as Joel can see. A school of viper snakes with fish-like heads wriggle and worm below his feet. Drifting beyond them is a colossal squid. The monstrous creature, a legend in its own right, sends shivers down Joel's spine as it motionlessly drifts through the perfectly still depths.

Joel glances towards the surface. He has sunken down far enough to be out of the harsh weather's reach. Kicking his feet, he rises back towards the surface. He breaks through to find that the approaching storm has come. The sounds of the torrential downpour is unending and apocalyptic in nature. Joel turns his head from left to right in a desperate attempt to find the plane, but the rain is thick like walls of stone.

Another wave takes Joel under the water's surface. Caught off guard, he breaks the seal of his lips around the apparatus and inhales a mouthful of saline water. He chokes and gags, all the while wrestling with the heavy wave. The pyramid below flashes once more as Joel breaks free of the current and rises again to the surface. He breaks through to find a clear, star-filled sky. The storm is nowhere to be found, and the ocean's waves are gentle and tame. A full moon shines overhead; it watches Joel from above as he spits out the apparatus and coughs up a mouthful of seawater with his weakened lungs. As Joel chokes down the night's cool, crisp air, he hears the distant sound of a dog's bark.

Spinning around in the water, Joel frantically searches for the plane. The omnipotent aura radiates from the pyramid below. Joel pinches his eyes shut as he is blinded by the flash of light. He blinks his eyes into working order to find that the moon and her stars are gone. The night has again returned to day. Feeling blinded and confused, Joel stares up towards the heavens beyond a blue sky.

The barking continues.

"Lucille?" Joel calls out as he is pulled from his mesmerized stare.

He glances towards the direction of the sound and spots the plane nearby. The retriever is standing in the open doorway and barking at him from the distance.

Confused and afraid, Joel dives forward and begins to swim towards the plane. His legs are weak and his stomach churns. His insides feel like they are devouring him from within. A white flash in the water suggests the pyramid is still pulsing below, but he continues to swim towards the sound of the canine's bark.

A wave slams down into Joel from his blindside and he is quick to wrap his lips around his breathing apparatus. He swims back towards the surface as another flash of light pulses from below. He fights his way to the surface and listens for Lucille, but only the heavy thumps of rain can be heard as they splash into the sea. Another storm has appeared out of nowhere, and a wall of rain shrouds any visibility forward.

A colossal wave devours the man; he kicks and rises to a stormless surface. As his head comes up out of the water, he notices the plane directly ahead. The surface of the aircraft is covered in brown streaks. The dog is hunched over and silent.

"What the hell?" Joel calls to the canine as he swims towards the plane's entrance. "You are supposed to let me know if we come into trouble," he adds with a hint of sarcasm, relieved to be back near the safety of the aircraft as another burst of light radiates from below the depths of darkness.

Fueled by a fear-induced adrenaline rush, Joel pulls himself up into the plane. The flooring is covered in water that sways with the waves that rock the plane from side to side. The stench of rot lingers in the air and sticks to Joel's taste buds as he struggles to breathe the noxious air.

"Lucille?" He calls, but the canine doesn't move.

Joel slips his arms through the air tank harness and drops the empty tanks into the ocean. His insides scream in agony and he feels weaker than before. His eyes close as his mind goes dark and he collapses to the floor. A moment passes before the man comes back to. He awakens, feeling weak with bones that scream out in agony under the weight of burning hot skin. In the corner of the aircraft lies a mound of wet, putrid fur.

"Lucille?" Joel cries softly as he crawls forward across the floor. His voice is distant and frail.

The interior of the aircraft is rusted, and water continues to slide across the uneven surface of the plane's floor.

Joel struggles to stand. He grabs hold of a rusty bar and pulls himself up on his feet. The bar snaps and the rusted metal slices through his wetsuit with ease. He loses his balance and stumbles towards the cockpit. Landing against a panel of levers and dials, he lifts his head to greet his own reflection in the windshield. The man staring back forces Joel to do a double take, and he reaches a hand up to a sun visor so that he can pull down a tiny mirror. The mirror is cloudy and worn, but Joel can see his reflection within nonetheless. The face of the man staring back at him is covered in dark liver spots. He slowly raises his hands to the edge of his wetsuit and pulls it down. His eyebrows have turned white in color, and the hair on his head is gone. Frightened, Joel looks to his hands. The veins along the backside are risen. The skin is wrinkled and uneven, like a deteriorating piece of crepe paper. The watch on his left hand has stopped ticking, and the sensation of warmth suggests that he is bleeding.

Joel tears off his wetsuit and glances to the gash in his side. His skin is wrinkled, and blood runs freely through the chasms of uneven skin. He raises his eyes towards the man in the mirror. The man staring back is well into the later century of his life.

Joel tries to form words, but he is speechless. He looks down at the dashboard of the plane. Most of the exposed bits of metal are completely rusted over.

"I don't understand," Joel forces out. His tone is brittle and weak.

His spine crumbles up and locks into an arched position as another pulse of light can be seen beyond the aircraft's window. His sense of fear devours his train of thought and his upper lip begins to quiver. He looks towards the faded photo of the woman for comfort. Lightning strikes the ocean in the distance and the object in the sea again flashes in the water. As it does, Joel's face shrivels up, and his insides succumb to the pain of oblivion. He lifelessly slumps over and falls face first into the dashboard before tumbling to the ground. As the plane continues to gently rock on the waves, the water on the floor washes over the decaying, motionless corpse of a man aged beyond recognition.

Creation Story

Locked away within the eternal darkness of a prison that we now call the universe, a young goddess by the name of Mikirhu lived for many eons on end.

Mikirhu had an older brother named Sakarah and a sister named Virshari, to whom her father's kingdom was promised.

Because Mikirhu's mother passed during childbirth, both her father and older sister had grown to hate the young goddess. It was only her brother who had felt sympathy towards the youngest born, and, as a show of this Sakarah would risk his life and sneak into the den of the blood god Luscious so that he may steal the souls of the damned. Luscious would collect these souls and feed on them, so taking from a god what he considers to be nourishment was a risky endeavor for Sakarah to partake in. Nonetheless, Sakarah would acquire the burning stars and pass them unto his sister. The stars would brighten her dark prison and keep her warm while she served out her sentence of exile and entrapment.

Mikirhu would often commune with the stars. She would confide in them and grow emotionally attached, but the souls of the damned made for diabolical company. While most of the stars had repented for their sins and merely existed as hollow shells of their former selves, there were some who clung to their identity of evil.

As the goddess discovered her own age of sexual maturity, her body, mind, and soul yearned for procreation. As if being locked within the confines of her eternal prison wasn't punishment enough, she now had to also abandon herself and the needs of her subconscious.

One of the stars, malevolent in its burning soul, took notice of the changes in the goddess's behavior. He began to whisper unto her thoughts of love, affection, and madness.

It didn't take long for Mikirhu's mind to break further. After spending a couple hundred years listening to the star, she finally gave into a radical idea that the star had devised- one that would serve to both free the star from its eternal damnation aflame, and also bear a child of Mikirhu's very own.

As per the star's command, Mikirhu reached out into the endless array of space and plucked the star from where it burned brightly. This she did with both ease and grace. It was as if the star was merely a fruit that was ripe and ready to be picked from a tree. With the star in her possession, Mikirhu used her free hand to spread the lips of her vagina. She carefully inserted the star inside of her and placed it within the protection of her womb.

In the coming months, Mikirhu's belly became warm, and a soft glow could be seen through the surface of her pale skin. She placed her hands over the warmth and then closed her eyes. For nine years she slept.

When the day of awakening had finally arrived, Mikirhu opened her eyes and remained perfectly still. Her stomach had grown to four times its normal size, and it was pulsing with a heartbeat of a child.

Overcome with joy and excitement, Mikirhu's face brightened with a smile that illuminated the darkness of her prison. She placed a hand aloft her palpitating womb. Through her skin, she could feel the face of the child, and in the coming days, she gave birth to a hideous infant that she named Tierra.

Blinded by elation, the goddess didn't notice the many imperfections of her baby girl. After Mikirhu spent a few months with her child, her brother Sakarah entered the prison. He came to warn his sister of the betrayal that had occurred in their father's kingdom. Their sister, Virshari, had forged an alliance with the blood god, Luscious, and together they murdered the king, thus claiming the kingdom for themselves.

Mikirhu didn't seem to care. She showed her brother what she had done and explained that she had found peace through the love of her newborn child. Sakarah was aghast to look upon the face of the infant. Tierra was a monstrosity. The child's skin was callused over, and at times, the infant looked to be in pain.

"Mikirhu," Sakarah said softly. "What is this?"

"This is the only thing that I have ever loved," Mikirhu explained as she pulled her baby close. The infant raked one of its stone-like claws against its mother's barren chest, and then it fed. "And this," Mikirhu added, "is the only thing to have ever truly loved me."

Sakarah could find no words to say. He knew that this was his fault. Gifting stars unto his sister was a mistake, and Tierra was a byproduct of that foolish blunder.

In searching for Sakarah, Luscious unexpectedly entered the penitentiary. He espied the souls of his collection that were now lingering in Mikirhu's prison.

"You have stolen from me," Luscious hissed. "I was under the impression that you were to heel to your newfound master."

Sakarah looked to his sister and her child. He then bit into his lip as he contemplated for a moment on the actions of the future. Without saying a word, Sakarah wrapped his fingers around the hilt of a blade that he wore on his side, and then turned to face Luscious.

"Careful, boy," the blood god warned. "Some mistakes cannot be undone."

Before reason could take hold, Sakarah withdrew his sword and plunged the blade into the chest of the blood god. Luscious cried out and returned the unwanted favor by driving a dagger into the back of Sakarah. Again and again Luscious gored the backside of his attacker until Sakarah's life faded away.

Holding her child close, Mikirhu watched as both men died. She saw that the entrance to the prison had been left open, and the light of her father's kingdom was shining in.

After spending a lifetime feasting on the burning souls of the damned, Luscious' blood had fermented into something volatile, and as Mikirhu approached the door, the stars within the blood god's body exploded.

For trillions of parsecs in all directions, the prison erupted with a devastating display of conflagration. Mikirhu was all but obliterated by the powerful combustion. When the brunt of the destruction had come to pass, she forced her eyes open only to discover that Tierra was nowhere to be found.

Mikirhu spent the next hundred years of her life drifting through the cosmos in search of Tierra. Not once did she abandon hope, and eventually her perseverance paid off. She found her child, but her discovery was not in the manner that she had hoped for. A group of stars had ravished the child, and all that was left of the infant was the charred remains of a lifeless corpse.

Mikirhu cradled the body of her deceased offspring. She hummed a song as tears ran down the front of her face. In time, both her and her child were sopping wet from the days that Mikirhu spent incessantly crying.

Losing her own will to survive, Mikirhu's life faded and Tierra, drenched in the tears of her heartbroken mother, was encased in a solid, thick layer of ice.

The souls of the damned ravished the body of Mikirhu - much like they had her child - but because Mikirhu's skin was soft to the touch, they also devoured her body and flesh. Eons passed and all that remained was the solidified corpse of the deceased baby girl.

A powerful star who went by the name of Ra discovered the preserved corpse of the infant. He felt pity for the child and knew of her story.

"Not all are ready. In fact, most are not," he said in regards to the child's mother.

He then spent a thousand years thawing out the ice that encased the dead infant. As the ice on Tierra melted, oceans came to be and the elevated portions of her rocky skin began to take form. The bacteria from her body multiplied and evolved. After millions of years, the land masses turned green and quickly grew lush with many forms of life. Many species of plants and animals alike came to be and flourish.

Astonished by what he had done, Ra grew warm with pride,

but the minor increase in climate scarred the planet's surface. The organisms that called Tierra home were fragile; in turn, they quickly died and withered away. With everything on the surface of Tierra dead, the only thing left behind was a barren desert wasteland. Heartbroken, Ra returned to his normal temperature. He thought that he had ruined his own creation, but in time the earth rebalanced once again into a state of lush, green life.

Throughout space, the fallout from Luscious' death was still in motion. From this, a small bone fragment once belonging to the blood god streaked through the sky and pierced through the tip of Tierra's soft cranium. Dust and dirt ruptured from the planet's fresh wound. The debris shot up into the sky and blocked out the light from the sun, from which heat was drawn. The planet began to freeze, and in doing so, everything died once more.

Ra waited for thousands of years for the dust to settle, and when it did, he discovered that Tierra was again encased in ice. He delicately warmed her and watched as life slowly returned to the surface of the hearty planet. This time, Ra maintained a balance to ensure the survival of life among Tierra, and this time, life evolved into a collection of complex organisms that were capable of both thought and emotion.

Ra couldn't quite grasp how this was possible, but he continued to observe in utter astoundment. At times, Tierra would quake. Her body would split open, and it was then that Ra came to understand the workings of life within her atmosphere. Tierra's heart was still beating; she was still alive. Trapped in an eternal slumber, the spawn of the great goddess was bleeding souls from her core. Those souls were inhabiting the organisms that called her surface home, and in turn, they were evolving into something more.

Today, Mikirhu's elder sister, Virshari, searches the cosmos for Tierra, and because of this, Ra keeps the child a secret.

For thousands of years, fellow stars have looked to Ra in awe of the secret that he has bore. They too have banded together in keeping the child hidden and safe. They tell of rumors that soon, Tierra will come of age. With her newfound strength, she will awaken from her eternal slumber, and she will rise.

Below the Depths of Darkness: Sea Witch

Aboard a large, wooden vessel, I sail west for the new world. Harnessing the power of the wind via three grand sails, the ship's design is truly extraordinary. It takes dozens of men to crew a ship of this size, but I am not one of them. Disguised as a girl of noble heritage, I have secured passage to Boston. When I make landfall, I will venture towards a town called Salem in search of someone that I used to know.

The coldness of my brown eyes and the pallidity of my freckled skin, along with its scars, are masked by affluent lace garments. How easy it is to deceive man by simply wearing expensive fabrics and perfume. I normally despise this sort of over-the-top attire, but it is a small price to pay given that which I seek.

Most of the passengers on this ship are stowed away below the deck like the taxable bits of cargo that they are, but not I. I grow sick of being confined, so I break the rules of normality and restriction. Much like their weakened souls, the laws and traditions of man can be broken by coin. So, while staying out of the way, I linger on the upper deck of the great vessel as we sail through the thick seas of the Atlantic.

A peculiar-looking man with his hair pulled back into a ponytail casually walks towards me, and I begin to feel sick with anxiety. Typically, I avoid contact with men and women alike, as I despise almost everything about them, but given the circumstances, I maintain my sense of cool and stay completely calm. Without saying a word, the man withdraws two red apples from a satchel and offers me one of them. In order to keep up with my charade, I accept the fruit and silently thank him with a nod. He leans up against a wall of rope and bites into his apple whilst admiring the great sails above that serve to carry us through the waters of the sea. I am grateful for his silence. I slip the apple underneath my veil and bite into the flesh of the fruit. The taste is juicy and sweet. Rarely do I eat, and when I do, it is nothing like this.

The ship sways as the seas grow rough. The man finishes his apple and turns to face the ocean. He tosses the core of the fruit into the water and then turns to leave, but not before looking into my eyes and smiling. Men are so full of themselves. They think that the way in which they carry themselves may serve to seduce a lady. For most women, that may be true, but I have no desire, need, or lust for a man. I entertain the thought of pushing him into the sea and watching his smug look dissipate into one of hopelessness, but surely those aboard would save him. Perhaps cutting his neck prior to pushing him in would guarantee that he sink rather than float.

The man leaves and I immediately begin to feel better. All is going according to plan until the moment arrives when - abruptly - things are not. Seemingly out of nowhere, darkness falls like a veil over the face of a bride-to-be, and the light of the sun begins to wither away.

As the air and the sea fall eerily silent, so too do the men of the ship. Some of the crew is seasoned in the ways of the sail, but even the hardy at heart appear to be uneasy at how quickly this storm has appeared. After a moment of awkward silence, the men begin commanding one another to fasten down anything and everything in sight. They are swift in their actions.

The winds pick up and begin to screech like a harsh violin being played in the hands of a man befallen to madness. A rope snaps and a barrel rises into the air like a weightless feather. It slams into one of the members of the crew, who is quick to be flung overboard and disappear into the darkness of the storm.

The men yell. Though they are within earshot of each other, their screams are muted by the crackles in the air as chaos quickly descends upon us.

Lightning strikes down into the sea. The flash adds contrast to just how dark it has become. Black fog surrounds us, and it is in this moment that I realize what is happening.

Waves crash onto the deck of the ship and rain begins to blanket everything on the surface. Many men are quick to lose their sense of balance. It is usually the noobies - the greenhorns - who are not accustomed to the rough seas of a tremendous storm. This time, even the most seasoned of veterans fight to weather the chaos. Poseidon's plans are currently in motion to claim the lives of them all.

The men sound off and repeat one another like a caged parrot who is desperately playing games for a treat. They are all looking forward as they shout, "Brace! Brace! Brace!"

I glance to the bow of the ship and notice a wave that is approaching. It is not like the others. It towers high up into the sky, and with every passing second, it grows even taller. I remove my veil so that I may see clearly in the darkness and witness the moment of our untimely demise as it arrives at our door like an unwanted guest. The tower is so massive that we find ourselves drifting through the shadow that the wave casts. A great wall of stone lies before us, and there is no stopping the collision to come.

As the tip of the ship pierces through the belly of the beast, wooden planks across the deck begin to vibrate and snap. Time is slowed as our fate is foretold.

Men scream and call out to their God to save them. How foolish it is to think that any deity would stand up to the might of Poseidon.

I continue to stare straight up into the eyes of the beast. It tramples and devours the ship as if the vessel were an unnoticed mouse in the unfortunate path of a titan. A gust of wind lifts me from the ground like an enchanted broom between my legs and I plunge face-first into the darkness of the sea. The water is frigid in the veins of death's cold embrace.

Of all the self-proclaimed gods who live among us, Poseidon is the most gluttonous in terms of murder. Perhaps it is his unmatched rage and strength that starves him of his stamina; thus, the depleted sea must feed. I too hunger. Fighting with this champion over even the smallest of table scraps is an exhausting excursion.

I open my eyes to see the light of the surface fading away as I sink fast into the depths of darkness. My body is paralyzed and I cannot move. Death has me in its grasp, and there is no escape.

The water is frigid and lonely. The further I sink, the more opaque the light of the sun becomes. The gentle push of the ocean's underwater current is the only sign of life in the murky depths of the abyss. The sun and its shine are forbidden from this plane of darkness, and that is a law that has stood firm amidst the test of time.

I begin to feel the pressure of the depths against my chest and skull. It is painful to the point where I wish to be dead, but life … is my curse.

The ambient sounds of the sea grow increasingly strange as the waters become eerily still. I sink further into the underworld until all light has faded. A hazy, red glow appears in the distance. The illumination gets bigger, and then splits into two. I soon realize that these eyes belong to one of Poseidon's many pets, and it is drawing near with great speed through the darkness.

Just as soon as the hateful pair of eyes swirls towards me, I am again engulfed in shadow. The beast has swallowed me whole. Its belly is a cauldron of tortured souls. I cannot see them, but I can feel their presence.

The water recedes within the belly of the beast, and I cough up liquid as I inhale the stagnant-tasting air. Death and rot linger within these walls of flesh and bone. I try to climb up to my hands and knees, but am thrown off to the side as the creature turns. I crash against one of the walls, and then slide back down until I land into a pile of liquid rot. I press my hands into the blight and try to lift my chest up, but my hands only sink further into the wretched filth. I can feel the bones of a rotten corpse within the heap of decay. It is the only solid object in the goo, so I wrap my fingers around the sunken cartilage and push myself up. A wave of rot splashes into my face as the beast makes another sharp turn. I fall forward into the stinking heap of blight before being flung towards one of the nearby walls. I tumble and slide back down to the ground, landing on my back.

"Is this my fate?" I whisper under my breath.

Stomach acids burn away at my skin like the fires of eternal damnation. The pain is unbearable, and the corrosive acid's sting sounds like a pit of angered vipers.

It is useless to fight it.

I remain silent in the darkness as I listen to the water slosh around the chasm of my foul prison.

My still mind begins to rot as time blurs by like the moments of a forgotten memory. Minutes turn into hours and hours to days, but the weight of eternity is ever knocking against the walls of my skull.

Seemingly out of nowhere, the beast comes to a stop. It isn't moving, nor is it swimming. The sounds of water and waves are no longer present. A faint light can be seen in the distance. We have surfaced.

I try to stand, but my legs are broken, and the pain I feel for soaking in acid for days on end is beyond belief. A gurgling sound echoes from deep within the belly of the beast, and the light brightens further as its mouth opens. I claw my way towards the distant light's shine, but a wall of acid and rot silently blindsides me. It carries me towards the light with great speed until I am thrown from the creature's belly out onto the stone floor of the surface world.

A deep voice can be heard conversing with the beast, but the words are adrift to me as I struggle to regain lost sanity.

Covered in goo, I try to lift my head and open my eyes, but the substance is too heavy. I wipe some away from my face and take a moment to muster some strength as I observe my surroundings. I am in a cavern. Roaring torches illuminate the chamber. The grotesque stench of rot lingers. I am sitting in a pool of vomit: a bath of partially-digested flesh and meat.

"What have you brought me, Nerites?" the voice bellows from above and my spine begins to tingle.

My eyes dart towards the speaker, and my suspicion is confirmed. Descending from a throne of coral and stone is a naked, muscular man. With a beard as white as snow and shoulder-length hair to match, this man is familiar to me. He is the self-proclaimed owner of the sea.

The man continues towards me with his cock swaying from

side to side. I glance away and am immediately filled with rage. My body is broken, and escaping this cavern is a folly notion.

"A mortal plaything?" The man bellows with a laugh as he draws near.

The sea creature, Nerites, is beached beside me. I read the hateful eyes of the monster. Its expression softens as it looks towards its master, and it backs away with a bow of its head. The beast is bound to its creator by the chains of a deep sexual affection: one of the strongest forms of mind control and loyalty there is.

"Rise, child," the man commands from above, but I continue to remain within the footprint of his shadow. My skeletal structure from the waist down is mostly gone. Only bits of battered bones remain within the casing of skin that comprises my legs and feet. Trying to stand is like building a home with the entrails of a jellyfish.

"You are in the presence of the great Poseidon," Nerites squeals with a phlegm-infused hiss.

The false deity places the palm of his hand against the basin of my neck. He then lifts me into the air and inspects my battered body from head to toe. As he does, I get a taste of his strength. It is beyond immense.

"It seems your beauty is false, Witch," the self-proclaimed god cackles as he runs a finger across a collection of open wounds that line my cheek. "Your skin is a disguise you wear that the sea has washed clean."

I flare my upper lip in anger and try to suppress the agony that is my existence.

"Ah, yes. There it is," Poseidon exclaims with satisfaction. "A servant of Lamia, I see."

"What gave it away?" My voice cracks as I break my silence.

"The forked tongue of a serpent belongs not in the mouth of a woman," he responds, twirling my head towards a crystal mirror along the cavern's wall. The wounds across my cheek allow for a perfect view into my mouth, where I flick my forked tongue against the roof of the orifice. A habit of anger.

"Well, then," Poseidon says as he continues to restrain me in the air like a head on a pike for justice served. "Let's set you free."

He then raises a free hand into the air and a high-pitched whistle ensues. The sound is not emitted from his mouth, but rather something else entirely is to blame for the skull-splitting tone.

My eyes bulge as I make the connection. I begin to panic and my mind races with thoughts of escape. Before I can come up with a plan, the incoming object appears. A trident, the source of Poseidon's power, darts towards its master. The air squeals and cries as the weapon tears through the cavern's humid draft. With his eyes locked onto mine, Poseidon catches the trident and lowers it to my face.

Unspoken words linger in my mind and a pact is made between the trident and me. The deal would sever my immortality like cold steel pressed to the belly of a swine should I choose to double-cross the living weapon.

My eyes weigh heavy. I am to become a tool of Poseidon. My immortality will be bound to the will of his trident. The weapon tells me that I am to seek out Aethiopia and ravage her shores in the name of Poseidon.

"You are hesitant," Poseidon observes out loud.

Through the trident, the god of the sea can read my thoughts. I try to mask them, but my deception fails at the hands of ultimate power.

"You are considering a way out," Poseidon exclaims. "You even think that perhaps my brother Hades will help you. Foolish serpent. You belong to me now."

Before I have time to react, Poseidon spins me around with one hand. His strength is greatly unmatched, but my mind continues to race for a solution. I consider my options as I examine the cavern, but before a play can be made, the self-proclaimed god presses the tip of the trident into the back of my skull. I jerk as my body falls limp against the weapon. I am not dead, for immortality is my curse, but I can feel the impalement of my mind. My skull splits open, and brain matter drools to the cavern's wet floor. I try to scream, but I am no longer in control.

My spine tears apart and I shed my skin like a cocoon in the spring. As my body births from its pod, it expands and grows. I hiss and growl as I endure the greatest pain that I've ever known. My muscle matter bursts like pustulant wounds, and I grow into something truly grotesque. With the body of a seal and the belly of a blubbering whale, I have grown truly immense. My face is that of a cuttlefish, and my mouth is lined with the jagged teeth of a tiger shark. My skin is scaly like a dragon's, and my new form is a tribute to everlasting agony.

"Now your form reflects your thought," the trident whispers.

Poseidon leans in to stroke the tentacles along my face. "I think I will name her Cetus," he remarks with a smile.

Nerites leans in behind the master. His expression is a mixture of disgust and fear. Fear that, come day's end, the master may end up admiring me more than him.

"You know what you are to do," Poseidon questions in a way that insinuates.

I bow my head.

"Excellent," the vengeful god exclaims. "Then go, Cetus. Wreak havoc on the shores of Aethiopia and bring warning of my arrival."

Nothing Poseidon says strikes my interest, but my will now belongs to him. I lower my shoulders and pay tribute to my god before dragging my heavy body towards the water. As I turn my back to Nerites, I can feel his piercing stare. It penetrates the scales along my back like the sharp knife of a fisherman who is preparing a meal. The bottom of my belly scrapes against the cavern's stone floor, and the stinging pain of faint cuts can be felt. I wince, but continue towards the water in my less-than-desirable new form.

I have been reborn. Bound to my master, I submerge myself into the saline waters and venture forth. I am a ligament of my father's will, and I will serve.

Strange Places

Five dwarves, short and stout, gather around the warmth of a roaring campfire. All of the attendees have neatly groomed facial hair: beards that curtain their necks and thick mustaches that curl up around the edges of their plump cheeks. The men bring with them magnificent steins and genuine smiles. They sit on logs and drink ale as black as the clear night sky above. Within a matter of minutes, the gathering is ripe with laughter. Each of the five men wear a ring on the index finger of their left hand. The rings are carved out of wood, and each bears the symbol of an ancient order- a league of cartographers.

"Alright," one of the dwarves chuckles. "Enough imprudence. Let us begin while the moon is still young."

The men quiet down and listen. Some refill their steins with ale from a nearby keg, while others pull in a little closer to the fire.

"Who wants to go first?" One of the stout men calls.

The dwarves look amongst each other for a moment, and then a fire-headed man, largest of the five dwarves, speaks up with a grumble. "I've no quarrel with leading the night."

The rest of the dwarves look to the red-headed speaker and give him the silence he requires to tell his tale. The dwarf fiddles with a leather satchel and stalls before he begins.

"Well?" One of the dwarvish men complains. Dark scars run across the surface of his skin. His eyes are hollow and his expression is hardened. "On with it already, Gremmund!"

"Right," the fire-headed dwarf stalls as he continues to fiddle with his bag. "I spent most of the year on Monoclara. It's mostly a barren wasteland. Insects and sand dunes, you know? But deep within the ground resides something truly... awe come on, ye little bugger!" Gremmund loses his temper as he continues to fight with the contents of his satchel until his stumpy little fingers manage to withdraw a small rock.

"A rock?" One of the dwarves questions with a light-hearted giggle. "I find that most places have rocks in the earth!"

One of the quieter dwarves, sucking on the end of an oak-carved pipe, glances towards the chipper dwarf. No words are spoken as smoke billows from his mouth and shrouds his face. Silence again befalls the group. The piper looks back towards the large dwarf and gives a subtle nod.

"Not just a rock," Gremmund is quick to continue. "This boulder lives!"

The group looks to the rock in Gremmund's hand. Round and still, the rock appears to be no different than any of the others found on the ground beside the fire.

"Have you gone mad?" A bug-eyed dwarf wearing a pair of oversized goggles questions with an honest heart.

"No. Have a look," Gremmund says with an offer of the stone.

The awkward dwarf lingers over towards his larger peer and accepts the rock. Using his massive goggles, he examines the stone with observant eyes.

"By Mother's fury," the dwarf says in astonishment as he continues to look over the rock. "This one lives!"

The group gathers close and the stone is passed around as Gremmund continues to tell of its origin. "They are born of the earth and grow to the size of mountains. I don't know how long they live, but my studies have led me to believe hundreds of millions of years isn't out of the ordinary."

"That is truly something," a light-skinned dwarf comments as he fiddles with the rock. The stone moves in his hand as it appears to gently breathe.

"As magnificent as they are," Gremmund continues, "their way of life seems to be in danger. The planet's atmosphere is dying, and as it does, the minerals that provide these mountains with nourishment are leaking out into space. There is more work to be done in order to find the cause, and I plan on returning to Monoclara prior to embarking on my next expedition."

The dwarf with the pipe is the last to see the stone. He observes the rock through a conjured cloud of smoke before returning the rock to Gremmund.

"Incredible find," the scarred dwarf concludes. "So, who's next?"

"I'll have a go," the softer-toned dwarf with light-colored skin proclaims as he raises a finger into the air. The others shift their attention towards their upbeat peer as he clears his throat. "I spent most of my year on Omega-Nine. It's a fascinating planet that lies on the outer edge of the Salorian system." His words are soft but quick. "It's filled with many strange creatures: insects, plant life, intelligent beings, and even aquatic abominations! All of the Omegas are unique, but nine is by far the most active in terms of advanced lifeforms. As is the case with the other planets in 'er system, Omega-nine is rather young, and as such, most of the intelligent lifeforms are tribal in nature."

Gremmund quietly tucks his rock back into his satchel as he listens to the smaller, younger dwarf tell his tale.

"I spent a good deal of time studying one of the tribal races, a bipedal group of nomadic hunters. Similar to many other young races, this group lives in an age of stone. They use simple tools and have a rather basic understanding of life and the universe beyond their borders.

"Did you speak with them, Brumdrus?" The scarred dwarf questions.

"Course not!" The young dwarf says with a gasp. "I merely observed from afar. Anyway, one of the more fascinating observations of these people is the way in which they perceive birthing, age, and procreation. The people of Omega-Nine don't celebrate the day of their birthing, but rather, they celebrate the day of their conception within the mother's womb.

"So the day that the mother and the father conceive a child?" Gremmund asks.

"Precisely," Brumdrus confirms. "Procreation isn't a private or emotional event for them. It's a community spectacle that occurs thrice per month. The tribe gathers in an area they refer to as the eternal hunting grounds and then, from there, they sing and dance while many men take turns sharing a single woman."

"An orgy," the big-eyed dwarf with mechanical goggles gasps, coughing up a mouthful of ale.

"Yeah," Brumdrus says with a naive grin. "Sex isn't taboo or secret. It's celebrated and open. A different woman is honored to fulfill the role every three months and-"

"Nobody wants to hear your tales of infidelity and smut!" The scarred dwarf interrupts. "This is only your third year here, Brumdrus, and again you bring us tales of obscenities!"

The light-skinned dwarf finishes his ale and then smiles. "Well, I'm only telling the truth in what I've seen." Boisterous laughter erupts from the group as Brumdrus refills his stein. He then looks to the scarred dwarf and says, "What of you, Balryl? What've you seen on your travels this year?"

The fire's reflection can be seen in the glossed eyes of the scarred dwarf as he stares into the heart of the flames. He glances around to the other members of the group. They are silently watching him as they sip their ale and wait for his response.

"Oceana-Twelve," the dwarf begins in a raspy tone. "We already know much about the aquatic planet, but because of its toxic oceans and monstrous creatures, we dare not dive into the depths of darkness: thus the secrets of her inner depths remain mostly mystery."

"You actually went?" Brumdrus inquires with a curious expression.

"I did not," Balryl confesses. "I projected."

"You left your body?" The bug-eyed dwarf gasps.

"Aye, I did, Grilmor," the speaker acknowledges. "Had to if I was to break the surface of the water. The oceans are laced with toxic gases that seep into the pores of your skin and liquify ye' insides within minutes. On top of that, the pressure of the depths... strong enough to crumble a mammoth down to the size of a pebble."

Gremmund winces as he visualizes the scene.

"But water and vapor molecules often distort a projection," Brumdrus raises. "How did you break the surface of the water?"

"He entered another vessel," Grilmor assumes and Balryl nods.

"It wasn't easy at first. Everything you've ever known begins to feel like a lie when you're living in the skin of another. In time, I grew used to the vessel, so much so that I began to forget what living as myself even was."

"What vessel did you use?" Brumdrus inquires.

"A rather grotesque sea creature of sorts," the scarred dwarf answers, his voice echoing from within his mug as he chugs more of the alcoholic liquid. "A strange cross between a cuddle fish and a seal."

"Did you override or coexist?" Grilmor pokes.

"I coexisted."

"What does that mean?" The red-headed dwarf, Gremmund, asks the rest of the group.

"The pineal gland is a stargate," the dwarf with goggles explains. "You can project yourself from yours into another, provided the target is of lesser intellect. Once within, you can either overtake the subject's mind, or you can coexist within the pineal. If you coexist, you become the creature, but you refrain from having control over the vessel."

Balryl nods.

"Difficult thing to do," Grilmor continues. "Also, the mortality rate is far from ideal. It's *very* rare that someone astral projecting returns to tell the tale."

An awkward silence befalls the group.

"There was a time during my stay that I thought I'd never leave," Balryl admits. His words are heavy as he confesses this deep hardship. "Anyway," he lifts his head to face the group. "Collected a lot of data on the creatures of the depths, the ocean floor, and how the toxic gases are pumped into the sea. I have drawn a hypothesis on there being a biomechanical society that lives under the planet's crust, and I think that it is their waste that is the source of the toxins that leach into the ocean. I won't know for sure until I return to the planet for another year's study."

The group says nothing as their eyes wander to and from one another. The possibility of their friend's demise is a very real thing that lingers in the air like a living wind.

""Grilmor," the scarred dwarf calls.

The bug eyes of the dwarf with goggles glide over to greet his peer in silence.

"I believe it is your turn," Balryl informs.

Nodding, Grilmor begins with a crack in his voice. After clearing his throat, he recapitulates his disquisition more clearly. "I ventured out to the Plertaox star system where I made some interesting observations of the local fauna. If you count moons, there are fourteen planets in the system with plant life."

"Let me guess," Brumdrus rudely interrupts with laughter. "You are going to tell us that, for over a year, you simply watched grass grow."

Balryl is quick to silence the imprudence with a piercing, cold stare. No words need to be exchanged between the two dwarves for the point to be made.

"Sorry," Brumdrus apologies. "Had a bit too much to drink, suppose."

"Well here," Gremmund roars as he hands the pale dwarf another full mug of ale. "Have some more!"

The dwarves laugh and even Balryl can't maintain his serious expression for long as he too breaks into a chuckle. Grilmor maintains a polite smile on his face as he waits for the commotion to die down, and then he continues.

"Now then, the ecosystem varies greatly across all of the heavenly bodies, and as such, the plantlife *should* differ from location to location. That, however, is not the case. Not only are the plants of similar nature and design regardless of the planet that they call home, but also there is only one single, invasive species that stakes claim across all of the available territories."

The silent dwarf with a pipe continues to puff as his eyes focus on the speaker with the utmost concentration. No other dwarf within this group is more observant than the quietest of the bunch.

"I was lucky enough to witness the eruption of a supervolcano on one of these planets," Grilmor adds with a grin. He manipulates a slider switch on the side of his mechanical goggles and the lenses glimmer as an electronic component within the frame digitally focuses the dwarf's vision. "Such a rare treat to see firsthand. What tipped me off to the pending event was the fact that the plants, viny by nature, climbed away from ground zero prior to the event's trigger. This suggests that the plants are self-aware and intelligent enough to understand what is and isn't a threat. This isn't something new, but what's really interesting here is how the plants *mourned* the loss of their dead. Collectively, across the globe and other celestial bodies that they called home, the plants suspended all fruit production so that they could redirect their energy. For a week straight they vibrated and emitted a toxic gas from their vines."

"That's pretty wild," Gremmund comments after popping a handful of shelled nuts into his mouth.

"Hey, you got any more of those?" Brumdrus whispers as he leans in towards the heavyset dwarf.

Gremmund reaches into his pocket and withdraws some more of the peanuts. He offers them to the pale-skinned dwarf.

"Hush now," Balryl growls.

"That's not even the weirdest part about it," Grilmor picks up where he left off. "I've found a mountain on one of the planets. It isn't made of stone, though, rather it's a massive, living, breathing plant structure. I have a hunch that it serves to home the matriarch. I believe that these plants may very well be part of a group hivemind: a collective consciousness shared across the entire species."

A cold breeze washes over the camp as the night reaches out and whispers.

"Here's where things get really weird," Grilmor adds with a smirk. "There are many different types of animals spread across this system, but none of them are advanced."

"Because they're stupid?" Brumdrus giggles and Gremmund grins from ear to ear.

"No-no," Grilmor corrects as he plucks his goggles from his head. "Rather, they aren't allowed the time needed to adapt and evolve." He wipes the lenses with a cloth before returning them to his eyes. "The plants bear fruit and the mammals consume that fruit. Humans, apes, mammoths, cats, and more. All consume, but none have the stomach acid to properly break the vegetation down, or at least not entirely. The seeds take root within the stomach of their host like a parasite."

Gremmund looks to the nuts in his hand as his face wrinkles.

"The seed sprouts and the plants begin to leech nutrients from their host. The vegetation spreads through the intestines and slowly eats away at the body's organs. Be it liver failure, heart failure, or any other means, the mammals die at the hands of the plants that grow within them. The vegetation doesn't stop when the host is dead, either. It ruptures through the skin and consumes the body right down to the bone in a matter of years."

"Morbid," Gremmund gasps.

"So these mammals, they must reach sexual maturity at a very young age," Brumdrus assumes out loud and Balryl rolls his eyes.

"They do," Grilmor confirms. "In fact, it's almost rather sad to see how these animals are robbed of a full lifespan as they are forced to consume the plants that ultimately kill them."

"You'd think that the mammals would evolve in a way to properly digest these plants," the quiet dwarf speaks from behind his pipe.

"Agreed," Grilmor says. "I think that under normal circumstances, we'd see just that; however, the plants are smart enough to alter their own genetic code. They are always one step ahead of the mammals that consume their vegetation."

"That's insane," Brumdrus gasps.

"It's unsettling," Gremmund adds. "That's for sure."

"It's self-preservation," Grilmor corrects. "The hive adapts to ensure procreation within the host bodies."

"I wonder how the plants originally spread from one planet to another," Balryl, considers.

Grilmor nods as he reflects on the comment. "It's a great question. I have theories, but Lord of Forge knows it will take many years to prove or disprove them all."

"What's one of them?" Brumdrus inquires.

"Well..." Grilmor stalls as he begins to feel foolish for the proposition that he is about to give. "Again, it's only a theory, but maybe the plants allowed a species of mammal the opportunity to evolve to a point of interstellar travel? They could then hitch a ride to anywhere they like, and from there, they could spread."

"Interesting theory," Balryl comments with a slow nod of admiration.

"But, yeah," Grilmor shrugs. "That's what I've got on the year."

The group takes a moment to refill their drinks and empty their bladders. When they reconvene, all eyes fall upon the quietest dwarf of the lot.

"I suppose it's my turn, then," the dwarf begins as he puffs a mouthful of smoke from his wooden pipe.

"Yes, Morduhr," Grilmor says with a smile. "I'm eager to learn of what you've seen."

"I ventured out towards the edge of the Milky Way cluster," the dwarf begins. "Perseus formation to be precise."

"Perseus?" Balryl confirms. "You went to Terra-Sixteen, didn't you?"

Morduhr nods as his upper lip twitches and releases a plume of smoke from the ridge of his mouth.

"We are banned from going there," Balryl states.

The group says nothing as an awkward silence washes over the camp. After taking a sip of his ale, Morduhr continues.

"I remote-viewed a trio of human families across the planet. Despite geographical differences, war had staked its claim over the lives of each and every one of the three families."

"As is the nature of the planet and its inhabitants," Balryl points out.

"With chaos came death," Morduhr continues without missing a beat. "Death led to disease, famine, starvation, and an overall sense of hopeless throughout the lives of *every* family." He puffs on his pipe as the words settle among his peers. "In ten months' time, a single war evolved into two wars, and two into three. It didn't take long for man to forget what exactly it was he was fighting for."

The dwarves share a serious expression as they ponder the tragedy.

"Still they fought - even under the banner of a forgotten cause," Morduhr explains. "Now we all know the importance of our order. It is our duty to preserve history, and what I've witnessed over the course of a year is a testament to the importance of our work.

You see, today, life on this planet is no more."

"No more?" Grilmor gasps with a foam-covered beard as ale drips down the front of his face. "What does that mean?"

"It is exactly as it sounds," Morduhr clarifies. "Man didn't just kill one another for ten months straight. The conflict reached a point where weapons were used that eradicated nations and vaporized continents."

"Trees, bugs, fish?" Brumdrus stutters with his mouth hanging open as he trips on his words.

"Everything. Gone." Morduhr snaps his fingers. "In the blink of an eye."

Grilmor turns his gaze to the fire, where he reflects in silence.

"We've witnessed many extinction events," Morduhr continues, "be it at the hand of a dying star, comet collision, bacteria or fungi takeover. The list is pretty long, but what's most troubling here is that this one is by no random act or natural imbalance or takeover... this event has occurred because of the ignorance and hate that lies within the hearts of a single evolved race."

"Humans," Gremmund draws the line out loud.

"Yes and this is the reason that contact is forbidden," Balryl clarifies.

"Because they can't be trusted," Brumdrus adds with a frown.

"Because it's like clockwork, and it happens every single time." Balryl presses a thumb against a deep scar across his left eyebrow and gently rubs the skin. "Man cannot evolve beyond its industrial age. It's really our only saving grace."

"That's actually not true," Morduhr injects softly and the group collectively shifts their gaze back towards the quiet dwarf with a pipe. "It hasn't been confirmed, but there is talk of a blue planet in the far reaches of space where man has broken beyond the industrial age."

"Fairy tales," Balryl groans.

"Could be," Morduhr agrees. "But rumor has it that the men who walk this planet have made it into the digital age, and if that's true, well... I just don't know... it's either an encouraging sign for things to come or ... it's something that's truly horrific..."

Abram Orlav

A small, awkward-looking boy with a broad set of shoulders and lengthy-looking arms climbs up over a mound of smoldering rocks. His pale skin and black hair is covered with a thick layer of dust. Fire claims victory over the horizon, and smoke veils the evening sky. It's hard to tell for sure, but the ruins of destruction look to be the remains of a once great city. Behind the boy is a labyrinth of metal pipes that protrude out of a collection of shrapnel and stone. Ash and dust covers everything in sight.

Reaching the top of the mound that he is climbing, the boy begins a descent down to the other side. He loses his footing and falls face-first into a heap of jagged rocks. The weight of his awkward figure adds to his momentum as he continues to tumble down the mound of debris. He tries to regain his balance but fails. The boy is wearing a backpack, and as he rolls to the ground the contents of his bag fall out. Antibiotics, medical supplies, and cans of food disperse in all directions across the ground. As he slides to a dusty stop at the bottom of the mound, he smacks his face against a large hunk of metal. Had he landed but a fraction to the left, a shard of shrapnel would have pierced through the boy's face. He opens his eyes and his pupils dilate as he fixates on the sharp edge of the shrapnel before him.

After collecting his thoughts, the boy sits upright and spits out a mouthful of blood. His body cries out in agony but he quickly presses on. He scoops up the goods that he has dropped and secures them within his torn backpack. As he begins to walk forward, he sticks a couple of his dirty fingers into his mouth and tries to comfort the pain that he feels. He withdraws his hand from his face. Pinched in between his index finger and thumb is a bloody tooth. A thick trail of blood and saliva is quick to drip from the side of the boy's mouth. His hand, covered in dirt but a moment ago, is now painted red.

It wasn't very long ago that the boy's father had taught him about the value in blood. *If life were a game of chess, blood would be king. It stains and claims over all else. It is the single universal language of all of Earth's creatures.*

"No one understands death, but everyone heels to blood," the boy reminisces out loud.

The words live within his mind as if they are still being spoken today. It is impossible to remember the phrase without also dwelling on the actions of his father that followed.

The boy reflects on the memory for a moment. He could see his father's angered eyes looking into the pit of his very soul. The words came from his lips just moments before he drove the head of a pickaxe into the skull of an unarmed man. The muffled screams of the man race within the mind of the child as he reflects on the kill that his father had forced him to watch.

"This is what we do to traitors, Abram," his father had said on that October night of many moons past.

A pair of high-tech hellcat fighter jets streak across the sky. As they hiss and squeal overhead, the boy's mind is forced back into the present. He is sharply reminded that he must continue to make haste on his journey home. He zigzags down an alleyway of rubble and picks up his pace as explosions can be heard in the distance.

By the time the boy reaches his destination, the blood on his fingers is dry and covered with dust. He slows up on his jog as he approaches a warped sign that reads 'Moscow Metro.' He then walks into a hole between two heaps of rubble. Once inside the ruins, he approaches a wooden door and pushes it open. Fine bits of debris shower his head from above and he steps inside.

Through much destruction, the ruins have taken the shape of a small cavern home. There is a makeshift table on the far end of the room that is constructed out of plywood and scraps of oddly-shaped lumber. A metal burn barrel sits in the corner beside the table. Above the barrel, lodged in the cement, is a massive pipe that serves as ventilation for when a fire is lit. Along the back wall is a pile of wood. In the opposite corner is a stack of canned goods and a broken filing cabinet with clothing stuffed into the drawers. With a mattress on the dirt floor and a bucket of dirty water beside it, the area is both shelter and home.

The boy glances from one end of the room to the other. Wooden beams have ruptured through the cement of one of the room's walls. He walks over to a blue tarp that is hanging from one of the beams and pulls it back. It leads into another section of the home. The remains of a broken cot linger in one of the room's four corners. A dirty old mattress is pressed into another corner, and an old broken dresser lies directly beside it. A crimson red patch stains the center of the mattress.

The boy takes off his backpack and sets it on the floor. He then walks over to the dresser and withdraws a book of matches from his pocket. He strikes one of the matches against a brick and lights the wick of a worn-down candle. Shadows dance in the room as the candle comes to life. The boy then picks up a wooden pair of rosary beads. Dust falls from the beads as he wraps them around his forearm and sits down on the edge of the bed. He falls back with a heavy sigh, and in no time at all, he drifts off to sleep.

While he slumbers, the boy dreams of a steam-powered train. It accelerates along a track that wraps around the bend of a beautiful lake. Nestled in the heart of a valley, the lake plays host to an assortment of wildlife. With the reflection of the train glimmering in the water, the boy can see himself sitting in the driver's seat. He pulls down on a rope and the train's horn bellows through the valley. He sticks his head out of the cockpit and smiles as the fresh air washes over his face. A flock of birds flee from a nearby tree. In perfect unity, they sail across a cloud-free sky. Together, they are family. The boy watches them and then looks to the sun. The great star is out and shining its warm rays down over the earth.

"Abram," a faint voice calls out.

The words drift into the mind of the boy and pull him into the present. His eyes bolt open and he sits down on the mattress.

He is still alone in the room.

The boy stands to his feet and looks to a nearby wall. Doodled in chalk is the faded image of a rose. It is detailed in design. He leans in and presses his forehead against the image. The cold stone gently vibrates against his skin and rubble begins to shower his hair from above. The muffled sounds of explosions can be heard echoing in from above. The boy closes his eyes and then looks to the floor with a hallowed expression.

As the walls continue to vibrate, the boy reflects on a moment: a memory of the not-too-distant past.

The vision begins with himself entering the abandoned home, but this time it is occupied. The burn barrel is lit and a woman is standing over it, trying to keep warm. Hearing the boy enter the room, the woman turns to greet him. She is wearing the filthy scraps of a once-white linen dress.

"Abram," she says with glee.

Her face is brightened by the sight of her son. Her smile is the only thing of beauty or value to be found within the room.

"How was school?" she asks.

"It was okay," the boy says without much emotion. "Melina's district was bombed last night and the other kids think she is dead."

The mother's smile is quick to fade away.

"The Kuznetsov brothers have stopped coming to class, so now I don't have to worry about them bullying me anymore at least," the boy adds with a faux smile.

"How many are left in your class?" The mother asks.

"There are five of us now."

"What did you learn?" She inquires in a desperate attempt to lift the spirits of the conversation.

"Well," the boy stalls. "Mrs. Sokolov never showed up. Most of the guys left after an hour, but I stayed and waited."

"You stayed there all day? Alone?" The mother gasps with shock in her eyes.

"Yeah, well, I still did school work," Abram defends. "I went ahead and read up on World War II and how the battle of Stalingrad was won."

The woman raises her cheeks and nods. She tells her son that she is proud of him and that he is a fine young man.

"The world will need men like you when all of this is over," she assures.

The comment is lost on the boy as he fails to comprehend its significance. The words resonate with him and embed their way into his mind for use on a later day.

Abram's stomach growls. It is loud enough for both he and his mother to hear.

"Get a fire going," the mother instructs. "I will heat us up some beans."

Abram obeys his mother and heads over to the burn barrel in the next room. There are embers at the bottom of the makeshift stove that are still warm and glowing. Abram picks up a rusty, bent pipe and pokes the embers. Cinders rise from the barrel like the fairies of a tale that is no longer spoken. Abram's eyes soften as a smile forms at the edge of his mouth. Bound not by gravity or war, the cinders have been freed by his hand - liberated from the prison at the bottom of the barrel. Abram continues to watch them as they burn up and fade away. His smile returns to a frown and he sets the pipe down. He then picks up a handful of wood from a nearby stack. He places the kindling into the barrel and then uses the pipe to blanket the wood with embers.

The boy's mother approaches the table in the room with a rucksack in hand. She removes a single can of beans and a sheathed hunting knife. She then sets the can down and unsheathes the blade.

"Want me to do it?" Abram offers.

"No, it's fine," she assures him as she uses the knife to stab at the top of the can.

The silhouette of a man leaks into the room and captures the attention of mother and son. The bearded face of a man peeks in through the open entrance.

"Father!" Abram shouts as he rushes to greet the man.

"Hello, son," the man says as he accepts the warm embrace.

The man is outfitted in military garb. He has a rifle strapped to his back and grenades are draped across his chest. A pistol hangs from his side.

"Boris," the woman says half-enthusiastically.

"How are you guys holding up?" The man questions as he sets down a bag of gear and approaches the table.

"We are down to one can of corn and three cans of beans," the mother explains.

"Well, I can bring you guys more food in the morning," the man assures. "How about you, kiddo? How's school?"

"Good," the boy lies.

"Yeah?"

"Abram said that when he went to school today his teacher didn't show up," the mother corrects.

The man scrunches up his face as he tries to recall the name of his son's teacher. "Sokolov?" He says with uncertainty.

"Yeah," the mother confirms.

Her husband slowly nods as he processes the information.

"She lived in the Tverskoy District, didn't she?"

"I think so," the woman says.

"Entire thing got leveled in last night's air raid," Boris casually informs them as he withdraws a tin can of tobacco from one of his jacket's many pockets. "Egorov's wife can take over teaching," he adds as he opens the can and scoops up some of the tar-like tobacco with two of his fingers. "I will talk to them about it in the morning when I go over there for supplies."

"His entire class is down to just himself and four other boys."

The father jams the wad of chewing tobacco into his mouth and says nothing.

"Boris," the woman says softly. "When are we going to stop lying to ourselves?"

The comment serves to annoy the man like a stinging bee at the basin of his nape. His nostrils briefly flare.

"I will stay here with you," she says. "You know I will, but Abram, he deserves a future."

Boris turns his head to the left and flares his teeth. His expression isn't that of concern, but rather one of anger as his temper sizzles like the fuse of a black powder cannon.

"Brussels will take him," she adds. "They are starting a new education program for children and everyone is welcome!"

"Those pigs are just rebranding the new world order," Boris spits, breaking his silence. "I'll be damned if they are going to take my son and feed him through one of their indoctrination camps!"

"What about Poland?" She is quick to counter in desperation. "They are accepting Russian refugees. Please, Boris."

"His place is by his father's side," the man says calmly with his eyes now closed. He is trying not to lose his calm, but the fuse of his temper has already been lit. "He is coming of age, anyway. Soon he will help to fight off these scum."

"His education is important," the mother says as her eyes begin to water. She is desperate, but her husband is stone.

"He can stay home and learn. He has his textbooks."

"Boris, please-"

Before another word could be formed by her tongue, Abram's father slides an open palm across the face of his frail-looking wife. A crack can be heard in the bones of her face and Abram yelps. It is then that the boy's father remembers that Abram is standing in the corner of the room.

"Head off to bed, Abram," the man says coldly.

"But I am hungr-"

"Do as I say, boy!" The father roars, cutting off his son.

Abram looks to his mother, who has tears in her eyes as she holds the side of her face. She nods slowly and the boy retreats through the tarp. He then heads over to the corner of the second room and sits down on the broken cot. It cracks under his weight, so he is extra careful about laying back on it. He curls up in an attempt to capture the heat of his own body.

Pebbles fall from cracks in the ceiling and they shower the boy like a heavy rain. He opens his eyes but continues to lay still. The ground begins to tremble, and the sound of explosions boom to life outside. The muffled noises of destruction from the world above pale in comparison to the fight that ensues between husband and wife. Abram tries to tune out the argument, but it is difficult to ignore. He pinches his eyes closed as he listens to the scuffle beyond the blue tarp. Something breaks and then his mother begins to weep. The father yells. Sharp smacking sounds ensue.

The high-pitched crack of a supersonic bullet being fired from a gun echoes into the room and Abram's eyes bolt open. He pitches forward on the bunk and it caves in underneath him. Abram ignores the broken cot and rushes to the tarp. He pulls it back to find his father standing on the other side of the room. He is facing away from Abram and doesn't notice the boy enter the room. Hunched over on the floor is the boy's mother. She is holding her stomach as her stained dress turns red.

In a volley of incoherent Russian phrases, the father yells down upon his wounded wife. He presses the barrel of his pistol against the skull of the woman and continues to yell a collection of hateful words.

Abram's mind goes static as his emotions collide in a swirl of foreign thoughts. Giving into a primitive power, he rushes for his mother's knife on the table. It is still lodged in the can of beans, but with ease he withdraws it and then leaps towards his father.

"Get away from her," Abram cries.

He runs the blade across the basin of his father's spine before the man can react.

The father spins around and pulls the trigger of his pistol. He sprays the ground with three shots before falling to the ground. As his father squirms, Abram dives onto him and drives the knife into his chest. Fueled by confusion, frustration, and fear, the boy stabs into his father again and again until the man who brought him life is forced to embrace death.

With bloodied hands, Abram lets go of the knife and leaves it stuck in the chest of his father. He loses control of his breathing at the hands of a panic attack and climbs across the floor to his mother, who is paralyzed with a look of horror.

With swollen, red eyes, the boy cries as he looks to his mother for comfort. He helps her up to her feet and escorts her to her bed.

Bombs sound off directly overhead and Abram is pulled out of his vision. His eyes water as he grits his teeth. He begins to thump his forehead against the chalked art on the cement and the rhythm of self-destruction allows for a moment of clarity. Again, he focuses on a vision from the past. This one picks up a few days from where the last one left off.

Abram is standing over his mother's bed. Using chalk, he is drawing out the detailed image of a red rose.

"Is that for me?" The mother's voice inquires. Her question is followed by the sound of wheezing.

"Yeah," the boy says with a voice that is on the verge of tears.

"Because my name is Rose," the mother points out.

Abram forces a faint smile and nods.

"Thank you, Abram. It is beautiful," she admits as her eyes water and her smile protrudes like the sun through the clouds of a dark and stormy day.

"Come. Sit with me," she says softly.

The boy sits on the edge of the mattress. The dim candle beside his mother's bed illuminates the corner of the room.

The woman struggles to raise her hand to the boy's face. She is dripping in agony and the gesture only adds more pain. She gently runs her fingers across the child's cheek and forces a faint smile.

"You must go," she says softly.

The words detonate tears in the boy's eyes. He begins to sniffle and tries to open his mouth, but his lower jaw quivers a bit and he is quick to clamp his lips tightly shut.

"Press on, my son. You are destined to do great things," she reaffirms before succumbing to an intense coughing fit.

"No, I am not," the boy chokes out as tears stream down the front of his face.

His mother lifts her cheeks and tries to smile. Her attempts to comfort her son are a well-played charade.

"I have seen it," she says calmly.

Abram gasps as he struggles to prolong an oncoming panic attack.

"You must get to Brussels, Abram," she says with certainty. "Get into a school and never give up."

Abram shakes his head as he tries to breathe.

"Listen to me, Abram," the mother orders softly.

The boy regains control of himself and looks into his mother's broken eyes.

"The time will come when God will speak to you," she continues. "The Lord will call for you, Abram, just as he came to Abraham and Moses." In watching her son cry, she too gives in and allows the tears in her eyes to silently fall down the front of her face. Regardless, she continues to speak with a sense of confidence. "One day, he will ask you to carry the weight of humanity's salvation on your shoulders. You must be strong. You must answer the call when the time comes."

Abram wipes his eyes and tries to process the information.

"But how will I know?" He asks, his voice cracking under the strain of fear and helplessness.

His mother returns her hand to her chest and closes her eyes. She winces in pain as she begins to yelp like a puppy who is lost at sea.

The boy's pupils dilate. He is frozen: stuck in place, watching as his mother dies.

Abram's mind drifts back to the present and he opens his eyes. He is alone with his head against the cement wall. With his eyes open, he watches as a tear cascades from his face. It falls into the abyss of rubble and stone below.

He raises his arm and pulls his mother's rosary beads up close to his mouth. He then presses the symbolic tool of worship up against his chapped lips. For a brief but significant moment, he knows peace as he is comforted by the lie of his mother's presence.

Abram lifts his head up and looks to the chalked image of the rose. It is now distorted and mostly unrecognizable. With tears in his eyes, the boy presses the palm of his hand up against the image. The wax of the lit candle runs out, and the light fades away. Alone and in the dark, the boy cries as bombs continue to assault the surface world above.

In Bloom

A girl is led down a lowly-lit hallway. She is being escorted by someone whose identity is shrouded by a dark cloak. The usher's face is covered by a mask that appears to resemble the face of a lion. As she follows, the girl stares at the floor with a set of eyes that are a little sunken in, and despite trying her best to maintain an optimistic-looking facial expression, she is not very good at being a liar.

Beneath her black dress and pale skin resides a soul who is tormented by the reality in which she lives. Day in, day out - her life is built upon a fabricated truth, and as such, the foundation of her soul has never quite been whole. If a home is constructed atop a basin of stone to ensure its structural integrity remains intact for decades to come, this woman, though true at heart, lives in a house that sways from side to side when the wind blows. And now... the season of storm has arrived.

As the lady presses forth through the corridor of cold stone, a dim torch brightens the side of her face. She has tried her best to forget her hunger: that which brings her to these lonely halls. Weak and malnourished, her exhaustion and unease is on display like the expression of a lie on the face of someone who is truly naive at heart.

As it has many times before, her mind cracks under the pressure of starvation and she is forced to remember why she has given into temptation and come to this place.

The two stop at a massive wooden door. The escort places a gloved hand against the entrance and pushes it open. With a loud creak, the door swings and the usher gestures the woman inside. As she steps in, the masked man closes the door behind her. She flinches in reaction to the sound of a metal lock being engaged on the other side, thus trapping her in.

The woman continues forward. The dimly-lit entryway leads into an enormous room with a marble floor. Though her bare feet are cold, she is warmed by astonishment as she gazes across the grand room. With ancient paintings framed on the stone walls and assorted artifacts belonging to the old world scattered beautifully about, the area is a testament to the spoils of conquest and greed. In the center of the room is an elongated table with a buffet of food strewn before a man who is sitting at the far side of the table.

As the girl draws near, she sees that the man is naked and gorging himself on the food that is prepared for him and him alone. He is sitting in a large golden chair that is upholstered with blue felt padding. The throne appears to be an antique from humanity's Victorian era.

The nude man is mouthing at a large leg of meat. He rips and tears into the flesh of what looks to be a cooked hog; bits of lard cake his fingers and drip down the side of his face. The oils find home within the crevices of his flabby neck. His bloated belly, lined with stretch marks, shines with the grease of many meals. The speed to which the man shovels food into his mouth outpaces the rate to which he can chew, and particles of his meal drip down, falling to his stomach and lap.

To the left of the man is a large television set on top of a portable metal stand. A live news broadcast is airing. Images of death and destruction are shown on the screen and a reporter begins to chime in with a bit of narration. "Spring is here again, and with it comes another round of peace talks between the UIGN nations and the rebel extremists who are hiding under the protection of the Russian Federation. As was with last year, talks got cut short with a bombing at a UIGN outpost today, and the Russian government was quick to condemn the act of terrorism."

More images are shown on the television; bodies trapped within a sea of debris look like ants who are stuck in molasses. Some are still alive, but escaping the wreckage that had befallen them proves to be an impracticable task. The video feed grants insight into a building that is on fire, and people- some being burned alive- are screaming as they flee out into the streets below.

The girl, now standing at the far end of the table, can feel the pain as those on fire seem to burn right through the screen of the television. "Well, Jake," the reporter continues, "The Russians are in a state of PR control. They don't want anything to do with these rebel groups, and who would? This behavior is cowardice and barbaric, but there is no question that a majority of the resistance is stemming out of Russia." A map of Europe is shown on the screen and a few areas are highlighted in red. A note in the corner of the image explains that the red areas are those where terrorist cells have strongholds. Russia has the most red pockets of any other country on the European map. "The attack today marks the third year in a row where a bombing has targeted peace talks. This time, an estimated six-hundred people were killed, but these numbers are early projections."

As the broadcast fades over to a commercial break, the naked man at the head of the table readjusts himself in his seat. He has moved on to inhaling little yellow pastries about as quickly as he can wrap his short, chubby little fingers around them. He then notices that the girl has entered the room. He stuffs one final pastry into his mouth before greeting her. Muffled by the food that he is chewing, he says, "Come a little closer so I can have a better look at ya."

The girl says nothing. She slowly walks her way towards the far end of the table. Her nose catches the scent of the food before the man. Her eyes drift towards the direction of the smell and her stomach begins to growl. She hasn't eaten in days. She is weak, but she tries to focus.

As the girl steps into the light, the large man reaches for a chalice; from it, he gulps hefty mouthfuls of red wine. His eyes are full of hate as he examines the girl's physique, and just as she begins to fear that he will not want her, he calmly expresses, "You will do."

The girl quietly exhales a sigh of relief. Though she is fairly attractive, she is also malnourished and exhausted. Darkened circles around her eyes make it seem as though she is wearing makeup, but she is not. She is far too poor to eat on a regular basis, let alone own nice clothing or fine cosmetics.

The girl shuffles forward and the man reaches out with one of his greasy index fingers. He brushes back her amber-colored bangs and observes her pale face.

"Pretty little thing," he observes out loud before reaching for a white grape and popping it into his mouth.

She can sense the fraudulence in his voice. His words are nothing more than a meager attempt at making the situation feel less awkward.

"Mmm," the man sighs with delight. "These are fresh," he adds as he begins to gorge himself on the grapes.

The girl's stomach growls, but she tries to stay focused. She knows all too well why she is here and figures there is no reason in wasting any more time. She slips off the straps of her thin black dress and the clothing falls freely to the ground. As she unmasks her chest, the man begins to laugh and she is filled with doubt.

"What, no foreplay?"

The girl is unsure if he is serious about his inquiry. He didn't appear to hold much value in anything. He simply lives in the moment, and from what the girl was led to believe, her only task assigned for completion on this day was to be the recipient of this lord's seed.

The girl's glossy brown eyes remain still for a moment. She then begins to stroke her bare chest, but the man's attention drifts away. He begins to mouth at the grease that cakes his fingers. His attention span is that of a child, and he is now paying no mind to the woman and her attempts at seduction.

"Why don't you take a seat over there," he commands, gesturing to a filthy mattress on the floor. He then slides his chair away from the table. The throne squeals under the weight of the man and the wooden legs buckle.

The girl glances to the mattress and immediately tries to press the sight from thought. Once white, the bare padding is now brown with patches of red stained about. She obeys. Wearing only lacy underwear, she takes a seat on the grotesque padding.

The man groans as he lifts his bare ass from his throne. A

collection of dark scars cover most of his rippled gut. This man has been under the knife many times. In standing, he is winded as he shuffles towards the woman. His manhood is but a nub between his legs. It wiggles slightly under the pressure of the rolls that comprise his hairless gut. He quickly drops down onto the padding. His scaled knees absorb the fall and then he lunges forward and reaches for the woman's hips. He then proceeds to tear off the girl's underwear. The force in which he pulls at the cloth causes friction to burn her skin. She winces but keeps her sense of cool. The moment has arrived and her role has been called.

She leans in towards him and presses her lips against the basin of his neck. Covered in grease, the surface of his skin is slick as if wet, but she works her way up towards his chin and then mouth.

He is hesitant to kiss her. It is in his reluctance that the girl is reminded that there is no love to be found in this moment. She is merely here as an object to serve a purpose.

The man grunts as he shifts the weight of his body away from his knees and sits on his bare ass. Once comfortable, the man takes the back of the girl's neck and plunges her head between his legs. He lifts a roll of belly fat and presses her face further where she is greeted with the man's flaccid cock. The smell of the area is unbearable, but she accepts his gift with her mouth and works quickly to inflate his manhood.

"Yeah," the man sighs from above. "That's good."

Once hard, the man pulls the girl by the hair. She squeaks in pain as she is flung from his cock and cast down onto her back by force.

The man then proceeds to make strange sounds as he struggles to straddle onto her. Once in place, he slips his cock into her and then releases his weight into her. The bones of her ribcage are quick to crack under the tremendous pressure and she lets out a screech. The man ignores her cries as pain shoots through her nerves and she is stricken with a sickness. She vomits in her mouth, but with her lips firmly pressed together, she swallows her sick and tries to regain control of her mind. The man seems to be further aroused by her agony and she can feel the hardness of his manhood strengthen within her. He thrusts harder and begins sweating profusely. Droplets of stinking perspiration drip down his face and rain down onto her as she is baptized by the foul liquid of her lover's dampness.

She tries to suppress the thought of her misery and clenches her eyes tightly shut as the man continues to have his way with her. *It will be over soon,* she reminds herself as the man begins to snort like a pig that is excited about its chow.

The horror lasts for a minute or two, but every second of the endeavor feels like a lifetime as the scent of blood begins to linger in the air. He is tearing her apart: ravaging his toy with the cock between his legs, but as he releases his fury, he groans like a whale and collapses into the woman.

The beast of a man coughs up a collection of phlegm and discards it to the floor beside the woman before sliding his cock out of her and standing to his feet. Sweating and out of breath, the man says nothing as he wipes his brow and glances down on the destruction he has caused. With a blank face that tells of nothing but exhaustion, he simply returns to his throne, gripping his chest. He exhales loudly as he sits and spends a moment regaining his breath before returning his attention towards the television with a slab of meat in hand.

The woman cannot feel the prostatic fluid that is deposited between her thighs. She knows that it is there, but she is troubled by the severity of a throbbing sting. Her hymen has been torn in a slaughterous sort of way. She winces, trying to mask her pain, but it is overbearing on her senses and she succumbs to a faint cry.

The girl rolls over onto her stomach and her ribs throb in agony as she slowly moves. She tries to suppress her cries, but her body is broken. She remains silent while tears flow forth from her face. In a desperate attempt to ease her agony, she places a hand between her legs. Wincing in pain, she quickly withdraws her hand and looks at her fingers, which are now painted red with fresh blood.

The great door to the banquet hall is pushed open and the man wearing a lion mask enters. He approaches the girl and then reaches down to help her stand. She whimpers as he touches her, but -nonetheless- she stumbles to her feet. As she rises, she moans and grips her side.

The usher takes one of the woman's arms and wraps it around his back so that he may better help the girl to walk. The girl freezes at the sound of droplets splashing to the marble floor. She looks down to see that she is leaking blood like a human faucet. Her eyes bulge and her upper lip begins to quiver. The escort drags the girl along as tears run down the side of her cheek.

As the two make it to the door, the girl looks back. She has left a faint trail of blood behind that leads back to the mattress. Preoccupied with his food, the grotesque man does not watch her go.

The usher leads the woman to another wing of the castle. As they travel through a corridor of stone, they pass by a collection of jail cells. Each cell is occupied by a stranger. All of them are either eating or sated. With swollen bellies, all of the strangers bear a child. None of them make eye contact and the unease that the woman feels forces her to look away. She stares at the stone floor as she continues to limp with the escort down the corridor until, at last, they reach an unoccupied cell. It is a small, windowless room with nothing more than a cot for sleeping and a hole for excretion. Some may call it a jail, but in truth, she has come to this place by choice.

The masked man extends a hand gesturing her inside, and she obeys. She steps in and a cold draft wafts in from behind her. The door is shut and the loud, mechanical sound of a lock engaging echoes within the chamber.

For nine months, the woman is confined to the room. Twice a day, a healthy assortment of fruits, vegetables, and meat is brought to her chambers. Her eyes would often roll into the back of her head as she consumed the delightful collection of food. For nine months, she is fed well. She doesn't have to hunt, nor does she need to beg. She doesn't have to plant, nor does she need to sow. All she has to do is exist within her cell and host the growth of a child that she will never know. She abides by the rules and allows her belly the time that it needs in order to grow. In time, her stomach inflates to the size of a pumpkin, and she spends her time alone whispering in the dark. The only company in her endeavor is the gentle kick of a child against the walls of her womb. Faint cries of forgiveness are muttered and she soon comes to regret the pact that she has made.

The cells are organized in such a way as to conceal one's neighbors. Often, though, the woman hears the cries of childbirth. It echoes down the corridor like tormented souls searching for a past that no longer exists. She watches the masked man take the newborns away. Concealed in cloth, the faces of the children are never exposed. A few days after a birthing, one of the women will shuffle by. Hollow and broken, the women are escorted to see their master. They return a few hours later only to be sealed away for another nine months. They exist within reality to serve their God, and bearing children is the currency for a night's stay in this palace of pleasure.

A few more weeks pass and then the woman awakens from a feverish dream to the feeling of something wet between her legs. She has soiled herself, but it is not urine she finds in her sheets. Her water has broken and contractions begin. For eight frightening hours, the woman painfully struggles to birth the child. With no guidance or help, she grits her teeth and squeals until the moment of birthing ensues.

She pushes and screams, then opens her eyes to notice the masked escort lingering in the shadows beyond the cell. Sweat beads down her brow and she continues to work in delivering the child until she hears the faint cry of a newborn.

With tears and sweat pouring forth from her face, the woman lifts the child from between her legs and pulls its naked body up close to hers. She forces a smile and a laugh escapes as she examines the innocent face of the newborn. She wraps the infant in a small blue blanket and then cradles him close. For a moment, she is filled with guilt. The fate of the child was decided long before it was ever conceived. She has given birth to a lamb who is destined to be slaughtered.

A mechanical lever is pulled and the door of the cage is unlocked. The masked man steps inside and reaches for the child, but the mother pulls away. Cast in doubt, her mind races for a solution.

The lion mask tilts in an eerie-sort of angle as the usher cocks his head in disgust. "The payment has already been made for the organs. The price of one's redemption is the life of another."

She glances into the glittering blue eyes of the child. Its innocent eyes linger, and it is clear that the infant holds no knowledge of its surroundings. The child is trying to form sounds as it fights to hold its young eyes open. It yearns to gaze upon its mother, but it is too weak to maintain any sort of stare.

"Okay," the woman says as her eyes begin to tear up. "I will buy this child."

The masked individual retreats into the hallway and then gestures for someone to accompany him in the cell. An old woman shuffles in. Her skin is wrinkled and her hair white. Within her frailty exists the rare appearance kindness.

"This one is free to go," the masked escort explains from where he stands behind the old woman.

The mother extends her hands and presents the child. With a nod, the elderly woman accepts the infant into her arms, but leaves the blue blanket in the mother's hands. The child begins to cry, and the old woman gazes into the eyes of the mother. Her expression is one of sadness and despair.

The masked escort withdraws a dagger from beneath his cloak and steps forward. He quickly severs the umbilical cord that links the infant and its mother. The old woman then simply exits the room with the child in hand.

The mother's tears begin to stream down her face as she drops the blanket to the ground and watches her baby go. The escort, with dagger in hand, flips the blade around and offers the handle to the woman. She reaches out to accept the blade.

"Avoid the harvestable organs," the man orders in a raspy tone before taking a step back and observing in silence.

The woman runs the tip of the blade gently across her index finger. The skin is quick to split open and bleed. She watches as blood runs from the fresh wound like a river undammed. Her cries begin to amplify until she shrieks out with a boisterous scream. The escort watches as she turns the dagger onto herself and plunges it deep into her stomach. As her legs buckle out from under her, she collapses to the ground and moans. Blood oozes from the woman's belly and seeps into the cracks of the stone floor. As her body slumps, she begins to breathe heavily. Though her will to survive is dead, her body struggles to live. Her eyes look past a tray of discarded food on the ground and focus on the blue blanket that served to warm her newborn child. As if catching fire via an open flame, the blanket absorbs the blood of the dying woman. Her heartbeat begins to slow and the blanket turns from blue to red.

With her eyes wide open, the mother's consciousness fades and the masked escort reaches down to the still corpse. He flips her over onto her backside and withdraws his dagger from her belly.

Wiping it clean against her torn dress, he sheathes his blade and exits the cold, dark, prison.

So Foretold

Alone and outdoors under the umbrella of a cloudy grey sky, a man sits at the table of a French cafe in downtown Paris. There is a cappuccino before him that grows cold alongside an untouched souffle in the center of a white plate.

The man is dressed in a slim black suit. Although he is sitting, his blazer remains buttoned. His mouth hangs open as if he is in shock. With a pale face and dry lips, he looks sickly and concerned. He remains perfectly still. His eyes are sunken in and out of focus. Although he almost appears to be dead, his mind is far from feeling quiet or deceased. Within, he can hear the screams of the damned. Millions of souls cry out to him in pitches so sharp that they cut through the man's nerves like Damascus steel pressed up against the flesh of a small child.

The world around the man is very much alive. People go on with their routine lives as they pass him by. Some speak on their phones, while others look to the ground and avoid eye contact with one another. Although the scene should be boisterous in sound, the man is deaf to his surroundings.

Seemingly out of nowhere, the man leans forward and grunts. Overcome with the dire sensation of needing to vomit, the man rolls his lips inward and tries to suppress the feeling. He fails and quietly spits up into his cappuccino. He wipes his lips against the sleeve of his jacket and then nervously looks from side to side. Through one of the cafe's windows, a young, albino-skinned boy stares at him in disgust. No one else notices and the man looks down to his cup. The liquid pulses as if someone was tapping against his table. As he continues to watch, the dark skin of a leech can be seen twisting and twirling in the cup of vomit and coffee.

The man is quickly distracted as his gut begins to swell and he winces in pain. He slips his hands under the cloth of his unbuttoned blazer. He then places his palms flat up against his bloated belly and tries to comfort himself.

The grey sky darkens further and the smell of sulfur manifests in the air around the suited man. He closes his eyes and raises his nose into the air. Some people stop in their tracks as they too are overwhelmed by the strange scent of hydrogen sulfide. His heartbeat is slowing, and his breathing is becoming increasingly loud. He tries to say something, but his tongue fumbles with the words.

A lady at the table beside the strange man glances over with a concerned look on her face. She presses her spectacles up against her nose before leaning in a little closer and saying, "Excusez-moi?"

The man's stomach grows increasingly bloated. His insides are pressing up against the basin of his spine, and this causes tremendous agony. He frantically works to unbutton his blazer and, in doing so, tears the top button completely off from the coat. The jacket's sides recede. He then tears open his white shirt and plants his hands over his bare stomach. He squeezes his eyes tightly shut and tries to mentally combat the pain that has arisen out of nowhere.

The index and middle finger of his right-hand twitch and his eyes bulge open in response. Slowly, he glances down to gaze upon his hands and stomach. The pupils of his eyes dilate as he comprehends the sensation that he has just felt in the pit of his stomach. A bead of sweat drips down through one of his bushy eyebrows. It lingers above his left eye for a moment before disengaging. The droplet plunges through the air and lands on the ridge of his left knuckle.

His heart skips a beat as he continues to watch and wait for confirmation. A moment goes by and then it happens; another kick occurs against his hands, and this one is far more painful than the last. Something is inside of the man and, whatever it is, it is moving. Losing control, he begins to scream as fear collides with pain.

Startled by the screams, a waitress drops a pan of porcelain teacups. They shatter upon hitting the stone floor. People stop and stare, but no one dares go near to help.

The man's eyes roll back into his head and his high-pitched screams take on a much deeper, coarser tone. He mumbles something that is completely incoherent. The words are harsh and sound like something out of an ancient dialect from long, long ago.

The man drops his jaw wide open and hunches forward. He begins to moan loudly. As the hairs raise along the backside of his neck, his incomprehensible babble morphs into words. His voice cracks under the pressure of a sudden anger as the words drift through the air like a pale horse dragging an old chariot.

"Mon âme! Ça brûle!"

Just as soon as the phrase is spoken, people within earshot begin to combust into flames. Screaming ensues as the stench of burning hair and bubbling skin wafts through the air.

Everyone not on fire begins to panic and scream. They flee in terror as the man screams out another phrase, "Épargne-moi de ce tourment!" His stomach ruptures and a beast of unimaginable terror rises from the open sack of flesh and meat. The man goes limp and drops to the ground. He is quick to die. The child that he has birthed stands to its feet and stretches. Its skin is like tar and its face looks like that of a moth. It has many extremities, all of which look like rotting flesh and drip a thick, black goo. Before anyone can really make out much more, it leaps forward and begins to devour anyone within reach.

After consuming a dozen or so bystanders, the creature opens its mouth and silently vomits a plague into the air. Visibility becomes blurred as locust swarms begin to frenzy. Some squirm their way into the mouths of the living while others press deep into the ears, noses, and eyes of others. That is where they begin to breed and lay their eggs.

People drop to the ground and dig at their faces.

Accumulating blood beneath their fingernails, they continue to scratch and dig at the orifices of their heads as they panic and succumb to madness.

Some of the survivors try to scatter like roaches under sunlight, but gravity has a new master now. Although they flee, they rise up into the air and fall back down towards the beast as chaos transcends the realm of science and reality.

The screams of terror continue as dozens of bystanders are devoured by the beast. Its power grows with each victim ingested, and soon even stone buildings begin to tremble under the power of its presence. A tremendous quake ensues and all of Paris crumbles into the earth.

The beast snorts and then screeches. Its sound is like nothing ever heard before. Sharp and piercing, it tears through the air and slices through all beings that can hear it. The skulls of animals and humans alike split from ear to ear. Within their own minds, the locust eggs burst and the larvae spawn dig their way to the surface of the skin. Once free from their prison, the maggots dine on the cuisine of dead corpses.

Together, the beast and its spawn feast. The stench of rot and death linger and dance as the scar on the earth spreads further across the lands and the seas.

In the blink of an eye, all returns to prevalence. In the streets, people pass by as they partake in their daily set of routines. It is as if nothing out of the ordinary has even occurred.

The man is still sitting in his seat at the table. His nose is hemorrhaging blood. He twitches before lunging towards a stack of napkins on the table. He frantically tries to attend to the severe nosebleed.

The man stands up and walks into the street, where he blends in and vanishes amongst the ranks of the crowd. Left behind at his table is his untouched food and drink. One of the crimson-stained napkins falls to the ground as he leaves. The clouds above begin to unleash an assault of heavy rains from the sky. As people scramble for shelter, they neglect to notice the napkin as it bursts into flames. Just as the red stain catches fire, it squeals like a pig being slaughtered; skinned alive.

Through the window of the cafe, the pale boy continues to

stare. His pupils are swollen and his eyes are obsidian marbles that bleed a concentrated ink. He smirks as his eyes return to normalcy. As lightning cracks across the darkened sky, the boy snickers and then disappears.

He Has Risen

The heavens darken as the sun turns its back on the earth.

The moon stays true to a blood pact that was made long ago. She plays witness and offers what little light she has as the drums of chaos and conflict begin to sound in the sky.

Lightning and rain assault the lands, and the earth begins to tremble in fear. The crust breaks and tears. Splitting like the dehydrated skin of a hairless mammal whose corpse has been left to rot under the blistering heat of an oppressive sun, the planet swells and cracks. Fire erupts from the wounds, and an endless sky of soot blankets all life.

The earth keels over in agony. As she tilts forward, the howling wind of the future arrives from the west. It withers away the relics of old as it washes over the land with the lungs of contention. Mountains crumble as the earth's skin is peeled back to reveal the pulsing heartbeat of a child within her womb.

The winds cease as frigid temperatures bleed from the sky. The heavens collapse under the weight of hell's expanse, and angels squeal in death as the thumb of oblivion smears their flesh against the planet's surface like paint to the canvas of eternal damnation. The rains turn to ice, and lakes become solid as stone.

Devouring his mother's insides, the child escapes from the womb. The mother dies giving birth to her son. Her lifeless body separates as the beast of gravity and chaos rises to sit upon the throne of creation.

An endless sea of devils and demons bow before the one true king.

Within minutes, all life on the blue planet has been put into perspective. No longer are the insignificant creatures of history in control. Their lies are scrubbed from the slate of eternity in the blink of an eye. It is almost as if they never existed at all, but the moon plays witness to the events of the past. She will live on to tell the tale of man and its ultimate creation: the birth of the allfather. Through chaos and sin, he is born. The antichrist has risen.

The Wolf Who Cried Man

The static hiss of a television set can be heard as a viewer flips through a series of mind-numbing channels. The flickering halts as one of the video feeds are given a second chance. The image on the screen depicts a deep blue sky, and the viewer is brought up over a mist-covered mountainside.

"Ah yes," an unseen narrator speaks. "Lavera."

The mountains are painted green, and the inner workings of life within the foothills are obscured by a sea of plants and fog.

"For the better part of a century, the Marcuda clan has called the forest-covered mountains of Lavera home."

The scene cuts away to the inner workings of a small forest town. Bipedal wolves glance towards the viewer with welcoming expressions.

"Lavera is renowned for its seclusion. A living sanctuary."

A flock of doves wash over the sky and a grey feather twirls in the air as it falls from one of the birds. Warping with the feather, the scene transitions into the image of colorful leaves being blown in a late autumn breeze.

"Encumbered souls, looking to get away from their hectic urban lifestyles need not look any further than Lavera. Give yourself the gift of felicity, and wash your soul in the calm waters of tranquility. Book your trip to Lavera today!"

A grey paw fiddles with a remote control. The television shuts off and the reflection of a wolf can be seen on the inactive screen.

***

A silver-haired wolf entered the confines of a beautiful cabin. He dropped his backpack at the door and had a look around. The cabin was warm and welcoming. Designed with minimalist expectations in mind, the retreat possessed very little in terms of furniture or clutter. Only the necessities were included in this temporary home.

The wolf walked outside and inhaled a breath of fresh air. With a smile on his face, he approached a small hammock and climbed inside. Swinging from side to side, he removed a pair of reading glasses from one of his front pockets and fixed the spectacles to his face. He then returned to the same pocket for a small, black notepad. The phrase 'An English Werewolf in Europe: The Autobiography of Lykos Migail' was scribed out across the cover. The wolf flipped through the pages until he landed upon one that was free of words. He then set the pad down on his chest so that he could look up towards the sky above.

A cool breeze gently rocked the hammock and Lykos couldn't help but close his eyes. The ambient sounds of the countryside were subtle and natural. The moment of bliss was simplistically beautiful, and the wolf felt the desire to live in these mountains for the rest of his days.

The afternoon turned to dusk, and the blank pages of the notepad remained untouched as Lykos nodded off into a peaceful slumber. He eventually woke up to the sounds of a growling belly.

The wolf reentered the cabin and looked within an icebox for something to eat. The expression on his face was that of disappointment as he closed the lid on the box and exited the cabin.

Making way towards a small town, Lykos approached the

staircase of a small shop. A meat cleaver carved into a wooden sign hung above the shop's entrance. Pressing his way inside, Lykos was greeted by another wolf - this one with peppered fur and glossy white eyes.

The shopkeeper was restocking a glass counter with an assortment of meat. A pair of skinless rabbits hung from the ceiling above via twine.

For a moment, Lykos drifted out of his body as the hunger in the pit of his stomach dictated where his thoughts may lead. Licking his lips, he tried to compose himself, but failed.

"You've got a little something," the shopkeeper said, motioning towards the rim of his own mouth.

Lykos broke his uncomfortable stare with the meat and reached up towards his snout. His fur was sopping wet and he had been unnoticeably drooling on himself.

"First time here?" The shopkeeper questioned as he reached for a wet rag and cleaned blood from his paws.

"Yeah. I arrived earlier today," Lykos admitted.

"What brings you to the mountains?"

Lykos wafted in the rich scent of exotic blood as the butcher stashed his red rag under the counter.

"I am working on an autobiography," Lykos confessed. "The fresh air helps to clear my head."

"A writer, you say?" The shopkeeper asked with a peaked sense of interest.

"Well... not really," Lykos confessed. "This would be my first and only title."

"But you are writing it yourself," the butcher complimented. "That's impressive, no?"

Lykos nodded as he considered the words. Most books of the modern age were written by ghost authors. It was always cheaper and faster to purchase written words from another than it was to compose your own.

"So what do you think?" The butcher asked. "Of the mountains?"

Lykos widened his eyes and nodded his head in awe. "I've never seen anything as breathtakingly beautiful."

"I hear that," the shopkeeper agreed. "I thank Fenrir every day that I'm blessed to live another day in this sanctuary." The twinkle in his eyes conveyed the truth in his statement. After a short pause, he continued, "So, what'll ya' have?"

"How about one of those rabbits there?" Lykos questioned, nodding up towards one of the hanging carcasses.

"Sure thing," the butcher said with a smile as he reached for a stool and climbed up into the air. "Anything else?" He added as he untied the rabbit and climbed back down with the lagomorph in hand.

"Not sure. Perhaps you have something I've never tried?" Lykos questioned as he looked towards the glass counter, where an assortment of exotic meats were on display.

"Ah, yes. Always embrace new things," the butcher said with a smile as he reached for a sheet of wax paper. "Let's see here... you've got an English accent, so I'm sure you've had your fair share of fish and lamb?"

"I have," Lykos chuckled with a smile.

"Have you ever had sapien?" The butcher asked as he tightly wrapped the skinless rabbit within the sheet of wax paper.

"Can't say that I have," Lykos admitted with a raised brow. "That was outlawed for a while, wasn't it?"

"Yeah, endangered species" the butcher admitted. "Little shits can be violent sometimes too, so they can be a challenge to raise. Legal here, though. My brother runs a farm out in the plains. Feeds them a drug that keeps them nice and docile while raising them."

The butcher placed the enveloped rabbit on the counter. He then walked down towards the far end of the glass enclosure, and Lykos followed.

"They are supposed to taste similar to pig, no?"

"They can be fatty," the butcher nodded. "But if raised right, you can get cuts more along the lines of steak."

The shopkeeper reached into the case and pulled out a strip of meat. Blood dripped from the filet as he withdrew a fine blade from his belt and sliced a piece off one of the steak's edges. "Here," he passed the sliver to Lykos. "Give it a try."

Lykos accepted the gift and sniffed the meat. The exotic scent was divine and he wasted little time in devouring the chunk of muscle. Immediately, the wolf's eyes rolled up into his head and his expression reflected bliss in its purest form.

"Pretty good, right?" The shopkeeper said with a chuckle as he returned the filet to the glass display.

"By Mother Moon," Lykos gasped, savoring the juices in his mouth as he continued to chew the meat. He swallowed and then nodded. "Alright." Closing his eyes again, he reflected on the ecstasy of the moment. "How about a full leg?"

"Sure thing. Preference in breed?"

"Preferably whatever that was," Lykos said in reference to the trial he had ingested. "What about loin cuts?"

"I am all out of veal," the butcher confessed with a frown.

"Yeah, I wouldn't know the difference anyway," Lykos admitted.

"Veal cuts come from the younger sapiens," the butcher explained as he disappeared into the backroom for a moment. "The meat is lighter in color and more on the tender side," he shouted from the backroom.

"Yeah, doesn't matter to me," Lykos muttered as he licked the paw he had used to hold the meat just a moment ago.

The strong scent of sapien wafted in from the backroom and Lykos sunk a canine into his lower lip. He picked up the wrapped rabbit carcass and then pressed his snout against the packaging. Inhaling the scent of the lagomorph, he tried to press the thought of the sapien from his mind.

"How's this one?" The butcher asked as he popped his head out from the backroom with a leg in hand.

Lykos set the rabbit back down on the counter and wandered over towards the butcher. With wide eyes and an open mouth, he marveled at the sight of the muscular limb.

"Thing is bigger than *my* leg," Lykos gasped.

"Aye," the butcher said with a smile. "My brother really knows how to raise them."

Lykos silently nodded.

"So I'll just go ahead and wrap this up for you?"

The wolf continued to nod as he forced a smile. His mouth watered and he found it hard to speak.

"Alright then," the shopkeeper chuckled as he returned to the back and proceeded to wrap the meat.

Pressing the thought of hunger from his mind, Lykos spun around and glanced down at the floor. The wooden planks below were withered and scuffed.

"How long have you been in business around here?" Lykos asked in an attempt at small talk.

"Shop has been passed down for many generations," the butcher called from the back.

"Decades? Century? Millenia?" Lykos offered as he began to fiddle with his paws.

"My family has been around these parts since the founding of Lavera," the shopkeeper said, now standing directly behind Lykos.

Lykos jumped, startled by the silent approach of the butcher.

"Great grandad loved to smoke his meats. Ended up burning the damn shop to the ground at the turn of the century. The only thing left standing was the foundation, so these walls aren't really that old."

Lykos nodded but ignored the words as his eyes fixated on the wrapped leg in the butcher's hands.

"That gonna be it for you?"

"That'll do. How much do I owe ya'?"

"Notta," the butcher said with a smile. "They set you up with an account phrase for your stay, right? Everything gets tallied and charged to your account when you leave."

"Ah, that's right. Reaching for oblivion."

The butcher scrunched his snout up, confused by the phrase.

"My account phrase," Lykos clarified. "An old book I'm rather fond of," he explained.

"Alright," the peppered wolf said with a shrug, jotting the words down on a receipt. He then plucked a yellow copy out from behind the slip of paper and set it on the counter before taping the original receipt to the wrapped leg of meat. "Rabbit's gonna be on the house," he added, handing both of the meats out for Lykos to take.

"Very kind of you," the wolf complimented as he accepted the meats with a subtle nod.

Lykos left the shop and scurried back to his cabin. The sun was quickly dropping over the horizon, and a chilly breeze accompanied him on his walk home. As he made it back, he entered the cabin and quickly rushed over towards the icebox. He deposited the packaged rabbit and then wandered over towards the fireplace with the sapien leg still in hand. The wolf set the leg down for a moment and got a fire going. Once the fireplace was lit, the cabin grew warm as shadows bled from the crackling flames. Lykos dragged a large chair - upholstered with red velvet - over towards the warm fire. Retrieving the leg, the hound took a seat by the fire and tore into the wax paper.

The wolf discarded the wrappings to the wooden floor and then examined his prize. The enormous leg was fresh, and the scent of the meal forced Lykos into a barbaric frenzy as he sunk his teeth into the flesh. Tearing off a chunk of tendons and meat, the wolf was suspended in a state of eternal bliss.

With a mouthful of flesh, Lykos mumbled a collection of incoherent words. Blood dripped from his snout and seeped into his fur. He closed his eyes and nodded as he chewed, swallowed, and returned for more. The exotic taste was so intoxicating that the wolf worked straight through the night devouring the feast until he was left scraping his teeth against the bare bone. He licked the cartilage until his tongue was raw and his belly was swollen. He then discarded the bones to the floor and slid down in the chair. Resting his head against the soft velvet, Lykos drifted off into a sated slumber.

The wolf opened his eyes to find himself standing on the edge of an open plain. Snowflakes gently fell from the sky and fresh powder littered the ground for as far as he could see. A skinless rabbit - alive, yet in agony- wobbled by and the wolf gave suit. Lykos embraced a feral lust as he dropped to all fours and gained speed. As the lagomorph weaved in-between shrubs, the wolf lost sight of its prey. He was left following a bloody trail in the snow.

Time melted inwards as the vision warped into a static plane. The cries of an animal could be heard, and Lykos turned his head to find a legless human hopping away from him. Unbalanced, the man fell to the ground and proceeded to sob into his hands as a river of blood ran freely from the open stub where his leg used to be.

Lykos licked his lips and approached the man, but as he drew near, a herd of naked sapiens attacked from out of nowhere. With makeshift knives and rusty blades, the humans brought Lykos to the ground. When the wolf was prone, the men and women pounced on top of him. They then proceeded to skin the wolf alive.

Pitching forward from his slumber, Lykos woke to the sound of himself screaming in terror. He gasped for air as his consciousness returned to the present and he struggled to regain control.

Panting, the wolf glanced around the room. He was still alone in the cabin. The warm embers of the fire had all but gone out, and a chilly draft whistled into the darkened home from thin cracks along the cabin's wooden walls.

Lykos stood from the chair and made his way outside. The fresh air washed over his anxiety and he looked up towards the night sky for comfort. The moon peeked out behind a veil of soot-colored clouds, and the wolf began to howl up to his goddess.

After spending some time in worship, the wolf retreated to the hammock and climbed inside for a night of restless slumber under the stars. His lingering thoughts of fright prevented a full night's rest, but when the sun came up, he pressed the horrific vision from his mind and tried to embrace the new day.

The wolf's stomach, however, began to growl, and he looked down to his belly with confusion. The taste of man was ripe in his mind and his stomach craved more.

"I just ate... twelve hours ago," Lykos huffed out loud to himself as he pondered the queerness of the hunger. He didn't eat often because he didn't have to, but his stomach continued to ache and growl as though he were starving to death where he stood. "Alright, breakfast then," he assured his stomach as he set forth towards the town.

Lykos licked the dry blood from his fur as he traveled back into town. He caught the shopkeeper just as the wolf was unlocking the door for open business hours.

"Back so soon?" The shopkeeper questioned as Lykos drew near.

"Yeah," the wolf giggled awkwardly. "Was a ... strange night."

"The sapien, how was it?" The butcher asked as he fiddled with the lock on the door.

Lykos kissed his paw and raised it in the air with a gesture that expressed his delight.

"Good. Glad to hear it," the butcher chuckled as he opened the door to the shop and gestured Lykos inside.

Lykos entered and the butcher quietly followed. The shop was cold and dark. The elder hound went around the open room and drew the curtains from all of the windows. The natural shine of light was bright and Lykos squinted, as his eyes had quickly adjusted to being within the dark room.

"Say, has anyone ever said anything about sapien meat inducing visions?"

"Inducing visions?" The butcher questioned with a furrowed brow.

Lykos silently nodded.

"Can't say that I've heard that one before," the butcher chuckled, walking behind the counter and tying an apron around his waist. "So, what'll it be this morning?"

"More of what I had yesterday!" Lykos blurted out, eager to get on with the purchase.

"Alright," the butcher smiled. "Same cut?"

"Traditionally, what are considered the best cuts?"

"Rack of ribs are good smoked or raw. The brain makes for a delightful stew, but it's fairly expensive. Fingers and toes are always a good snack food. Skin jerky and-"

"Yeah, sure," Lykos interrupted. "The ribs will do." He licked his lips at the thought.

"You got it," the butcher assured. "Single rack?" He added, gesturing to the left side of his chest. "Or full cage and breast?" He motioned towards his sternum and then ran his paws out across both sides of his torso.

"Full," Lykos spit. The kindness in his tone was no longer present.

The butcher went into the backroom, and Lykos began fiddling with his whiskers. He combed through them with his paws, but then as the agony of hunger lingered, he started to pluck at the ebony bristles. It felt as though he had been standing there waiting for a lifetime before the butcher returned with a hefty parcel. The wolf's eyes widened as he accepted his prize. Like a child, he cradled the package in his arms. He inhaled the sweet scent of the meat and a twisted smile formed across his face.

"Reaching for oblivion?" The shopkeeper asked as he placed the tip of a pencil down against a slip of carbon paper.

"That's right," the wolf confirmed. "No need for a receipt."

Lykos bolted for the door with his prize in hand. He wasn't

sure if he had thanked the butcher for the goods, but then also, he didn't really care. Nothing could be more important than returning to the cabin and digging straight into the sapien.

Lykos made haste with his journey back. Taking a shortcut through the yard of another vacationer, the crazed wolf waddled with his hefty prize at an awkward pace. Reaching his camp, he set the heavy package down on a nearby wooden picnic table. Continuing with the spirit of his frenzy, the wolf tore open the wax paper and withdrew the ribcage. The carcass had been skinned, but the breasts remained.

The wolf gazed upon the meal with lust in his eyes. A feral groan vibrated from his vocal cords, and he lunged down towards the table. Snapping and tearing at the ribs, he broke the bones and began stripping them of their savory meat.

Lykos continued to feast as the vibrant sun drifted across the sky. The bones were picked clean within a matter of hours and Lykos, still under the influence of an ancestral feral lust, had moved on to licking bloodstains from the wooden picnic table.

As the sun's shine withered, the wolf came down from his high. He sank to the ground and cupped his bloated belly. Famished, he closed his eyes as his mind sailed with the sun towards darkness.

A collection of incoherent whispers could be heard through the hazy fog of insanity. Lykos bolted his eyes open to find himself bound to a branch by rope. He tried to speak, but his mouth was gagged with an apple and a strip of tattered cloth held the fruit tightly in place.

A tribe of humans danced around a nearby bonfire and a man, wearing a wolf pelt, approached the subdued hound. With a wicked smile, the man spit in the wolf's face, and then the tribe approached. In a bizzare, ritualistic display, the men in the group took turns spitting on the wolf. When they finished, the women of the tribe took turns licking the wolf's fur.

Lykos watched in silent horror as the ritual continued, and then the men united in lifting the branch and the wolf. They moved the hound over towards the fire. Time skipped and agony ensued. Lykos had been skinned alive and his body was running red as he hung over the immense fire. The heat sizzled his muscle matter and he tried to scream, but his muffled sounds were drowned out by the roaring crackles of the fire below.

Lykos pitched forward howling.

He had awakened to find himself still on the ground outside the cabin. The midday sun confirmed he had slept clean through the night and his deep slumber had carried him into a new day.

The wolf rose to his feet and immediately ventured back into town. His better half questioned the horrific vision, but the need - the hunger - for more outweighed all reason.

The hound reached the town and approached the butcher's shop. He tugged at the door, but the entrance didn't budge. A sign on the door read 'closed for the new year.'

"The new year?" Lykos muttered. "The hell is that?"

The wolf spun around to see that the small town was completely barren. All of the shops were closed and not a single person was around.

Lykos growled as he pondered his options. There weren't many, and even if there were, he didn't dwell on the matter for long. He leaped from the shop's porch. Landing on all fours, he made haste towards the back of the shop.

The hound approached a window. After ensuring that the coast was clear, Lykos took three steps back, lowered his head, and then ran at full speed towards the glass.

The wolf broke through the window with ease. He landed on the shop's wooden floor and tumbled to a distasteful stop. As Lykos stood to his feet, shards of broken glass caked his fur. He ignored the inconvenient pain and glanced around the room. A collection of metal tables lined the walls of the backroom, and chains with hooked ends hung from above. The metal links swayed under the breeze brought in from the broken window.

Spotting a large metal door in the corner of the room, the hound scampered headfirst towards the vault. He threw himself against the freezer and then contemplated how exactly the handle mechanism worked. After fiddling with the doorknob for a moment, he managed to open the door, and a gust of frigid air blasted out from the walk-in refrigerator. Through the haze, a collection of fully-intact bodies hung from chains along the ceiling.

Lykos didn't bother picking a prize, but rather went for the closest corpse. He bit into the leg of a naked woman and wrapped his paws around her hips. Tugging at her body, he tore the corpse from the metal hook and dragged the body out of the freezer.

The wolf tossed the woman out of the window. He then exited the room, cutting himself further on bits of the window's broken glass as he took leave. Ignoring the wounds, the hound dropped to all fours and sunk his teeth into the body.

Lykos dragged the corpse over towards a nearby treeline. Fully intact, the sapien was far too heavy to carry all the way back to the cabin, especially given the circumstances of the hound's hunger-induced fatigue.

Once shrouded behind the camouflage of a tree and her saplings, the hound pressed his snout to the corpse and dug into his meal. Caked in blood and glass, the wolf worked through the day feasting on the body. Again, Lykos was suspended in ultimate bliss as he devoured the corpse in a feral fashion and, again, once the wolf had consumed his fill, he succumbed to a deep sleep.

Awoken by the flames of an inferno, the hound was transported into a reality of smoke and fire. Much like with his last vision, Lykos was still in the presence of the tribal folk, only this time, dinner was served. The tribe was surrounding the wolf and the fire. Twisted smiles were accompanied by the cynical sounds of hideous laughter as the tribe used their fingers to tear into the hound's flesh. Lykos tried to howl in pain, but his body was deceased and only his soul remained. Stuck within a motionless prison, the hound was subject to the torment for hours on end as his body was torn apart and consumed in full.

As the tribe finished devouring the wolf's core, the leader of the group approached. The wolf pelt that he was wearing seemed familiar, but through the chaos, Lykos couldn't place it. As the tribal leader glared down into the eyes of the deceased hound, a glimmer across the iris suggested that the man knew full well that the soul of the wolf lingered within the frayed vessel. The man said something in a foreign tongue and reached for Lykos. He plucked the wolf's heart from his chest like a ripe fruit from a tree, and the shackles of silence were lifted. Lykos opened his eyes and jolted forward, screaming as his mind exited one reality and entered another.

The hound was back to the present. He tried to scramble to his feet, but his muscles felt sore and he fell back against the basin of the nearby tree. He yelped in pain as he heard something snap and felt the sharp, piercing sting of a branch penetrating his backside. Darkness filled the sky as the night had arrived. Stuck leaning against the tree, Lykos glanced over towards the shredded corpse of the woman. Her innards were strewn out across the ground, and only a small portion of the meal was actually consumed.

With his chest rising and falling at a panicked rate, Lykos pressed his paws to his face and covered his eyes. He tried to calm his fear-induced sense of despair.

As the wolf struggled to understand it all, the sound of something ruffling through the forest captured his attention. The hound's ears perked up and his heart skipped a beat as he slowly removed his paws from his eyes. Standing in the distance was a cloaked figure. The intruder pulled back a green tunic to reveal a sheathed sword hanging from his waist. He then planted the palm of a gloved hand against the base of the blade's hilt. Lykos could hear the sound of leather being stretched as the figure slowly wrapped his fingers around the weapon's handle.

An authentic fear bled over from the wolf's visions as more cloaked figures silently stepped forth from the shadows. Writhe with panic, the hound's emotions took hold of his spine like a vice grip, and Lykos was frozen in place. He tried to form words, but his jaw was locked and his mouth felt like it was full of hardened cement.

The hooded figures simultaneously approached Lykos from all sides. The sharp sound of steel being drawn followed as the figures removed their hoods to reveal the faces of men and women alike.

The wolf's cries cut through the air as butchery ensued. The liquid sounds of overly efficient murder echoed out under the blanket of a howling wind, and a blood red moon shone down from the abyss of a nightward sky.

Reaching for Oblivion

A series of red LED numbers are counting down. With sixty seconds to go, I grow warm with excitement. I have been living in a dropship pod for the better part of two weeks. Alone, I've drifted through the coldness of outer space as my pod sails towards the unexplored planet of Kepler-62E.

The only acquaintances I've made thus far in my travels are the series of numbers on the clock before my face. I speak to these friends often, but they serve to be a poor form of company. They have burned into the core of my memory. I see them when I close my eyes. I think of them when I sleep.

Once I have completed my month's stay, I will return to the pod and a recovery drone will scoop me up. I will then spend another few weeks traveling back to Outpost Seventeen, where I will relay the information that I have gathered. My return is a dreadful thought that I bar myself from dwelling upon further.

The numbers on the clock plummet through the teens and the pod begins to vibrate as we enter into the atmosphere of the new planet.

I grit my teeth and close my eyes. An impractical praxis to think that blindness could somehow save me from a disastrous landing. Outdated human instincts.

The pod's vibrations quickly become violent as it continues to plummet.

"Three... two... one."

My feet sink into the floor as the dropship slams into the planet's crust. I jerk forward in my seat and groan. My harness keeps my body in place as my insides painfully shift within. The clock reads zero. I have landed smoothly. With no time to waste, the hydraulic door lifts and the air of my new world surges into the stuffy cabin of my pod. I am eager to exit and explore.

I slip out of my harness and stand to my feet. My legs feel like gelatin but - fueled by ambition and excitement - my strength is quick to return. I puncture the airtight seal of a storage locker and reach my hand inside. I have been given a backpack with diverse contents that are essential for my survival during the stay. Under the backpack is a magnetic rail gun. The rifle is military grade and should suffice in taking down even the biggest of game that Kepler-62E has to offer.

After slinging the rifle and bag over my shoulder, I exit the pod, but not before kissing my hand and planting my palm against the surface of the clock.

"See you soon, old gal."

The oxygen-rich atmosphere is pure. It almost feels synthetic. The planet's natural beauty is intoxicating. I am overwhelmed with a mixture of excitement and joy as I exit the pod's open door. The ground is blue and the grass purple. Lush like the Amazon of the old world, the landscape before me is a living, breathing ecosystem of estranged and wondrous diversity.

I have landed on the outskirts of a marsh where a small mesa meets the edge of a thick forest. I cautiously make my way towards the rocky plateau so that I may scout out the area from a natural vantage point.

There is an ambient hiss that drifts through the air as foreign bugs carry on with their daily existence. While this planet is unexplored by man, early scannings have detected a plethora of life.

A flock of birds erupts from a nearby tree. They look similar to crows, but the color of their feathers is a deep purple. Startled, I raise my rifle and disengage the safety with my thumb.

As the birds sail off and out of view, I am left feeling embarrassed for my moment of unjust cowardice. I re-engage the weapon's safety and sling it back over my shoulder so that I may carry on with a false sense of courage.

I reach the basin of the plateau and begin to climb. The rock is mostly smooth, withered by time, but there are many angles available for me to take advantage of when climbing, so I scale it with relative ease. Once I reach the top, I stand to my feet and take a moment to examine the horizon.

To the south beyond the marshlands, there are open plains under clear, bright skies. Directly west, a dense and colorful forest shrouds the land beyond with limbs and branches that reach for the sky. To the north lies a tremendous mountain range that the plateau leads towards like a clear path on a bright and sunny day. Lastly, to the east is more swamp, but unlike the colorful nearby marsh, the swamplands to the east are darker in color and rotting in stagnant lakes of water. The mountain's shadow alters the swamp's horizon in a way that darkens the view.

"Alright. Eeny, meeny, miny, moe," I say with a raised index finger to the wind, tapping it in the four separate directions.

I then leap across a minor divide in the plateau. Landing on a lower platform, I now have a clear path for miles north. My journey is mostly quiet as the sun slowly drifts through the sky. The days here are more like a three-day weekend back home, so I make the most of it and travel far.

I come across many bugs of queer shape and size. Beetles the size of a burly man's hand and ants with sharp, barbed backs are the common species to be found along my path. The terrain grows difficult, though, as the sun continues to sail and the path begins to wither. Jagged rock formations force me into some thorny brush. Unsure if the spines are poisonous, I make way through a patch of waist-high grass. Silence befalls the area as I notice that the constant hiss of insects has vanished entirely. I take caution to the warning and move slowly forward. A lingering scent of lemon is strong on the senses and my eyes search for the source, but nothing seems exceptionally out of the ordinary.

I walk for a few minutes before I notice something move in

the grass. I freeze in place like stone as I watch the bulb of a flower silently rise from its slumber. The flower's bulb rolls up from its stem and then blossoms into something horrific. The pedals are of a disorienting color combination and their innards are lined with jagged spikes. As I begin to understand the danger, the plant lashes out at me with a snip. I stumble backward through the grass where a second bulb rises. I back away and watch as both flowers reset back into a trap-like position. Once clear, I continue to stand perfectly still as I glance around the small field. The small bulbs can be found everywhere when I look hard enough. Perhaps more troubling is the existence of larger bells, bulbs the size of a man's head, scattered across the field and waiting for their shot at a meal. Goosebumps line my arms and I look back towards the way I came.

I slowly backtrack through the field, setting off bulbs along the way. I'm careful to keep a safe distance until I trigger one of the larger bells. Its speed is slow, but its face is immense as it lifts its head into the air. The petals blossom and I bolt, running with all the strength that I can muster. Plants come to life across the field's entirety as I begin to run. Then... the mother rises.

In the center of the field, a single bell towers over all of the other plants. I quickly piece together the frightening hypothesis that this entire field is a single-hivemind-being.

I don't bother stopping to examine further, but instead keep running back towards the plateau. A cluster of barbed spikes drifts past my head with great speed. Another bunch can be seen flying through the air and landing ahead of me. I cock my head to find that the mother is built differently than the rest of her spawn. She lacks petals and instead has enormous stalks and leaves below her tremendous bulb. Some of the stalks have pink, bushy tips that wiggle and worm as they fire arrow-sized projectiles towards me.

I continue to run, but am soon thrown to the ground, impaled by a volley of spikes. The grass flooring is dense and moving. I run the tips of my left hand across the backside of my right shoulder. The fingers don't go far before discovering the cluster of spikes that are embedded into my skin. I try to pull the knot out, but it's lodged too deep and I end up slicing the tips of my fingers. I yelp and retrieve my hand.

I'm fueled by adrenaline and I can feel the crash in energy as I linger on the ground, so I stand to my feet and continue my run as quickly as I can. I make it out, but don't stop running until I make it back to the plateau. The sun is beginning to take shelter behind the mountains, and a menacing shadow lingers over the horizon.

Panting and out of breath, I drop to one knee and lower my head to the ground. The pain of my wound begins to set in as the adrenaline fades. I withdraw a thin piece of carbon fiber cloth from one of my pockets and wrap the fabric around my left hand. I then reach for the cluster of bulbs in my back and pry them out. The pain is excruciating, but the organic matter gives way and slides out. I wrap the cluster in the fabric and then stash it away in my pack. The matter may be useful under the lens of a microscope.

I stand back to my feet, take a long, deep breath, and then laugh out of nervous habit. My shoulder aches, but the wound isn't deep enough to be of too much concern. A more pressing matter is the finding of wood so that I may light a small fire. I remove my backpack and rifle, then set them against a nearby rock.

Going back into the grass isn't an option, and the thorny nearby brush is too thick to hack through within a reasonable amount of time. I scavenge small shrubs from along the plateau's surface. They are flimsy and dehydrated, so they should serve well in lighting a flame, but I still need thicker wood if I'm to keep the flame lit through the coming night. I wander down below the side of the rock, where a piece of driftwood catches my eye. I kick the basin of my booted foot against the dry log. The wood creaks and slides closer to the rock, but it doesn't go far.

I hear the flickering hiss of something scream. It is followed by a moment of silence before the unnerving seethe returns. Unearthed by the log, a serpent dwells with fangs exposed. Its size is enormous, and the log only served to partially conceal its face. The rest of the monster's body was camouflaged along the basin of stone, and I had failed to notice it until now.

I stumble backward and look up towards my backpack on the rock. I try to run, but my legs are going numb. It is then that I realize that the serpent has already struck, and my pant legs are stained red. I lunge forward and drop to the ground as I begin to crawl. It takes all of my strength, but I pull myself back onto the rock, and my mark is left in the form of a crimson-stained trail.

As I claw my way towards my backpack, a sixth sense begins to tingle at the basin of my spine. It feels like a hundred needles are being pricked into my skin: a barrage of overwhelming concern.

I am being watched.

I remain perfectly still as I begin to consider my options, but there is no moment of defining clarity. Rather, I feel something sharp dig into my backside. I feel it scrape through bone as the attack ruptures through ligaments and muscle with ease. I am thrown forward and pinned to the ground before I have time to realize what has happened.

I try to jerk away, but as I twitch, a wall of scales crashes down and encases me. I am trapped in an organic prison. The pressure is immense, and my blood circulation slows. There is a type of burn that pulses through my body and I grow increasingly stiff. My blood is heavy and boiling. I cannot move and my screams are suppressed as I now find it difficult to breathe.

A cold shimmer of pain manifests along my back as I feel the fangs of my attacker slide out from under my skin. The serpent slowly rises to greet my face.

The snake tightens its grip further. My ribs crack and I continue to moan, but even trying to choke down air is painfully difficult. The small breaths that I manage to take fall short of even being considered a wheeze. I begin to feel lightheaded and dizzy as my mind races with panic. For a moment I think of home. I think of my mother, who is back on Outpost Seventeen, and I call out to her with the voice of a child.

I am then pulled back to reality with the piercing sting of a whip's crack.

My eyes begin to dilate and I watch as the serpent draws near with its forked tongue flicking from its mouth.

I moan, but my cries are muffled by a wall of solid muscle.

The snake then begins to disengage its lower jaw. It wraps its mouth around my head and then proceeds to loosen its grip on small sections of my frame as it works its way down, consuming everything at a slow and steady pace.

Within a matter of minutes, I am consumed alive. I manage to clench a fist and thrust it forward, but there is no momentum in my swing. The blow is absorbed by a sea of unyielding matter just moments before everything goes dark.

A light awakens me from the slumber of purgatory. There is no pain or fear - only confusion and blindness as I begin to hear the sounds of chatter.

It takes me a moment to piece together, but I am not yet dead. Rather, I am alive, being digested by the snake as the numbing venom and its slumber-inducing coma begins to fade.

Something has punctured through the snake's skin, and the light that trickles into my prison of agony comes from the sun beyond my tomb. As my mind shifts back to the present, my body is freed from the serpent. Covered in stomach acids, I try to see amidst the brightness of the sun, but my eyes are burned badly and my vision is a blur. My palms feel wet and coarse, and I try to look down at my trembling hands. Dissolved by the acids of the serpent's stomach, most of my skin has been burned away and digested.

I moan as I remain perfectly still on the floor like a newborn struggling to lift its head. My sounds capture the attention of a nearby entity, and I am lifted up from the ground by a pair of red-skinned creatures. I can only make out partial detail, but the creatures are naked and have the anatomy of women. They make strange hissing noises as they fasten my broken body to a long, severed branch. Once I am bound to the wood, the monsters lift me into the air and carry me away.

I again succumb to a slumber that teeters on the edge of madness and incoherence as a pair of realities descend upon my soul with the weight of oblivion.

Time fails as my consciousness fades- deteriorating into little more than silence and darkness.

I am then viciously pulled back through reality as I awaken to find myself hanging above a lit fire. I have been nailed to a cross and my body is slowly roasting. A cloud of black smoke lingers above my head. It reaches towards a darkened sky, where a collection of stars silently watch my eyes as they scrape against their sockets.

The enormous carcass of a snake hangs nearby. Split from head to toe, the serpent's corpse is fresh. There is movement behind it, and then one of the red-skinned women appear. Her face is a blur of cackling darkness, and I can only make out pieces of her figure as she draws near. She is clenching what looks to be a stomach sack that is filled with an unknown liquid.

I feel as though I am basking in the unseen smile of a truly wicked force.

The creature sinks its teeth into the stomach sack and tears away a small section. She then holds the sack over my melted face and empties the contents of the organ. A dark liquid drains from the puncture wound and drenches my face. It is an oily liquid that drips across the surface of my skin and seeps into my open wounds.

The creature then reaches for my abdomen. With ease, it pulls one of my legs from its socket as if tearing into the flesh of a pulled pork.

The fire below is fueled by the oil and the flames climb up to my face.

The fabrics of my essence are tossed into the blast furnace of eternal damnation, and my agony is eternal.

The Hunger

My stomach aches and growls, twists and turns. The pain echoes through the hollow walls of my insides. Beyond physical starvation, my desires - my need for mental nourishment - painfully lingers and consumes my thoughts. It is a guest that pounds at the door of my skull and splits through the walls of my head. It gets worse with every second of every day gone by. It is a lust, much like that of a sexual desire, but far more taboo in the eyes of a mortal. I must feel the touch of another's skin against mine. I must use the claws of my fingernails to dig into their flesh and tear open wounds. I must press inside, to feel the warm blood of another. It is a divine love that can be matched by no other.

Sitting in the corner of my study, I watch the embers crackle in the heart of a fireplace. I stare into the flames and try to control my thoughts. For a moment, I dwell on my surroundings. Fine art hangs on the walls of my archaic-feeling, 17th century home. Cobwebs have claim over much of everything in sight. Much like the views in my head, the books on my shelves have collected a thick layer of dust. I have no strength - no ambition - to do much of anything, and thus, I neglect myself.

I do not own any mirrors. To possess one would be folly, for I have no reflection. Through my sense of touch and peripheral-based sight, I know that my body is malnourished. My muscle mass is all but gone, and my pale skin outlines the bones in my ribs and chest. My breathing has become irregular, and the neural tendencies of emotion are sporadic at best. I jump from love to anger and anger to hatred within minutes. It doesn't take much of anything at all for my rabid emotions to return full circle.

I close my eyes and listen to the sound of the fire as it continues to crackle and roar. Visions of past cuisine are quick to manifest, and I succumb to the temporary comfort that nostalgia provides. A child, no older than ten, hangs suspended from the ceiling of my cellar. I lay naked on the stone floor below him and smile as blood leaks from a wound in the center of his head. Some of the droplets land in my mouth, while others splatter onto my face. This memory serves as a reminder of the last time that I can actually recall truly being happy. Though decades old, the vision is clear down to every last bit of detail.

Three quick knocks pound on the wooden door of my home and I am pulled from my dream. My heart skips a beat, or so it would if it still had a pulse. The fire has gone out, and all that is left in the center of the hearth is a cold pile of ash and soot. The room feels strangely stagnant and cold. I second guess myself and stay put in my old Victorian chair as I await confirmation... Again, three knocks pound against the door, and this time a greater sense of urgency is conveyed.

With bloodshot eyes, I go from sitting to standing in a meager fraction of a second. Confused, I stare at the door on the other side of the room. A final trifecta of knocks barrages against the entrance and I blink forward.

I try to speak but my vocal chords crack under the strain of omission. Afraid, I force only a single word.

"Yes?" I squeal.

"Hello?" The intruder shouts. "Can you help me? Please!"

My guest sounds like a young woman. The tone of her voice is saturated with an authentic fear. I press my face against the door and listen very carefully. I can hear her gasp for air as she tries to reclaim control over the irregular pattern of her breathing. I pull my head back for a moment so that I may think clearly.

Is this a trick?

Stimulated by the wickedness of my sickness, I again throw my ear to the door. I can hear her heartbeat from within her chest. It is young, and thus perfect for circulating the blood that her body stores inside. The sound is erotic, and I soon find myself trapped in the indulgence of daydreaming.

"Hello?" She cries.

I snap out of my momentary mesmerization and slowly wrap the fingers of my right hand around the door's brass handle. I turn the knob and crack the entrance slightly ajar so that I may peek a single eye through the sliver of a gap. The hour is late, and with the sun slain, the girl's face is lit by the light of the moon. She is quick to glance over and gaze into my eye. The authenticity of her terror is confirmed with the expression on her face. She is desperate. With long blond hair and soft-looking skin that is olive in tone, she is beautiful. Her lifeforce radiates all around her, and I can see the millions of particles that make up the nucleus of her soul.

"Please," she pleads. Her voice is sweet and comforting.

My eye darts across my estate and my misunderstanding goes hyperbolic. Full grown trees tower over the courtyard. Consumed by plantlife, statues of my lineage are now hidden relics of an ancient time. Squinting further, I notice that the metal gate that leads to the manor is rusted over and ajar.

Confused by a present that no longer resembles the past, I swing the door open and continue to examine the world beyond my home.

"How can this be?" I mumble softly.

The girl catches sight of me, and immediately her fear amplifies further. She shrieks and stumbles backward, but the uneven terrain of my unkempt yard forces her to lose her footing and she tumbles to the ground.

My train of thought is lost as a powerful vision overtakes me. A red rose blooms. The silky petals of the flower are torn away by an unseen hand. With only the pistil remaining, the ravaged blossom bleeds. The scent of its pollen is euphoric.

The girl frantically scrambles to her feet. A crimson trail of iron leaks from the crown of her head. At first, the open wound seeps into her golden hair, but it doesn't take long for the paint to run further down the side of her face.

Like a flash of lighting, I lunge forward and pounce on the young woman. She kicks and screams and tries to fight me off, but the blows of her fists are soft and delicate like her sweet, sweet scent. It doesn't take me long to overpower her, and I drag the girl into my home with relative ease.

I drop to the ground and straddle my victim. She continues to scream up until the distinct sound of a crack echoes through the air as I cleanly snap her neck. Her legs continue to twitch like a beheaded chicken's, but her eyes go out of focus. This moment is exhilarating. I roll her limp head to the side and press my face down against the surface of her warm skin. Wafting in the scent of my victim, I quickly become aroused as I open my mouth and sink my fangs into her neck.

It is then that I realize that this moment is a memory. My neurons twitch within my head, and I awake from this dream of insanity to find myself sitting before the hearth and its flame.

My stomach makes noises as it feasts on the contents of itself. I lean forward and regurgitate my insides. Chunks of various organs are ejected from my mouth, and I begin to wail as blood, black as the night sky, drools from the side of my face.

Falling to the floor, I crawl towards one of my home's windows and slip up under the silky red curtain. The sunlight burns my flesh if I dare step outside, but the moon is out, and thus, under normal circumstances, I'd be relatively safe. If it weren't for that *cunt* of a witch, Amelia, I'd go outside and satisfy my eternal hunger. She has marked my soul with a powerful curse that stops me from ever leaving my home.

I scrape at the window. It sounds like nails on chalkboard. I claw up towards the great dark above like a greedy little infant who is reaching for its mother's breast.

Shrieking and screaming, I revel in my sorrow as agony wraps its leeching fingers around the core of my soul. It squeezes and wrings me dry of every last drop. She is a vengeful umbra who celebrates my torment.

Hearing whispers beyond the glass, silences befalls my home as I motionlessly rise to my feet. A trio of young children stands idle before an abandoned fountain. They whisper horrific and unjust rumors as they point and stare.

Bewildered by this rare opportunity, I quickly turn my attention to the youngest in the group. I focus on the pupils of his bright blue eyes. This is the doorway to which leads into his mind, and I silently whisper my song unto him. The other children speak words of fright as they back away, but I have the young one firmly in my grasp and I'll never let him go. He shuffles forward as his friends turn to flee. They cry his name, but he is lost in the vacuum of space as he continues to approach the house.

I glide towards the entrance of my home and greet my guest as he arrives on my front step. It isn't until he is left standing alone in my home does he snap out of the hypnotism spell. Unknowing of his location or how it is that he has arrived, the young boy glances to me with eyes of utter terror. His mouth opens but no words come out. His mind is broken, and this fear is a delightful garnish that rests on the edge of my served plate.

Revealing my fangs, I glide towards the boy and embrace him. I caress the back of his head as I blissfully soak in the occasion. Scratching my nails into the basin of his nape, I revel in pure ecstasy as the hour of nourishment has arrived.

I sink my teeth into the boy's neck, and my eyes roll back into their sockets. The front door of my home bursts open, but in this hour I am powerless. Suspended in euphoria, I tune out the sounds of shouting as a man barks at me from across the room and I continue to feed. I bring the child's carotid up towards the surface of his skin. I then pluck the artery from his neck so that I may sip the sweet nectar with ease.

My frail ribs crack into a hundred jagged pieces within my chest, and I am flung across the room at a tremendous speed. I crash into the floor and tumble to a bloody, decadent stop as I scream in both agony and anger.

I glare up towards the party's antagonist. Standing over my meal is a man dressed in black. His soulless eyes look down at me with disgust, and he is brandishing a weapon with both of his hands. He has struck me with the blunt end of an axe, and as I lift my head, he spins the weapon's edge around. Approaching me, the man lifts the axe well above his head.

My eyes dart down towards the boy. His body is twitching as he bleeds out on the floor and I am barred from being near during the moment of his ultimate demise. Angered with this disruption, I hiss at the man from where I lie on the floor, but he doesn't waver.

The axe rains down into my soft flesh again and again until the man becomes winded with his moment of slaughter. He leaves the weapon embedded into the wooden floor beneath my belly. My stomach has been split open and my insides have been spread out across the ground.

I glance towards the still, warm corpse on the ground and ignore my moment of despair. I pull myself forward. Pulling my weight against the tip of the axe, my upper body splits and tears away from my lower half. Free from the burden of flesh, I claw towards the dead boy with great speed. My entrails ooze out from my open ribcage as I continue towards my meal.

I can hear the man as he pries the axe from the wooden floor. Just as soon as I sink my face into the boy's open neck, the steel weapon impales the backside of my skull. My head implodes as my innards are further painted across the floor and eternal silence ensues.

Deathbringer

He feels their beating heart as if it were his own. A stink radiates from their bodies like fog over a lake in the early hours of the morning. They try to mask it with perfumes and colognes, but he is very good at seeing through their lies. Their time has come, and he has arrived to serve as their escort into the afterlife. They always deny the inevitable right up until they take their very last breath. Some kick and scream, but he feels no pain and does not listen. Most whimper and plead, but he only offers his hand in walking them down the aisle of eternity.

It is only when they accept their fate that they turn to a deity. With no time to spare, they cry out to God and pray that he is listening, but there are many gods, and each of them knows better than to interfere with death and his work.

He places one of his grotesque, rotting hands on the left arm of his date, and she stops what she is doing so that she can ponder what this foreign sensation may be. Her eyes bulge and she grips her chest as she collapses to the floor. Those around her shriek and call for help. It is only when she is on the floor does she see him. A long, rotting beak protrudes out from a thick, black cloak. Her eyes lock and she tries to scream, but all she can do is moan. Her heart has stopped, and within seconds she will die. It is in this moment that death decides to play a game. He lets go of her arm and she closes her eyes. As he silently drifts backwards, her heart begins to beat again.

Some time goes by and she awakens to find herself in a hospital bed with loved ones by her side. He floats in the corner and watches them as they tear up with joy for her return. He is unseen and still. Although she bears the memory of him, she too forces a smile and welcomes the embrace of her family. *This* is his queue.

He drifts down towards her and again grips her by the arm with one of his rotting hands. His image is unveiled to her and her alone. Her heart stops and she shrieks as she grasps her chest once more. Her family cries out for help and doctors rush into the room. Everything they do is futile as he continues to grip her arm tightly. This time, he has no intentions of letting go. A moment goes by and then her soul drifts out from her body. He inhales it like the smoke of an exotic drug. He then lets go of her arm and her lifeless body falls limp. The room goes cold and the doctors sulk. The family weeps and mourns their loss, but all he does is smile. He is just getting started with a long day's work.

The Gateway to Damnation

Amidst a storm of apocalyptic resolve, lightning struck the highest point of a great, leafless tree. The limbs of the ancient timber cracked under the force of the tremendous torment. A man, who was frantically trying to piece together shelter at the time of the strike, was befallen by the sudden crash of debris. He was quickly buried alive.

The ranger's lips moved as he cried out in a mixture of both pain and terror, but the wind and the rain drowned out the lesser sounds of the man and his mouth.

The heavy pile of debris trembled like a cowering dog before its master as the man struggled to climb out from his tomb. Just as soon as he managed to scramble to his feet, he again fell to the ground. Crippled by a newfound injury, he pulled back his cloak to discover that his leg was badly broken. His pants were torn, and at the center of the fray was a crimson-stained patch of mutilated skin. Protruding from the husk was a thin sliver of bone. The man could feel the pulse of his heart as it thumped at the base of his throat. He pressed the palm of his hand against the piece of jagged bone. His eyes rolled back into his head, and he winced in agony. With rain pouring down on him from the heavens of an angry god, the man went on to tear up strips from one of his lighter shirts so that he may tie the cloth firmly around the injury and prolong the event of bleeding out.

After addressing the wound, the man looked to the ruins of his makeshift shelter. Everything he had managed to do over the course of an evening was destroyed by the fallen tree. He glanced up towards the darkened sky and tried to gain his bearings, but the stars that he had used for navigation were blocked out by the overhead storm.

Breathing heavily, the man limped away from the wreckage of the tree. He hopped through the forest under the weight of his sopping-wet clothing. Feeling woozy, he slouched his back up against the soaked base of a leafless birch. He couldn't see it, but carved into a section of the white bark above were the markings of an ancient and truly foreign dialect.

The man's breathing slowed as his mind begged his body for rest. Closing his eyes would be a death sentence, but weakness began to prevail. He slid down against the base of the tree and pinched his eyes shut as agony ensued. As his eyelids touched, he forced himself awake at the sight of a dim light through the forest. A warm sense of hope festered in the pit of his gut and the ranger clamored to his feet. He limped through the forest and endured the storm until he reached a small, wooden home. Sitting in one of the cabin's windows was a fully-lit candle: the source of the light that he had seen from out in the distance.

The ranger stumbled up to the door of the home and knocked three times.

"Hello?" He shouted. His voice was limited in contrast to the chaotic sounds of nature.

Again, he banged on the entrance, but nobody answered.

The man planted a hand against the door to stabilize his balance. In doing so, he noticed that the candle in the window was no longer lit.

"Please," the ranger begged, his voice cracking under the strain of his pain. "I know you're there. I saw the candle in the window."

Lightning lit up the area with a brief but saturating strobe of absolute power.

The man pressed his forehead against the door. Feeling helpless, he sighed and began to ramble. "My name is Oliver Allure. I was tracking a pack of wolves out this way when the storm came out of nowhere. I think that I broke my leg. I am just looking for a place to sleep through the night until this storm passes."

Feeling dizzy, Oliver swayed back and forth like one of the trees being blasted by the torrenting winds.

"I do not have any coin on me," he admitted softly, "but I could return in a fortnight to repay you for the trouble. I just … just need…"

Struggling to finish his sentence, the man collapsed against the door and a sterile darkness ensued.

A faint, pixelated light appeared through a still veil of total darkness. A pure silence draped the horizon. As the faint glow continued to manifest, the glimmer retreated back into the footprint of total darkness.

Oliver painfully opened his eyes. He was indoors and on his back. The flames of a nearby fire cast shadows on the ceiling above. The obscured crevices of the twig ceiling played the game of shadows well.

Forcefully blinking his eyes, Oliver came to from a deep, groggy slumber. He regained his sense of intellect and quickly pieced together the equation of reality. It took him a moment, but slowly he came to terms with where he was and how he'd gotten there. He was tucked into an uncomfortable wooden cot via a tattered green blanket.

"Quite the nasty break," a raspy, feminine voice said.

Oliver turned his head to lay eyes upon the speaker. His neck was stiff and difficult to manipulate.

Standing at the far end of the single-roomed home was a naked woman. Her spine was twisted and arched in such a way that forced her head to droop forward. She wore a single piece of tattered cloth over her waist, which veiled the organs between her thighs. Her skin had a bluish hue to it, and her bare breasts sagged from her blotchy chest. She was working with a stone pestle. Her bare breasts swayed in the chilly air as she churned an assortment of unknown ingredients within the stone bowl.

Wanting to not stare or be rude, Oliver looked away from the naked woman. "Thank you," he tried to force out, but his words were lost under the strain of a forgotten voice.

"You've been asleep for some time," the old hag added.

Oliver said nothing. He glanced down at his leg and pulled back his cloak. His pants had been removed and his privates were exposed. The wound on his leg was covered in a collection of small, strange looking leaves, which were secured in place by a single white bandage. A dark patch of blood stained the center of the cloth.

"Said you were hunting wolves," the old woman stated. "Didn't say where you are from, though."

Oliver's eyes drifted back towards the hag. She was still working with the mortar.

"A little over twenty kilometers to the east," Oliver forced with a dry mouth. He noticed his torn pants were folded on the floor beside him. "It is rare for a pack to lead me out this far, but these dogs have been known to do strange things when winter is upon them," he added as his eyes wandered about the small home.

The cabin consisted of a single room, which was cluttered in a chaotic sort of way that seemed to also be somewhat organized. There was a table off to the side with hundreds of different candles of various lengths and widths. Large puddles of wax covered the table's top, and the different colors of all the candles seemed to blend together to paint an image that raised the hairs on the back of Oliver's neck. He was unsure as to how exactly a collection of dormant wax could trigger a discomfort within the pits of his stomach but, somehow, it had.

"It's dangerous in these woods," the old woman asserted. She was now facing Oliver and had a ram's horn in one hand and the stone bowl in the other.

Startled by her silent movement, Oliver looked away and agreed. "Aye. Our village is poor and the pelts can go far." The image of the woman's bare chest was branded into his mind. He continued talking in a desperate attempt to offset the awkwardness of it all. "We can keep them for warmth or trade them for food, so it's often worth the risk."

The hag knelt down beside Oliver and handed him the horn.

"Thank you," Oliver expressed with a nod.

The horn was cool to the touch, but the liquid within was warm and smelled of peaches. Parched beyond belief, Oliver didn't question the contents, but rather sipped the tea at an excelled rate.

"Have you ever been bitten?" The hag questioned as she pulled back Oliver's cloak.

"No. More often than not they bleed out in a trap before I retrieve the pelt," Oliver explained, his face blushing at his exposed privates.

The old woman set down the stone mortar and then used her crooked fingers to delicately unwrap the bandage on Oliver's leg. She plucked the leaves from the dry wound and Oliver looked away in agony. When the leaves were clear, the woman retrieved the mortar from the floor and proceeded to smear something warm over the injured area. Oliver glanced back down to discover that a couple dozen stitches held the fresh wound together, and the hag was brushing a brown paste over the damage. As she did, her bare breasts grazed against Oliver's skin and again his face blushed.

"Are you a witch?" Oliver blurted out. The question had been on his mind, but asking it felt rude. Why he'd gained the courage to ask it now was beyond him, but he immediately regretted the decision after the words departed from his lips.

"I've been called that before," the old woman admitted with a face of stone.

"I'm sorry," Oliver offered with regret. "I didn't mean to offend."

The hag said nothing as she finished smearing the paste across the wound.

"What is your name?" Oliver asked.

The old woman hesitated for a moment. She wrapped a fresh bandage around Oliver's leg. "Amelia," she announced at last, avoiding eye contact.

"Well, thank you, Amelia."

Oliver pondered the reason for the hag's choice in location for a home. There could've been a handful of reasons for an old woman to retreat deep into the forest to live out her days, and Oliver figured it wasn't his place to question a single one of them, so he pressed the thought from his mind. The hag stood up and returned to the far end of the room. She cleaned her hands and then began plucking feathers from a decapitated hen. Oliver remained silent as he observed the inside of the home.

Hanging on the wall behind him was a sizeable collection of glass vials. In them were liquids that seemed to defy logic and understanding. Some had the appearance of gel, and others a water-like substance, but all of them had abnormal traits about them that forced Oliver to wonder what exactly they were. Oliver sat upright on the cot so that he could get a better look at one of the vials. There was one in particular that glistened from within with nebulas and stars - a living galaxy within a glass vial. As his eyes fixated longer, he could hear faint screams within his mind. He felt as though the vial was calling out to him and his soul was departing from his body.

"You should be resting," the hag informed.

Oliver flinched, startled by the words. He glanced over towards the witch to find that she was still plucking the feathers from the bird and that her eyes were still trained on the task before her. Oliver slouched back down and closed his eyes.

Heavy rain continued to assault the land beyond the cabin and, in time, Oliver again succumbed to a deep slumber. While he slept, he dreamt of his wife. He could see her face as her soft lips caressed the rim of his mouth. He could feel her warmth as he slipped a hand up under her skirt. Her skin was soft like silk, and it didn't take Oliver long to become fully aroused. The couple proceeded to make love and the climax of their adventure led to his sudden awakening.

Oliver opened his eyes to find himself still lying on the cot in the old woman's cabin. The nearby fire was lit low, and Amelia was nowhere in sight. The rains had stopped and the storm had passed.

The ranger removed the blanket to confirm a suspicion. The area beneath the wool was damp. He had ejaculated on himself in his sleep.

"Fucking hell…" Oliver muttered as he glanced around the room.

He sat upright and groaned in pain. Oliver wanted to dress himself, but he knew he couldn't do so alone. Embarrassed, he wrapped himself in the blanket and stared at the dirt floor.

"I'll never make it back like this," Oliver complained with a sigh.

He then lifted his head as he considered the notion of designing a crutch. The man growled as he struggled to stand. Once up from the cot, he swayed from side to side as he wrestled with the pain and overall lack of balance. Slowly, he put some weight on his injured leg, but there was a sudden point in leaning where the ranger simply crumbled to the floor in agony.

Oliver cried out as he fell. Smacking his face against a nearby table, the taste of iron was quickly on his tongue as he landed on the dirt floor.

The ranger opened his eyes, but his vision was out of focus. The world before him had fractured into two, and the parallel realities teetered on the edge of madness as they collided and retracted again and again. Oliver closed his eyes for a moment; doing so only served to make matters worse.

Keeping his face flat against the dirt, Oliver blinked a few times as the duplicate visions slowly melded into one. With his head still spinning, the man watched as something moved at the far end of the room. In time, his vision would return to normal, but the movement across the way continued and Oliver furrowed his brow as he contemplated what exactly he was seeing.

A faint smoke seeped from the cracks of what appeared to be the basin of a doorway. The entrance across the room was veiled in a dark blue blanket, but the disguise failed to cover the object's lower half.

The longer Oliver remained on the ground, the more curious he became as to what exactly he was looking at. The smoke continued to billow, but the shadows dissipated as they lingered away from the object. As Oliver continued to fixate on the hidden entrance, everything else in the room began to slowly vanish until only he and the door remained.

Oliver could feel his heart beating through his chest as he remained on the ground and watched from afar. He could hear the faint sound of a rhythmic thump coming from the door. The closet had a pulse of its own that beat like the heart of a dying fawn. Struggling to survive, the heartbeat withered as it throbbed through the cracks of the door.

Butterflies mingled within the belly of the man, and a hard lump soon formed in his throat. He felt as though he were being drawn towards the door and - as he glanced down into the dirt - he noticed that he had, in fact, moved forward.

As the second pulse stopped, the crackling sound of embers could be heard beyond the wooden entrance. The distinct sound of a door creaking open followed. Slow and offkey, the noise cut through the room like a rusty knife pressed to the spine of a murder victim.

Oliver slowly lifted his head. The entrance before him was cracked ajar, and the blanket that encased it was flapping under the weight of a foreign gust. The scent of sulfur wafted into the room, and a distinct growl reverberated from the object. The sound was both complex and abnormal. It was like nothing Oliver had ever heard before, and he couldn't place it amidst his fright.

A soft glow appeared in the shadows as something approached the open entrance from the other side. Through the smoke, a beady pair of red eyes appeared, and Oliver's throat fell deep into his stomach. He continued to fixate on the creature that lurked in the shadows of the wardrobe. His heart skipped a beat, and then the organ stopped beating entirely.

Oliver gripped his chest and groaned. His eyes were still locked into the standoff stare with the creature while his body jerked and flailed under the strain of a heart attack.

The eyes receded back into the darkness. A second growl ensued; this time, the cry was louder and more distinct than before. Accompanied by the sound of phlegm and decay, the howl was a subtle cry of chaos and destruction. A pair of horns scraped against the crack in the door as the creature pushed its way out and the blanket that encased the wardrobe tore under the forceful stretch. A small, lanky creature with black, leathery skin and magma-colored eyes drifted forward from the wardrobe. Its face was the animated skull of a bull. Bits of muscle and skin melted from its snout as it snorted a gust of red-hot air.

Oliver groaned as he watched the creature linger. His heart had restarted, but the pulse was heavy and his chest felt tight. His eyes dilated as his jaw hung open and he clenched the dirt below out of both anxiety and fear.

The creature's eyes pierced through the ranger like a needle through fabric. The skin below its neck was twisting and warping as it shambled forward on four legs. Oliver remained frozen, suspended within a vial of liquid terror. He watched as the beast lingered near. Faces, lumped under the creature's flesh, lifted and pressed expressions of horror against the barrier of their prison. Doomed, they retracted back into the muscle matter beneath the skin as more faces rose to press against the walls of eternal damnation.

Oliver whispered a collection of incoherent words. The hour of judgment had arrived, and he was lost in a sea of conflicting thoughts.

The beast approached the man and its vocal cords began to make a series of clicking noises as it exhaled a warm breath into the face of its victim. The belly of the beast shifted with the faces of a thousand souls as cries for salvation stretched out towards the ranger.

Oliver's mind broke, and he began to stutter as sweat poured from his face and his eyes embraced the fate of total helplessness.

Arms reached forward from the belly of the beast. One of the limbs tore through the flesh of its captor, and black rot oozed from the open wound. An authentic heat radiated from the decrepit ligament as it cupped Oliver's face. The ranger screamed out in agony. The sizzling sound of charred flesh outweighed his cries as the hand sunk deeper into the flesh of the man's head. Oliver's eyes rolled back into their sockets as he screamed and flailed under the torment of his new god.

The hand receded back into the belly of the beast. A deep depression of cauterized meat and skin was imprinted across Oliver's face. Oliver returned his gaze to the monstrous creature. Its presence was statutory, and it demanded an audience.

Agony and terror collided within as the meld of chaos festered within the pit of the mortal man. He yearned for an end to it all, but this bringer of torment was not giving gifts. Oliver wanted to slip off into the eternal night. Only the finality of death could sever the spinal cord of torment that he felt.

The creature spun around to face the wardrobe. From its backside, another arm ruptured through its skin. The rotting limb grabbed the ranger by the foot, and Oliver face-planted into the dirt as the beast dragged him away. His charred wounds ran deep to the bone, and he cried as the beast dragged him towards the wardrobe.

Oliver didn't fight it. It was useless to even try. He simply whimpered and cried as he was hauled through the dirt. Once within the door, the texture of the floor changed to stone.

As Oliver glanced from left to right within the closet of darkness, he was suddenly thrown forward. He screamed as his soul plunged to an unimaginable depth. For weeks on end, he continued to sail down into the abyss, screaming in agony and terror for every second of every minute of his dark endeavor.

Splattering against the ground, Oliver's corpse split open and dispersed across a jagged stone floor. The ranger struggled to lift his head. His organs and flesh were fused into the ground.

Oliver was still alive despite his disfigured new form. He tried to lift himself up, but the pain was eternal. He pressed forward with his desire to stand and continued to struggle, but only the inner skeleton of his splattered corpse rose from the floor. Ligaments and bone popped under the strain of the carcass as it stripped itself of its fleshy body. Dripping with meat and blood, the ruined skeleton shambled to its feet and swayed under the stagnant breeze of damnation.

Dissonant whispers of torment littered the cavern's halls in all directions. Oliver, in his new form, helplessly glanced forward while the fiendish shadow of his new master loomed overhead in the eternal prison of despair.

Inked

Locked away in the depths of a musty, dark cellar, a creature lives his life in solitude and pain. The steel bars of his cage suggest that he is a prisoner, yet the scars along his leathery skin tell a different story. Perhaps he is safer here in this confinement than if left to face the bigots who live beyond the stone walls of his home.

The inmate is naked and its human-like body is covered from head to toe in a thin layer of mucus. The creature has hundreds of small, translucent tentacles protruding from the surface of its purple skin. With circular suckers covering the minor limbs and a bulbous sack in place of where the head should be, the creature is a monstrous hybrid of both octopus and man.

With no windows from which to shine, the sunlight is forbidden from entering this dungeon. A pair of lowly-lit torches hang near the entrance of the cell. The soft flames cast shadows along the walls at all hours of an endless, eternal night.

The monster shakes uncontrollably as it hunches in the corner and stares with marble-black eyes into cracks along the stone wall. Shadows seep into the fractured bits of rock, and the illusion of company is all the creature knows.

The squid forms sound with its mouth as it speaks to the silhouettes. Its voice is soft and distinct, like bubbles being blown into the gentle current of a mostly-still creek.

A wooden door, unseen from the vantage point of the cell, can be heard opening in the distance. The distinct creak of something that is both heavy and old echoes along the chamber's walls.

The monster stands to its feet and dashes towards the far end of the cell as the sound of someone wearing chainmail can be heard approaching from down the hall.

A short, bearded man peeks around the corner. He then steps forward with a torch in one hand and a wooden pail of water in the other. He sets down the bucket and inspects the cell from the safety of the other side. The man is wearing a layer of chainmail overtop a tattered white shirt. A metal helmet hangs down over his eyebrows, and a pair of swords are draped at his waist. The sigil of a red key resting in the open palms of two hands is etched into the front of his helmet.

The creature gurgles a collection of strange sounds as it awkwardly tries to press its large body into one of the cracks along the stone.

The man plucks one of the torches from the wall and drops the flaming end into the bucket. The sizzling sound of the fire's demise is quick. The creature shrieks in fear as the sharp sound cuts through the air like the cry of a death that it is. The man then dislodges the second torch from the wall and drops it into the bucket. He withdraws a ring of keys from within his cloak. With his own torch still lit and in hand, the soldier approaches the cell.

"Alright," the man groans in a phlegm-covered tone. "Come on out," he adds as he unlocks the cell and opens the door.

The creature remains in place near the far corner of the prison. It trembles, trying to ignore the command.

"Well, come on, then," the man spits. "The flames are out, you know."

The creature continues to tremble and avoid eye contact.

"Listen, Kraken!" The man barks. "You make me come in there and you'll lose one of 'em pretty little limbs o' yours!" He places the palm of his free hand against the hilt of one of his two blades as he leans in towards the cell with his torch pressed forward. "Now come on out!"

The monster rises to its feet. Still trembling, it stumbles towards the guard and the man backs away from the cell. The creature wraps its arms around the steel bar of the cage and then proceeds to pull himself through. Its body compresses and then expands as it warps through the bars like gelatin. The faint hiss of smoke can be heard seeping from the pores of the creature's skin as the estranged maneuver is clumsily executed.

The guard lifts an eyebrow and snickers in disgust. "The door is fookin' open..."

The creature looks back towards the open cell. It then silently glances back towards the man.

Shaking his head, the guard turns to face the hall. "Let's go."

The two work their way through the corridor of stone until they arrive at an ancient wooden door. As they exit the dungeon, they enter the well-lit halls of a castle. With lofty windows that reach up towards the sky, the walls of the stone mansion are brightened by the sun. Elegant banners and vibrant fabrics drape the walls. The creature arches its back as it peeks up towards the wondrous banners. The sigil of a key within a pair of open palms is stitched into the flags.

The two traverse through the quiet castle. They are greeted by none, but as they turn a corner, the creature begins to make out the sounds of commotion. The muffled cries of a crowd shouting can be heard in the distance. The monster gets a little closer to the escort as its grotesque frame tenses up with fear. The man stops walking and peeks around a corner, but the creature continues to follow him right up to the point where it collides against the man's back.

Startled, the man leaps forward and spins around with his torch in hand. "Get the hell back, will ya!" He shouts; a mixture of anger and fright lingers in the tone of his voice. He sweeps his torch through the air with one hand and wraps the fingers of his free hand around the hilt of his sword. "I'll send ye' straight to hell, Kraken! By the gods I will!"

The inkling shrieks as it retreats back towards a nearby wall. The maneuver is uneven and the creature loses its balance as it collides into a stone pedestal. The creature crashes towards the ground with a small statue of a man, but in an awkward twist, the inkling catches the sculpture.

The man shakes his head with a mixture of both disappointment and disgust. He lowers his jaw, but his words are lost, adrift in a sea of loathing.

The inkling fumbles with the statue and then climbs back up to its feet with the sculpture in hand. It plants the artwork back on top of the pedestal and then turns back towards the man with shame in its eyes. A trail of goo leaks from the sculpture.

"Don't fookin' touch anything, uh?" The man groans as he turns back towards the entrance to another hall.

The two continue their journey in silence until they reach another open entryway.

"Order," a man calls from around the corner. "Order!" The rowdy crowd silences itself and the man continues softly, "Let her speak."

The escort presses forward around the corner and the inkling cautiously follows. This smaller corridor leads directly towards the commotion, and the escort stops when he reaches a vantage point into the grand hall beyond. The inkling peeks around the guard to see into the room where a woman, dressed in ebony-colored robes, is on her knees. There are specks of blood on the marble floor beneath her. Her long, messy black hair drapes a pair of shackled hands behind her backside. Her blackened eyes are closed and her lower lip is wet with blood. A crowd of well-dressed men and women stand behind her with anger and hate in their eyes. The crowd is silent as they stare off towards the far end of the room.

"What say you?" The unseen man commands from around the corner.

The woman opens her eyes and fights off a seething anger as her upper lip twitches. "I only ask that my death be swift, my Lord."

The inkling continues to lean forward until it catches a glimpse of the man who is speaking to the woman. Sitting on a golden throne, the man is dressed in exotic fabrics. A clean beard covers his jaw and a golden crown rests atop a head of short, blonde hair.

"I've considered this," the king responds. His jade-colored eyes pierce through the woman with a chilling sort of stare. "The gods know I'd love to watch you hang in the streets, but it's not up to me."

"Back up, will ya!" The escort whispers as he notices that the inkling behind him is lingering a little too far forward. The monster retreats, but his vantage point still allows for him to see the woman on the floor.

The girl remains perfectly still. With a face of stone, she awaits judgment.

"I don't expect you to understand, witch," the man on the throne roars with vigor. "For every day and every hour of your life, the gods have called your name. You, however, have chosen to abandon them. As such, a beheading is far too merciful a judgment for your sins."

The girl drops an eyebrow as she contemplates the meaning of the statement.

"Priests of Solumguard," the king calls.

A group of masked men steps forward from the silent crowd. Dressed in white, the men hold their arms up towards their chests as they walk. A hood hangs over their owl-like masks.

"The gods speak to you of judgment," the king begins. "Now tell me of their thirst. What is it that they demand?"

One of the robed men drifts towards the king and the inkling's curiosity leads it back around the corner. It watches as the cloaked figure whispers up towards the throne in a foreign tongue.

"So be it." The king nods with heavy eyes, and the priests retreat back towards the outer edge of the room. "Executioner!" The lord calls from his throne.

A hooded man approaches the throne and kneels.

"You may be dismissed," the king informs.

The executioner stands and bows before exiting the great room. The girl watches in silence as the man takes his leave. The expression on her face is that of confusion.

"The gods are merciful, even when judging the evils of our world," the king begins. "As such, you shan't die on this day, witch."

The woman's cheeks lift as a twisted smirk manifests across her face.

"You *will*, however, be branded," the king informs with a look of stone.

The woman's smile fades as her eyebrows sink with discomfort.

"It would be a disservice to the realm if we simply let you go," the lord explains. "You will be marked before you are banished from these lands so that those you encounter know of your crimes."

The king looks towards the hall, where the escort is silently waiting. The lord then gestures with a nod, and the escort turns to face the inkling.

"Let's go," the man whispers as he enters the grand hall. All of the eyes within the room linger over towards the kraken and a frenzy of whispers ensue.

"No!" The girl screams as her eyes bolt from the monster back towards the throne. She tries to stand, but a pair of guards dressed in plate armor approach the girl and restrain her. "No!" She cries again and again as she begins to panic.

"Silence!" The king demands.

The crowd hushes as the monster squirms forward behind the escort. As the man steps aside, he looks to the inkling and gestures towards the woman with a nod.

The woman kicks and cries, but she lacks strength and is bested by the two guards within the blink of an eye. The knights strip her of her robes. A blow to the face drops her back to her knees and blood begins to pour from her face.

"No..." she cries from down on the marble floor. "Please."

The inkling looks up towards the throne, where the king watches in silence. It then peeks over to the crowd, where concern and fear radiate from the eyes of men and women alike.

Again the escort silently gestures towards the woman. This time, he uses his eyes as his head remains perfectly still. The inkling looks down to the woman and glides forward.

Thousands of thin strands sprout from the tips of the creature's tentacles. The hairs seek out the girl as the inkling drops to the marble floor. The hairs then begin to wrap themselves tightly around her arm and the knights release her as they retreat. The naked girl fights back, but the hairs multiply, split, and spread out across the surface of her body until she is shrouded in darkness from head to toe.

"No!" The girl screams, her eyes and mouth being the only surface of her corpse that is free from the grip of the hairs. "No!" She repeats in a stronger, more desperate tone. This time, the word has been infused with the power of a deep magic. A gust of energy bellows from her vocal chords, but the inkling pays no mind.

The hairs work quickly in penetrating the girl's skin through her pores. She clenches her eyes shut and screams out in agony as the walls of her anatomy are breached with relative ease.

"Not once have you paid tribute to the gods!" The king narrates calmly. "Only now, on your day of death do you call for mercy... but no longer will they listen."

The girl continues to scream.

With the hairs submerged into the girl's skin, the inkling then begins to vibrate. The hairs expand and the girl's pores open further. Many of the watchers in the room are forced to look away, but the king continues to stare with the blank expression of a soulless leader.

The inkling puffs its body. At the steady rhythm of subtle breathing, it injects its victim with ink. Cries of eternal torment cut through the room and then the woman passes out. The inkling continues to discharge the fluid with ease. When finished, the strands of hair wither and die as they are separated from the limbs of the monster. Exhausted, the inkling stands and the escort shoos the creature back towards the wall with his torch in hand.

As the inkling collapses against the wall, its eyes catch sight of the naked woman. The girl's skin is black like tar. She awakens to a reality of agony as she forces her eyes open. Much like her body, the white within her eyes has been turned to ebony. Caressed within the open palms of eternal damnation, she dares not move her broken body. Her jaw hangs open and she silently cries alone on the marble floor before the kingdom and crown of Solumguard.

Love Potion No. 9

A young boy, no older than eight or nine, leans against the basin of a great oak tree. The tree's roots stretch far across the lush, green forest. Its thirst is quenched by a nearby stream. The stream runs around a collection of rocks before being fed into a lively pond. Children are playing with tadpoles and frogs at the shallow end of the lagoon, and the boy behind the tree simply observes from afar.

The watcher's clothes are ragged and torn. His face is dirty and his brown hair is tangled and unclean. His blue eyes continue to survey the other children's fun. In time, the other kids will notice the watcher. They will then chase him down like a pack of wolves. They will poke him with sharp sticks and they will bludgeon him with hard stones.

The poor boy's personality is a bit dull. His mind takes root in stagnant waters, and for this his peers despise him. He is slower than the other children his age, both inside and out.

As the years go by, the children get a little bit older. Despite physical growth, the mind of the poor boy never ages or learns. For some time he endures the torment of his peers, until one day, a beautiful girl arrives from far, far away.

The girl dresses in green silks and smells of exotic flowers. Her curly, golden hair reaches to her belly and with piercing green eyes, she captures the attention of all the boys around her. Her ears are oddly pointed and long. The light color of her skin has a warm but subtle glow. Her beauty is considered divine within the eyes of the children.

On the day of the girl's arrival, she witnesses the beating of the poor boy. She intercepts the attack and shields the boy amidst the assault. She fights the monsters with courage and words before healing the young boy's wounds with unseen magics.

The poor boy becomes infatuated with his savior. He is too shy to speak directly to her, but his heart beats a little bit faster when she is near, and his mouth turns dry when she looks his way.

Anxious thoughts take advantage of the boy's lethargic mentality. Visions of the truth become warped into something cynical, and the boy convinces himself that the golden-haired beauty despises him. His thoughts betray him further as whispers bang on the drums within his ears. He believes that the girl looks down on him. In his world, she finds him repulsive - nothing more than insignificant vermin.

The boy dwells in the shadows of the forest for many months. Alone with his thoughts, he marinates in fear and strife while his lust and desire for the girl turns into a minor obsession.

On the night of a full moon, the boy discovers a shack in the woods. It's located in an area he's been to, but he isn't bright enough to understand the queerness of this structure's sudden appearance. He approaches the shack with eyes of wonder. There is a candle that is lit aflame and glowing in one of the home's windows. The boy tries to peer through the glass, but the sound of someone stirring about redirects his attention. The door to the small home opens and a woman dressed in dark robes peeks out.

"A child?" The woman gasps in a raspy-sounding voice.

The door opens further, and the woman looks down to the boy, who is frozen in place.

"Tell me, child," she requests, looking from left to right and examining the woods around them. "What are you doing out here all alone?"

The boy says nothing as he continues to stare at the woman. Her face looks disfigured and her hair is a black mess. The long, ebony knots do little in terms of disguising the lesions and boils that cover her skin.

"Well, why don't you come in, then, and get out of this cold," the woman suggests as she steps back into her home.

The boy is hesitant at first, but he is willing to follow.

"How does a cup of warm cider sound?" The woman asks as she wanders deeper into the shack.

The boy skitters in behind her. Once inside, the wind slams the door shut, and the boy flinches, but he doesn't take his eyes off the hostess.

The woman reaches for a small, corked jar that rests on a flimsy shelf made of twigs and mud. She removes the cork and wafts in the scent of the brown liquid.

"A very delicious blend from last autumn," the old hag recalls out loud as she pours the juice into a small tin bowl.

The boy glances around the stuffy cabin. The walls are lined with branches and herbs that are hanging to dry. Plants and dirt litter the ground within the floorless shack.

"Perhaps after we get you warmed up, you'll tell me why you've come," the woman rambles as she sets the bowl in a pit of warm, burning embers. "Here-here, sit, my child," she adds, gesturing to a log beside the fire.

The boy approaches the log and takes a seat. The old woman then begins to dig through a pile of nearby things. The boy can't tell what she is going through, so instead, he diverts his attention towards the walls of the shack.

Small shelves are found hidden beneath the drying spices. On one of the shelves is a glass bottle with something trapped within. The remains of a small, blue imp are suspended within the jar. The creature's face is battered and broken, but despite being disfigured, the body is well preserved in a motionless jelly.

The old hag discovers what she's looking for and then sits down in the dirt across from the boy. Grasped between her broken hands is a chalice made of bone. She reaches for the hot tin bowl and then pours the cider into the chalice. The hot metal hisses in her hands as her flesh is burned. She flips the bowl over and leaves it to dry against a nearby branch and then offers the chalice to the child.

The boy accepts the beverage and then breaks his silence. "Are you a witch?" He questions softly in a frightened tone.

"I am no witch, child," the old woman seethes.

The boy sips from his cup and then observes more of the details across the cabin. A line of vials are hanging nearby. Within them are very strange liquids. One of the vials is red with a bubbling, boiling liquid within. Another houses a black tar that moves in unnatural ways, but most of the flasks contain a sparkling green goo.

"But you make potions," the boy states.

"Of sorts. Yes," the woman replies with a grin as she watches the boy inspect her home from his seat on the stump.

"Do you know a lot of potions?"

"I know of many and can craft a few," the decrepit woman responds, weaving through the awkward phrasing of the child's inquiry.

"Can you make ... a love potion?"

"A love potion, you say?" The woman repeats.

The child's eyes bulge as he considers the notion that he has said something wrong.

"I'm sorry," the boy apologizes. "That's not a real thing," he then assumes out loud.

"Well," the old woman cackles, amused by the boy's ask. "In a way ... it is."

The boy raises an eyebrow and listens for more as he finishes his warm drink.

"It is too serious of a thing for a child to have, though," the hag adds in a tone that slightly mocks.

The boy sets down his empty chalice and then stands to his feet. "Please," he says. "I can be serious."

"Can you?" The woman's voice purrs as it shifts in tone.

The boy quietly nods his head.

"Then you best listen," the old hag instructs.

The child's eyes dilate as he watches the hag lift up from her seat in a cloud of seeping smoke. Once standing, she grins from ear to ear and glides towards the boy. Her sudden shift in presence strikes fear in the child's face. As instructed, he is listening *very* carefully.

"You wish to take love?" The woman questions, her grotesque

face slithering closer towards the child. "You want to control one's will? Bend it," she flares, shouting down at the boy. "Force it!" she screams. "Take it?"

The woman's words have penetrated the boy's mind like an axe in the belly. His innocence has been stolen and left in its place is the mark of a deep, burning magic.

The old hag withdraws a jagged blade from beneath her robes, maintaining her ghoulish stare into the eyes of the boy. The weapon is curved with the tip of its edge forked into two. She rolls the dagger between her crooked fingers in a way that mesmerizes the child.

"Murder is the potion of love, my dear."

"Murder?" The boy questions, his mind lost in the deep haze of a lingering fog.

"Yes," the woman confirms. The letters of the word roll from her tongue like the hiss of a dangerous snake who is about to strike.

"Murder," the boy repeats to himself as if he's considering the suggestion.

"Yes," the woman repeats. Her voice cuts through the air like sharp steel against the flesh of a lamb as she offers the dagger to the child.

The child's eyes remain perfectly still for a moment as he considers the meaning of the price. He then glances up towards the offered weapon and his lips curl up the side of his cheeks as he reveals a nefarious grin.

"Murder," the boy confirms as he accepts the dagger with a subtle nod.

Treasure Goblin

It is something ancient. It is something old.
The treasure that I seek is almost mine to behold.
It glimmers on display while my soul remains grey,
But that doesn't matter now,
I've discovered the tatter of tao.

My mind has been made and I've slain off the resistance.
No longer am I blind. I am rewarded for my persistence.

Atop a mantle of stone and brass, lies a chalice of bone and glass.

I take hold of my prize and scurry away.
Like roaches in light, I worry that I'm prey.
Once inside and away from the sun, I withdraw my bride and prepare
for fun.

I wrap my lips around the crystal.
I become aroused and deflower my pistil.
My jaws clench tight as I press with all my might.

Crush this glass within my mouth. Blush at last, I bleed and strouth.

It scrapes and tears into my gums.
Blood drapes my cares and totals my sums.

I bear this pain for all the world to see, for owning this task is pleasure
for me.

Some may think it crazy, others say it's sadness, but in the end, it is
my choice:
to pursue a life of madness.

A Guide to Mapping the Universe

A video transmission begins to play and a tall, humanoid creature approaches across a cold, steel platform. The creature is standing on the bridge of a space station. A veil of stars and darkness can be seen out of a window behind him. Wearing robes from the waist down, the being's tone chest is completely bare. Its ivory-colored skin is tight and smooth. Its blue eyes are dilated to the point where they almost appear to be black. The skeletal structure of the creature appears to be thin, yet lanky. Although it's muscular and fit, the being is also skinny and scrawny. In place of where a human would have hair, the top of the creature's head is covered with elongated tendrils of a bluish hue. The monster also has a long pair of ears that blend in amongst the basin of its hairline.

A floating orb can be seen in the window's reflection. The sphere serves to be the source of the video feed's transmission. The creature focuses its ebony eyes on the orb and then begins to speak. His words can be heard, but his lips do not move. His voice is telepathically projected and silently spoken.

Greetings explorers, and thank you for your curiosity. I hope that this guide finds you well. The idea behind this transmission is to simply educate you in the manners of intergalactic mapping and how best to achieve it. Creating a map of the universe is a task like no other, and only together can we achieve such a paramount goal.

The creature blinks its beady eyes and then turns to escort the orb down a dimly-lit hallway.

Let's begin, shall we?

The narrator drifts down the hall. His legs are slightly out of view, but his body's motions are relaxed. It's almost as if the creature is gliding across the ground without actually moving its legs or hips.

The white-skinned being enters a large, dome-shaped room and the transmission orb follows. The escort then presses the palm of his elongated hand against a panel on the wall. It drags its ball-tipped fingers across the pad and draws a design-based code. The room darkens, and millions of holographic spheres appear above. The lights differ in size, and for every million that can be seen, another billion are hidden within the three-dimensional plane.

The creature inputs another code into the blank panel and then weaves its fingers. It is in direct control of the image that the spheres reflect. The lights in the room begin to accelerate forward, and the camera's point of view is warped through space and time. The holographic image transports the room through a digital map of the universe. Lightyears upon parsecs are displayed in minute detail.

Truly incredible, isn't it?

The journey continues as the room projects the images of a star and her system. Planets are flung by and sister stars are revealed.

And to think, we only possess a tiny fraction of this limitless map.

The holographic display speeds up and fires across a billion star systems. It expands beyond gas clusters and stars to reveal a universe that is truly horrific in size.

The map then fades away and the room returns to its poorly-lit state.

There are very few species of being within the known universe who can recollect the layout of the stars in the sky. It's a shame, really, given all creatures look to the sky many times over the span of their lives. However, all hope is not lost in this endeavor. Because various species do look to the sky with eyes of wonder, their subconscious memory stores that information in the form of an image through life and, sometimes, even death.

The narrator leads the transmission orb back out into the hallway and then proceeds to glide forward. The corridor opens up into a vaulted room. The ceiling is transparent with a natural sky of endless space. The proximity of floating rocks across the darkened atmosphere above suggest the station is located within a belt of asteroids.

The great machine. The wicked cultivator. Nemesis. This structure goes by many names across many nations, and it is where our journey begins.

The narrator raises a hand and gestures towards the center of the room, where a strobe of electricity coils around the basin of a colossal pylon. The odd structure reaches into the sky and blossoms into an intricate network of capacitors and cables.

If you are unfamiliar with soul harvesters, consider picking up Makarda's Guide to Harvesting Souls. Due to the text's controversial nature, it can be difficult to track down. Many governments have banned the book and threaten severe forms of prosecution for possessing such knowledge, but most Sin'de'kari traders keep it in stock.

Thunderous applause from the gods themselves can be heard roaring in the heavens above as a wall of lightning silently sinks along the walls of the pylon's outer silo. The harvester is electrified and energy is dispersed across the intricate blossom of network strength.

An incredible machine. Built to siphon souls out of dark matter, this particular harvester is up and running at all times. The power draw is immense, but the production outcome is well above average.

The white-skinned creature proceeds forward towards a pair of double-doors at the far end of the open room. The orb follows the narrator, passing by a wall of automated computers and displays. The machines hum an eerie sort of sound as they execute their automated command.

As the camera floats through the open pair of doors, lights activate and a series of liquid-filled tubes begin to dimly glow along the walls of the corridor ahead. Suspended in the nearest cylinder is the living fetus of a human child. The orb rotates to show many other tubes with similar test subjects suspended within their chambers.

One of them has a full-grown woman floating within. There is a collection of cables running into her mouth.

It is crucial that you keep your subjects sedated at all times. Even the slightest show of freewill can jeopardize the harvest process entirely, and such a mistake can not be corrected, thus forcing the untimely disposal of your clone.

A tube pumps oxygen down the woman's throat. Her bare chest inflates and deflates under the terms and conditions of automated design.

A drug-induced coma is the route we take, but given resources, your methods may vary.

The escort glides towards one of the artificial wombs. He then runs his ball-tipped fingers across the surface of the glass casing. A string of data appears and the woman's vitals are displayed.

The human brain is far from perfect, but its potential in the field of subconscious memory is vast. This truth, coupled with the fact that human cloning is relatively cheap, makes the species the ideal choice in regards to this sort of project. Of course, the mind of a Loresi archmage would be the perfect specimen, but the ingredients and time investment required for such a clone is difficult, to say the least.

The data fades as the alien double-taps a blue rune on the glass display.

This one's still a little too young, but we've got one that's ready for extraction in the next room.

The creature folds his arms behind his back and silently glides towards the next room. Muffled screams can be heard beyond a nearby door. A hydraulic entrance retracts as the narrator draws near and a collection of horrific sounds echo into the hallway.

Now you may be asking why it is we take the time to accelerate the growth of our clones. The answer is simple. Efficiency. The human brain doesn't require much time to develop fully, but it is an investment. It's crucial that you wait until your human reaches maturity before you dive into the depths of their mind. Harvesting the memories of a child is a costly mistake that's all too common in our field of work. Patience is something that you will have to understand as you begin your project. While both the child and adult vessel have the exact same memories of the stored soul's past life, the web that is a child's mind is tangled further by things like imagination. It makes data extraction difficult to the point where losing the mind in question occurs at vastly unacceptable rates. Luckily, humans respond well to growth serums, so keeping them suspended in the gel is a beneficial addition to the cloning phase.

With many doors to choose from, the narrator enters a small, closet-sized room and the camera slowly follows. Strapped to a chair in the center of this private gala is a naked man. Mechanical conduits run from his eyes into a nearby machine. The man's mouth hangs open as he teeters on the fine line between consciousness and madness.

Right over here, if you will, the escort suggests to the viewer in reference to a sophisticated, three-dimensional display on the backside of the room's wall.

As the camera swivels around, a thin piece of cable can be seen running from the basin of the man's nape that leads into the ground. The creature taps a command into the display and the man awakens. He is birthed into a moment of utter chaos. The display lights up and grows warm as the man begins to scream.

The subject is sedated, but no amount of liquid plasma can ease the agony of one's creation. The sting doesn't last long, but the entirety of their birthing sequence is painful. The moment the soul awakens is a truly magnificent sight to see.

The nearby display flashes an assortment of colors. The primary emotion across the panel is displayed in the form of a deep red. As the subject's screams begin to subside, the panel flickers. The red turns to yellow, and green pockets can be seen manifesting across the digital map. Unheard thoughts and unseen emotions are translated into the form of vibrant colors: an endless sea of pixels generated within a compressed, three-dimensional space. A sense of emptiness and hunger are reflected by means of sensory lights, and a seat of affection is constructed.

It seems that we are almost ready for extraction.

The caretaker slides his ball-tipped fingers across the display. A panel of runes appear and a code is entered. One of the room's walls recedes, and a hidden cable begins to slither forward. The end of the advanced piece of equipment splits off into a dozen sharp extensions, which then work to peel back the skin of the man's forehead. The sedated man begins to drool from his open mouth. His facial expression suggests that he feels a slight tingle. A negligible confusion manifests into agony as the probe punctures the soft, fleshy tissue of his brain.

There is no pain during this phase of the procedure. Even though the mind feels no pain, the muscle memory of their faces often depicts agony. An interesting flaw in human design.

The probe furthers its dig as tiny sensors are injected into the subject's brain matter.

Gaining access to the mind is rather simple. The delicacy comes in sifting through stored memories and locating the files that depict the native soul's planet. In particular, we are looking for subconscious stills of the sky.

The three-dimensional display begins to light up as the supercomputer navigates through a web of tangled data. A few moments go by where the lights strobe at an incredible pace, then the computing power simply comes to a stop. A string of code is projected across every surface in the room.

There it is. Now for extraction.

The escort swivels a finger around a yellow rune, and the room goes dark as power is diverted into the probe. The lights flicker back on as the cable becomes fully charged, then, in a violent and sudden burst, the subject's brain matter bursts from within its head. The flesh is spewed against the wall, and the probe begins to make a repetitive motion with its limbs. A synthetic orb is created out of a variety of matter, brain tissue included. The probe then delivers the finished data orb into the open palm of the narrator.

All of that for a little slice of heaven.

The escort clenches his fingers around the orb and then drifts towards the room's exit. He leaves behind the gory scene of the deceased man with his innards spewed across the white walls. The subtle sound of meat and blood can be heard dripping from the large wound in the man's head as the camera follows the narrator back into the hall. The creature quietly moves into the next room.

Now, for the final step. We have the data, but where does this puzzle piece fit, exactly? For this solution, we turn to phebs.

A nearby display wall shifts into a two-way mirror. Beyond the glass is an enclosure where a small octopus is playing with an assortment of toys. The animal lacks a skeletal structure. Its skin is transparent, and encased within its mandible is an enormous brain. A shimmering ooze coats the creature's limbs. Traces of slime cover most of its room.

Many are repulsed at the sight of such a creature, but the truth is that phebs are a species of tremendous value. While their basic needs and native tongue are both barbaric, their mind is superbly unique in that they are masters at problem-solving. Belonging to the mollusca family, phebtolocomostious, or phebs for short, are the advanced cousin to the common octopus.

The narrator feeds the data orb into a hole in the wall. A moment later, a ground-floor panel within the pheb's enclosure shifts open, and the data orb rolls into the pen. The creature freezes in place as it listens to the marble spin. Pockets of electricity manifest within the enclosure. Beams of lightning shock the monster and frighten it towards the data orb. The animal obeys the unseen hand that feeds and begins to pull its heavy-looking body towards the sphere.

If your space station or planet, doesn't have access to phebs, you may substitute their value with advanced forms of artificial intelligence. It will work all the same, but the problem may take longer to solve, and the power drain required will be tremendously expensive. Using computers to solve the puzzle is only recommended for class two or higher civilizations on the Kardashev scale.

The mollusca curls one of its arms around the marble. It then gropes the orb with its suckers. A thick coat of slime drips from the sphere as it's continuously fondled for a minute or two. The monster then deposits the orb into a tray and approaches a touchscreen display. It runs one of its oozing limbs across the pad, translating an unspoken language entirely through the sense of touch.

The slime-covered data orb sinks back into the wall. A sprinkler system above the creature's enclosure begins to spew a green-colored mist into the air. The mollusca falls into a motionless jelly-like state as it succumbs to an ecstasy that is incomprehensible through the lens of the video's transmission.

The wall of the tank shifts and the orb is spat out into the narrator's open hand.

And just like that, the encryption is cracked.

The escort glides down the hall and travels back towards the first room with the planetarium theatre. The recording orb follows. Once back inside the darkened showroom, the narrator places the data orb into the fleshy wound of an organic machine. The living apparatus digests the sphere and then disperses data along a wall of networked computers.

The human provided the data, we harvested and deciphered the code, then phebs solved the puzzle's equation. A simple journey, really, from start to finish.

Millions of orbs bleed from the theatre as the show begins. The viewer is slungshot through oblivion as the display travels to a darkened section of space. Dark clouds lift as the map is filled and the unknown area is brightened by a sky of galaxies and stars. The feed then warps through travel as the vantage point increases out and away from the network of everything that is known. Even at a distance, the map moves like an ocean: gentle waves confirm the existence of an unknown pulse.

It's endless in all directions, and so our work will exist beyond any mortal legacy or reign. From collecting the soul, to embedding the seed into the mind of a host, raising the clone to maturity, and harvesting the data, it took roughly six weeks- universal time - for this individual piece to be unlocked. Now that burden is, of course, lessened by the volume in which we operate, but even then we are limited by our resources. If we want to create a detailed map of the universe, we must work together. If you have any questions about this transmission or wish to join the cause, feed the following key into an encrypted gehouli machine, and someone will contact you in a timely manner.

A series of numbers, letters, and symbols flicker across the screen. It only lasts for a fraction of a second, but the detail in the code is complex and beyond comprehension. The image then switches back to the map. It zooms into a desert planet and then soars out to its moon. From there, the viewer is taken past an asteroid field and beyond a local star. Continuing on this journey, many stars are seen as the travel speed increases. Black holes, galactic gas trails, and pocket dimensions whiz by before the transmission goes static.

Lights, Camera, Action!

The ceiling of a dark room is removed like the lid of a pickle jar. Bright lights beam down into the perfectly still and abstract room. Grey panels line the basin of the white walls and, in the center of the room, a steel chair resides.

One of the wall's panels slides up. A pair of eyes glimmer in the darkness of the hidden entrance.

A deep voice says something in a harsh tongue, "drawrof emoc."

A young girl wearing a pink sundress crawls out from the opening. Her skin is smooth and pale. Her hair is black and her eyes are blue, yet hallow. She climbs to her feet and looks up towards the ceiling of the room.

"tis," the voice commands.

The girl approaches the chair and sits down.

"nigeb," the watcher instructs.

The girl's cheeks are lightly powdered and her baby blue eyes are outlined with a dark purple eyeliner. At first, her expression is blank. She is emotionless, but then she forces a convincing smile.

"Hello, friends," she says softly. Her voice is innocent and soothing. "I've been thinking a lot lately about-" she pauses and again looks up. "I don't know what that is."

"sdrow eht daer tsuj," the instructor demands, and the girl returns her attention forward.

"I've been thinking a lot lately about the soon and the stars-"

"Nus," the instructor interrupts. Although his tone is violent by default, he now seems deeply angered by the way in which the girl has pronounced the words.

"I've been thinking a lot lately about the sun and the stars," the girl repeats. "What do they look like? How are they laid out in the sky? I like to look at them. Don't you?"

A moment of awkward silence comes to pass, and the girl then looks up. The sinister silhouette of her handler towers in the sky. He is naked and hairless. The texture of his skin is like fresh tar, and the stench of sulfur lingers. The creature's face is obscured by the shadow of an artificial eclipse. He nods, and the girl then crawls back into the hole in the wall. The panel swings back into place, securing her within her prison. As the lid of the chamber is closed, the room fades to darkness.

Programming

Ambient screams carry down the darkened halls of an unknown location.

Within a nearby room, a delicate procedure is underway.

An obese man is naked and hanging in the air. Conduits and cables are fused into pockets of skin across his body. Ripples of fat bear the force of his weight against gravity. Eternal agony is fused into the core of his being, but a tube of liquid secretions eases any discomfort. The hose runs from the center of the room's ceiling. It feeds directly into the swine's mouth and down his esophagus. A headset is permanently welded into his eye sockets and - because of this - his known reality is purely synthetic.

The human swine groans for a moment and then defecates freely on the floor. The soft feces splatters on impact. The brown ooze seeps through steel grates, and the man is oblivious to his own defiling.

A hydraulic door opens and an immense, tar-skinned tentacle slithers to a stop. The husk of the colossal appendage begins to tear until a puddle of acid and puss is ejaculated into the room. After discharging the liquid, the monstrous limb continues to worm its way down the hallway. The door shuts and the puddle begins to swirl.

The pool of liquid heats up and smokes. A short, tar-skinned creature is birthed from the chaotic rift. With a callused, eyeless head, the monster begins to snort from a dozen orifices across the surface of its face. It sprouts stubbed limbs from its back and then hunches over as it pulls its awkward body towards a collection of electronics that line one of the room's four walls.

The obese man is oblivious to his guest and the plane of reality that the two share.

A colorful display of lights are projected along the walls as the creature begins to manipulate the console of electronics. The colors depict a pixelated image of what the man sees in his headset. He believes that he is at home, naked on the couch, and gorging himself on sugary snacks as he watches a television set.

The creature manipulates some of the electronics and the man's mind is warped to another location. The projection along the wall displays what he sees within his headset.

He is standing in a dark room. As lights begin to shine from above, a girl can be seen sitting in a metallic chair. She is glaring directly into the eyes of the man. Her piercing blue stare is a chilling cry for help, but as she smiles, the man's attention is pulled to the direction of the creator's design.

"Hello, friends," the young girl says softly. "I've been thinking a lot lately about the sun and the stars. What do they look like? How are they laid out in the sky? I like to look at them. Don't you?"

The tube that is rammed down the man's throat begins to vibrate, and a liquid secretion force feeds him a gel of blissfully delightful flavors.

The video feed stops and a new image is displayed. A three-dimensional projection of colorful data serves to graph out the man's thoughts and emotions. As the colors go dull, the readings confirm that the swine is sated.

The creature limps over towards the colorful projection and begins sifting through the endless data. The stream of code slows down as the drugs further their grasp on the man's mind. The creature slowly moves one of its stubbed arms back towards the console. It then places another stub against the man's forehead, and then a third limb is pressed to the backside of his skull.

Slowly, the data continues to tick. The holes across the creature's featureless face begin to swell as it absorbs and deciphers the stream of knowledge presented before it. Hairs silently sprout from one of the creature's spare limbs. The hairy ligament slowly drifts towards the man. The fine strands wiggle and worm as they enter the sated swine's nostrils. The obese pig begins to groan as the hairs climb further into his head, tickling his innards along the way.

The human lab rat sneezes and the creature glances back. Snot is dripping from the ligament that hangs from his nose, but he is still oblivious to the procedure. The creature returns its eerie gaze back towards the stream of code. One of the lines of text begins to ripple with purple vibrations. As if on cue, the grotesque creature shrieks and the submerged hairs dig through the subject's brain. The man tenses up and begins convulsing. The pockets of fat across his suspended body begin to ripple as he jerks in the air. He then falls silent as the creature's submerged limb ruptures from one of the swine's ears. Hanging from the tip of one of the hairs is a piece of brain tissue. The creature uses another limb to retrieve the organic matter. It then withdraws the submerged limb, and a trail of ooze (a mixture of blood and brain) leaks from the dead man's nostrils.

The creature crawls towards the exit and takes leave with the sliver of brain tissue in hand. The dead swine is left hanging from the ceiling. His motionless body gently sways as a thick trail of sticky matter slowly drips from his open nose. Like lingering raindrops on the morning after a torrential storm, the bits of blood and brain drip at the rhythmic pace of a steady pulse.

It's Only a Simulation

It's only a simulation. It's a simulation. This is a simulation. I exist within a simul-

"Dad?" A girl interrupts my train of thought.

The rapid sound of an agitated pulse comes to a sudden stop.

I open my eyes to see the pretty face of a young girl. In her teens, she is a spitting image of someone that I used to know.

"Are you okay?"

I remain calm and say nothing.

The girl walks over to a nearby window and tries to slide it open. A lock on the frame prevents the glass panel from moving. She uses her left hand to disengage the lock and then slides the window open. The fresh air wafts into the room. Spring is upon us... *Or so they would have us think.*

The girl takes a deep breath and then turns back to face me. "So, how are you feeling?"

I maintain my silence as my eyes focus on the world beyond the open window. A barren branch sways in the breeze and blocks a clear view. Small green buds are sprouting from the branch and I squint my eyes.

"Doctors say you are getting better," the girl says as she takes a seat next to me.

I continue to watch the buds sprout from the branch of the tree. Within seconds, the timber goes from being bare to harboring a blanket of fully grown leaves.

"They say you should be able to go home soon," the girl adds in a sweet and loving tone.

I disregard her words as I examine the leaves from afar. Though green and mature, something feels off about the foliage. I fixate longer to notice the lack of stems or veins. As I squint my eyes to confirm, the window begins to move. The entire backside of the room drifts away from me until the window becomes too distant for my vision to reach.

I attempt to stand and approach the distant wall, but the lower half of my body remains perfectly still. I glance down to see that my legs are concealed under a wool blanket. I remove the cloak to discover that my seating is, in fact, a wheelchair, and my legs are incapable of moving.

The girl watches. She is expecting me to lose my cool, but I remain calm.

I glance back to the window, but it is now gone. I can't be sure if it was ever even there. The white wall is bare, and the only source of light is shining from above. I raise my head to find there are no light fixtures, and that the source of this light is completely unknown.

The girl's eyes begin to water. A string of emotions swirl in the pit of my gut.

This actress is convincing.

"I just miss you so much, Dad" the girl chokes out. "We all do."

I examine my hands. The detail in my skin seems accurate, but I'm missing a scar on my left knuckle.

"From when a dog bit me as a kid," I accidentally let out.

The girl follows my gaze down to my hands. Her tears are a tempting distraction, but I do not break my stare. The girl places her soft hands over mine. I look up towards her to see the gentle tears that run down her cheek.

"Dad. I don't want to talk about money while you're ill, but your treatments are expensive, and I really need some help. It's hard for me to do this alone with mom gone, ya' know?"

At last, there it is.

"Do you remember our safe word?"

The girl sniffles and nods. She withdraws a pen from her pocket and uses her right hand to jot down a phrase on the inner wrist of her left hand. She then reveals the words that are written on her skin.

"You are right-handed," I observe out loud, ignoring entirely the phrase that she is trying to show me.

The girl looks down at the words with watery eyes and then glances back to me with a confused expression.

"Kalipso was left-handed," I add, the words barely escaping my vocal chords.

"Dad," the girl cries. Her heart is full of pain. The agony oozes from her skin like an oil, then a flame is ignited and the imposter who poses as my daughter begins to melt in her seat. Her skin bubbles and splits as she withers to ash. Her screams are authentic, and I endure the scene with slightly saddened eyes. Her death is hard to watch, even if it is only a simulation.

The room goes dark, and I can feel the burning rush of an injection coursing through my veins. In the real world, beyond my prison, they are upping my dosage. They are running out of time and they are getting desperate.

My mind goes dark as I succumb to their drug-induced coma.

I can hear voices in the distance as my consciousness drifts between two worlds.

"Dad! I need help! I can't do this on my own!" Kalipso cries from afar.

I try to see, but the veil of shadows lingers over me like a cool fog on a crisp morning.

"Dad! I need help! I can't do this on my own!" The words are repeated and, for a moment, I believe them to be true.

The lights return and I awaken to find myself sitting in a chair before a window. This time the tree beyond the glass is full of leaves, and the attention to detail is a little excessive. I glance down at my left knuckle and find that there is a scar that runs across the surface of my skin. They have hit the reset button.

"Dad! I need help! I can't do this on my own!" The voice

echoes in my head like the memory of a lingering nightmare.

I lunge forward and thrust my open palm against the window. I can feel the wet condensation on my fingertips. The glass is bolted shut from the outside. I pull my hand back and examine the details of wet skin. Droplets of water run along the dermal ridges of my inner palm.

I tug at the cloak that's wrapped around my waist. I roll my toes and feel their movement. I am no longer bound by a chair, so try to stand. I am weak, but my legs rise, and within a minute or two I manage to stand.

"Dad! I need help! I can't do this on my own!"

I begin to feel lightheaded as my thoughts race to discover the barriers of my reality. Behind me is a metal cot with white sheets. Beside that is an old computer from the early days of microchips and transistors.

At the far end of the room lies a metal door. I walk over to it and press my face against a glass viewing window. There is a hallway with bleached white walls. I can't see much beyond that. I glance up at the ceiling in my room. A string of fluorescent light fixtures radiate with a gentle hiss. This time they've coded in the sounds of magnetic ballasts.

I take a seat in front of the computer and rest the palm of my right hand against the mouse. The screen awakens to the backdrop of a snowy mountain. I open a run command and then input a string of code. The computer makes a connection with an encrypted wallet. This is what they're after. They want a key that only I can recreate.

"His mind has been fragmented," a man can be heard explaining on the other side of the door.

I quickly dive out of my chair and lunge towards the door so I can listen to the conversation beyond.

"A small piece of him lives within reality, but he is far from complete," the man adds.

They want me to think that I'm crazy. It's an easy way to cover up for their sloppy work.

"But I can see him," a girl says in a manner that comes off as more of a suggestion than a question.

"You know my thoughts on the matter," the man enforces, "but you also know that, legally, I cannot stop you from seeing your father."

The man peers into my cold room. His eyes burn with disgust as he notices that I am listening to him speak. He steps away from the door and whistles for some help. A pair of muscular men dressed in medical attire appear by his side. One of them then approaches the door and instructs me to step back.

I obey the command, retreating to the cot and having a seat on the edge. The door unlocks and a girl steps inside. Dressed in a blue button up blouse with a matching skirt, she wears the face of my daughter.

"You are older than I remember," I say with sass.

The words serve to bring a smile to her radiant face. She spins a chair around and then takes a seat directly across from me.

"Dad," she says, still wearing the radiant smile.

I say nothing.

"Doctors say," she pauses as she ruffles through a stack of papers on a clipboard. "Well... they say a lot of things."

I examine the many imperfections of my daughter's face. Her image is convincing, but not entirely true.

"How are you, Dad?"

I say nothing and, this time, my silence forces the girl to roll her lips inwards.

"I saw your sister last week. She helped me with some legal forms. She said she misses you, and told me to give you a hug for her."

I sink my teeth into my lower lip.

"Dad?" The girl questions softly.

"I'm not your father," I admit with cold words.

The girl's face begins to prune as she absorbs the statement.

"Kalipso died on the day I was taken," I spit.

The girl's eyes are quick to water as the words cut her deep like a fresh wound at the hand of a sharp blade. She takes a deep breath as she tries to reclaim control over her emotions. She then rolls the left-hand sleeve of her blouse up to her elbow. She reveals the skin of her inner arm, where a pair of dark brown scars run across her forearm.

My eyebrows stiffen as I glance at the healed wound.

"I don't hold it against you, Dad. I know you're not well, but I just want you to get better."

Memories surge to the forefront of my mind like the storm-induced waves of the ocean smashing against the rocky shore of a distant beach. I am reminded of the day I was taken. I can remember holding my wife as I ran the knife across her throat. I tried to do the same to Kalipso, a quick and mostly painless death, but as she squirmed to get free, I slashed her left arm and left her to bleed out while I frantically destroyed my hard drives. I can remember with vivid detail the image of her lifeless body. The moment her leg last kicked and when her life finally faded. Facedown in a pool of her own blood, she was wearing her favorite pair of black and white shoes. Her pinstripe socks were painted red with her mother's blood.

"Dad! I need help! I can't do this on my own," the girl exhales with a burst of tears.

I glance at the floor and cup my face. It all feels so real, but it's supposed to. It's a simulation.

They are running out of time, and they are getting desperate.

The sniffling sound that the girl makes pierces through my heart like a cold knife.

She's a simulation. This is a simulation.

Upset with the rebirth of memories that I wish to forget, I unleash a burst of violent rage. I lunge towards the girl and tear the clipboard out of her hands. I then snap the fiberglass in half. The broken edges are jagged and sharp. I run one of the shards across my daughter's neck and scream, "You're not real!"

A pair of doctors rush into the room. Their size dwarfs me, and their strength is unmatched as they grapple me and throw me to the ground.

"It's not real," I seethe. "She's not real!"

Kalipso slumps to the ground as she struggles to breathe. The choking sounds that she makes are disturbingly authentic. Her blood runs along the edges of the floor's white tile. My fingers soak in the warm fluid as I struggle to fight off the two men that have me pinned.

"It's only a simulation!"

It Takes a Village

At birth, children are immediately taken from their parents and placed into government infant programs, where they are raised until they are two years old. From there, a child will be sent off to live with an adult. All adults over the age of thirty are required by law to take in a child for two years. They must do this for a minimum of eighteen years. The child changes homes every two years until the age of eighteen is reached. Then, as an adult, the individual gets integrated into a military program, where eight years of servitude is mandatory. Once done with the military phase of their lives, they are placed into a state-run college until they are thirty years old. After college, people are free to live their lives.

The term freedom is controversial in meaning. Even after reaching the age of thirty, one is still required by law to raise the state's children for eighteen years. Then, after that, you may freely work and live as you choose. The private sector is dead. Your paycheck comes to you from the government and always in the form of credits. No one in society ever handles or owns money. Everything is owned and operated by the state. When you die, your belongings are liquified because you, technically, do not have any children. Outside of the uncommon bond of marriage, nobody truly has anyone that they can call their family. The state is your mother, father, daughter, and son.

***

A blue light begins to flash in the corner of a small, windowless room. As time passes, the light intensifies, shining faster and brighter. A screeching alarm annoyingly chimes in to accompany the lights.

Every square inch of the room is illuminated, and a dark-skinned boy in his teenage years is asleep, dreaming of the ocean. Waves crash into a rocky shore, and the sound that the water makes is powerful. It is natural. It is free.

The boy moans as the peaceful moment that he privately owns within the confines of his mind is tainted and ruined. He opens his bright green eyes and faces the reality that is before him. The time has come to wake and dress. Being forcefully pulled from within his slumber is a maddening experience, but he accepts the inevitable course of his fate.

The boy peels away the bland, grey sheets that served to bring him warmth throughout the night. He sits upright and sighs. As he does, the alarm is automatically deactivated. He stands up and walks over to a grey dresser. He then removes a pair of grey pants and a grey button-down shirt. After getting dressed, he makes way for a small sink in the corner of his bland bedroom and begins to brush his teeth.

The boy stares at his reflection in a mirror. After hunching forward and spitting out a mouthful of toothpaste into the drain of the sink, he sets down his toothbrush and continues to stare at his own reflection. The faint trickle of a peach fuzz mustache is coming in unevenly across his upper lip. He runs the tips of his fingers through his short, nappy head of hair, and then a knock comes on the metal door of the room.

The boy shuffles over and answers. A large, rough-looking man is standing at the entrance, and he is holding a tray of food. On the tray is a plate full of fruit and a bowl filled with warm oatmeal. The boy reaches out to accept the delivery. No words are spoken between the boy and the man. A simple nod is exchanged and the door is again closed. The boy retreats back into his room to consume the meal. He sets the tray down on a small table and then seats himself. Silently, he eats his food.

The wall beside him lights up and a school schedule is displayed. A nearby tablet computer illuminates and reflects the same image of curriculum that is planned by the hour.

"Good morning, Elijah," a robotic voice says over a hidden stereo speaker in the ceiling.

"Good morning, Alexa," the boy responds before spooning another mouthful of oats.

"I see that you are awake and dressed. Are you ready to start your day?"

"I'm eating breakfast," Elijah disputes.

"I'm sorry, Elijah, but that is an improper response," the AI explains.

The room flashes red and an X appears in the corner of the boy's tablet.

"Awe, come on," Elijah complains. "The day hasn't even begun!"

"When would you like to begin, Elijah?"

"When I'm done with breakfast," the boy groans.

"I'm sorry, Elijah, but that is an improper response."

Again the room flashes red and a second X is marked in the corner of the tablet.

"In five minutes," Elijah says, rolling his eyes.

"Okay. Timer set for five minutes."

Once finished with his meal, Elijah spends his entire day working with the robotic voice. The AI serves as a digital tutor for the boy and guides him through a series of academic endeavors. From mathematics to science, English, and Chinese, Elijah submerges himself fully into his studies. The curriculum is broad and mostly accurate, but history is written and told by the victors of time. What Elijah comes to know of the past is only what the masters of the world wish for him to know.

As the long day comes to an end, Elijah concludes his studies with a lesson in gravity. Alexa teaches him of Sir Isaac Newton and the studies he performed in order to prove gravity's existence.

Elijah puts his tablet away and sinks the tips of his fingers into his temples. His eyes ache and his forehead is throbbing. Every day is the same, and it is tiresome to be fed information with little to no reward. He sits down on his bed and falls back with a sigh. Not long after, a knock comes at the door. The man from earlier in the day opens the door without being welcomed or acknowledged. He stands near the open entrance and awkwardly begins to speak.

"Tomorrow is your birthday," the big man says with a grunt.

"Yes, I know," Elijah admits.

"That means we only need four more credits, and then we can retire," the voice of an unseen woman adds.

Yeah... that is exactly what my birthday means, Elijah snickers in his own head.

"Well, you will be transferring to another home in the morning. Since we will be out of town this weekend grabbin' the new kid, I reckon this evening will be the last time that we will see ya," the man informs.

Elijah says nothing. In truth, he can't wait to move on to the next home.

"So, take care of yourself, alright?" The man says, extending his hand.

"Yeah. Thanks," Elijah forces as he accepts the handshake.

"Remember what I told ya'?" The woman interjects as she enters the room. Her beady eyes bolt from left to right as if she is guarding a terrible secret behind a mouth of rotting black teeth.

Elijah nods and the woman lowers her head. Her skin is greasy and lumps run across the surface of her pale face. She looks into the boy's eyes as she awkwardly awaits for verbal confirmation.

"Don't ask my foster parents for anything, never leave my room unless instructed, and stay ahead on my school work," Elijah says.

"And with that, you will do fine," she says with a heinous smile.

The man and woman exit the room. Elijah rolls his eyes and gently closes the door behind them.

The boy takes a seat on the bed. With a blank stare, he glances towards his tablet, which is on and glowing. The text on the display is a study guide for a night's worth of homework.

"Alexa, who are my parents?"

"Your current parents are Michael and Tiana Harbour," the vocal assistant informs.

"No. Who are my real parents?" The boy rephrases.

"Your current parents are Michael and Tiana Harbour of seventeen Linden-"

"Stop," the boy interrupts. "Let's just get started."

Elijah proceeds to work through the evening. Trapped within his cube of conformity, he obeys and performs under the instructions of his unseen servant. He reads up on the distorted half-truths of history and writes essays on his learnings until his eyes are bloodshot and his brain is numb.

When the work is complete, the boy sleeps. Alexa wakes him up the following morning and instructs him to pack his things. He fills a black backpack with clothes and a toothbrush and then sits on the bed. With a hollow expression, he awaits further instructions.

The door to the room clicks and Elijah glances over.

"Your escort has arrived," Alexa informs over the speaker system.

Elijah stands and exits the room. The home beyond his cube is a mess. Nicknacks and trash litter the hall. He doesn't linger long, and instead makes haste towards the home's entrance. Tapping a finger against the front door brings up a touchscreen monitor. An integrated camera feed reveals a hallway beyond the suite. The display is encased in a solid red border. Within the frame is the image of a circular globe. With lights flashing across the metal chassis, the drone reflects emotion through color as it speaks.

"Greetings, Elijah. My name is Alex. I'll be escorting you to your new home today."

"Of course your name is Alex," the boy mumbles to himself.

Elijah plants a second finger against the touchscreen display, and the icon of a padlock appears. He uses his thumb to swipe at the abstract logo. The door's red rim flashes as it changes to green. A mechanical bolt is released and the display returns to its ambient appearance of resembling a fully intact door. The entrance recedes into the wall, and the chilly draft from the hallway beyond washes into the apartment.

The little spherical drone hovers in place. A burst of neon-colored lasers radiate from the chassis of the robot as it wirelessly scans Elijah's biometric data.

"Identity confirmed," the bot says as it drifts in towards the boy. "Shall we get going?"

"Sure," Elijah agrees. As he exits the home, the electronic door closes shut behind him.

The escort leads Elijah through his rundown apartment building. A constant drip can be heard as water pools in the hallway from the collapsed ceiling of an abandoned home. As the two reach a musty stairwell, Elijah looks back towards the hall and sighs. He reflects on how much he hated living in this place. Hopeful that the next home will be better, he follows the drone down the stairs, and the two exit out into the city streets.

The streets themselves are mostly barren. An electronic wagon silently hovers by, and Elijah glances over to see that there is nobody inside the vehicle. Men and women, dressed in grey, emotionless uniforms, shuffle to and from work. Their faces are expressionless and they avoid eye contact with one another at all cost.

As Elijah continues to follow the drone down the avenue, he passes by a robot carrying a screaming infant. The child is encased in a glass cage, which serves to muffle its shrewd cries.

After traveling a few blocks through the concrete jungle, the two arrive at the basin of a towering skyscraper.

"Is this it?" Elijah questions as he glances up towards the building's apex.

Cutting into the clouds of a sunless sky, the high rise tower is only one of many that litter the concrete block.

"Yes," the drone confirms. "We have arrived at the location of your new home."

A high-pitched scream cuts through the air, and Elijah turns back to face the street. Wailing around a nearby corner are a pair of spider-like machines. With great speed, the drones pull themselves forward as they exert a warning cry that is accompanied by flashing lights.

Elijah's companion begins to strobe red and blue colors.

"Please step aside, Elijah," the escort instructs as it ushers the boy back and away from the street.

"Are those hunter drones?" Elijah asks.

"Yes," the escort responds.

The two spider mechs turn the corner and disappear. Their sirens fade with the spread of their distance.

"Where are they going?"

"It is none of your concern, Elijah," the drone informs as it ceases its warning strobe of lights.

The two enter the high-rise building and silently approach an elevator. A touchscreen panel within the lift displays an assortment of options. The drone wirelessly communicates with the panel, and then the number six flashes on the screen before the two begin their ascension. The elevator rises and then halts. The doors open to reveal a chrome corridor.

The two exit the lift and pass by a series of cream-colored doors. They stop at an entrance that is marked with the number twenty-seven, and the drone wirelessly activates an electronic doorbell.

An awkward moment comes to pass as Elijah silently waits to meet his new parents.

The door recedes into the wall and a slim, fit man stands on the other side. With chestnut-colored hair and a clean-cut beard, the man is well kept. His brown eyes are soft and welcoming.

"Mr. Travis Conover?" The escort inquires.

The man nods as a smile forms at the edge of his mouth, and the drone washes over him with a series of analytic lasers.

"Hey, yeah," the man begins with a smile as he glances from the drone to the boy.

"Identity confirmed," the escort announces as the lasers disappear. "Mr. Travis Conover, this is Elijah Bennett. He will be your new foster."

The man maintains his smile for a little longer than he should, and Elijah begins to question the expression's authenticity.

"Right, well, come in," the man says through his teeth.

"That won't be necessary," the drone responds. It turns to face Elijah. "Farewell."

The boy watches the escort hover back down the hallway towards the elevator.

"Come on in, and we'll get you settled, kiddo," the man offers, and Elijah glances back towards the man standing in the open door frame. With the drone gone, his posture is relaxed and his expression relieved.

As the two step inside the home, the man withdraws a polymer pistol from his waistband. He then slips the weapon up under a hidden ledge over the doorway's frame.

Elijah notices the hiding of the weapon but acts as though he is blind to the action. He instead turns to face a wall of framed pictures to his right. Each snapshot is of the man and a woman. With gold hair, soft skin, and welcoming blue eyes, the girl is beautiful. The images tell the silent story of grand adventure shared between two souls.

A woman steps out from around a nearby corner. Her belly is swollen and she is cupping the bump with the palm of her right hand as she walks.

"Elijah, was it?" Travis asks as he escorts the boy further into the home.

The boy nods in silence.

"Well, kiddo," the man begins, "Welcome to your new home. That's Jeff," he says, pointing towards a glass orb with a goldfish inside, "and this is my beautiful wife, Leslie," he adds, gesturing towards the woman standing in the open hallway.

The woman blushes and rolls her eyes as a warm glow radiates from her soft skin. She is prettier in person than in the pictures.

"We didn't know that you'd be arriving today," the woman explains nervously. "I mean, we expected you to come sometime this week, but the state didn't tell us when exactly that would be."

"I'm sorry," Elijah atones.

"No-no," the woman eases, feeling as though she has offended the boy. "It's not your fault, and we are glad to have you. Please, come inside and have a seat!"

The woman leads Elijah further into the home, where she gestures to a grey couch.

"I'm fine," Elijah mutters as he continues to subtly examine the small apartment. The living room is like something from another time. There are no electronics to be found, and instead there are many old-fashioned books littered about.

"Are you hungry? I can make you something," Leslie offers as she wanders towards a small kitchen area.

"No thanks," Elijah objects. "I'm okay."

"Let him settle in," Travis chuckles.

The woman turns to face her husband. She is left hanging with an awkward expression that is embedded with a pleasant smile. The man laughs and then plants a gentle kiss on his wife's forehead.

"Pardon me," she says, taking an abrupt leave for the hall. Her departure leaves Elijah alone with the man, and an awkwardness comes to meet the present as the two find no words in the moment.

"She has to pee all the time now," Travis interjects, breaking the silence.

Elijah forces a stiff smile as he considers a way out of the conversation before it can begin. As the woman returns, he finds a way out.

"Where is my room?" Elijah questions softly.

"Um, right," Leslie says. "It is going to be down the hall and on the right. Would you like me to walk you?"

"No, I think I've got it. Thanks."

Elijah shuffles towards his new room. Indian tapestries line both sides of the hallway's walls. He arrives at the door to his room. The entrance has been left open. He steps inside and goes to close the door behind himself, but then stops and contemplates whether or not he needs to. He reflects on the past, where it was accustomed in every home for him to stay in his room with the door closed. He wasn't to exit unless summoned.

The details of the bedroom force the boy to lose hold of his train of thought. His eyes drift about the room and he considers the strangeness of it all. Every room that Elijah has ever lived in has looked exactly the same; a windowless white cage with a gray cot for a bed, two tablets for school, and a closet that also serves as a washroom with a sink, stand-up shower, and toilet. This room, however, is different. It has no washroom. The walls are painted blue, and there is a shelf nearby that is loaded with paper books.

Elijah sets his backpack on the floor and runs the tips of his fingers across the soft fabric on the bed. The sheets are a dark blue. The texture forces the boy to smile as he continues to caress the cotton blanket.

"Finding everything alright?" A feminine voice calls from

behind.

Startled, Elijah jumps to his feet and turns to face the open doorway.

"Lez'," Travis calls from out in the living room. "Leave him be."

"Right," the woman frowns. "I'm sorry, it's just that we've never had a foster," she admits, lingering in the doorway. "I just want to make sure that you feel welcome."

Elijah wanders towards the entrance and smiles. "I do feel welcome," He entertains. "Very much so."

The woman's face brightens with excitement.

"Great! Well, good, I mean," her tongue trips on her words. "Would you like to join us for dinner?"

"Out there?"

"Yeah," she giggles. "You don't have to eat in here alone." A frown forms as she realizes that more often than not, it is tradition for children to eat, sleep, and live in their rooms.

"I would like that," Elijah agrees.

In a matter of hours, a table is set and the boy joins the strangers for an artfully crafted meal. Elijah remains mostly quiet throughout supper, and Leslie jumps from one subject to the next as she talks like a radio whose power button has been snapped off. Following the meal, Leslie tries to convince the boy to try dessert. Wanting to not be rude, the boy tastes a slice of cherry pie. The flavor is both tart and sweet.

"Never liked cherries," Leslie confesses with a mouthful of pie, and Travis chuckles. "It's weird the things you crave when you're expecting."

"Expecting?" Elijah questions, confused by the phrase.

"Mmhmm," Leslie mouths at a juice-covered spoon.

"Expecting what?"

The couple looks at each other and laugh. Elijah then feels stupid for not getting the joke.

"A baby," Leslie clarifies with a giggle.

"Oh, you're pregnant?"

"I am," Leslie says as she gently cups the palm of her hand over the naval point of her large belly. "Could you not tell before?"

"I've never known anyone who was pregnant," Elijah admits.

"So you just thought I was a fatass!" Leslie gasps and her

husband swallows loudly in a joking manner.

Elijah grits his pearly white teeth and shrugs, nervous that he has upset her.

"Relax, kid," Travis eases. "She's only messing around."

The woman begins to laugh. "I'm sorry."

"When are you due?" Elijah questions as he sets his spoon down on his empty plate. Only crumbs remain of the pie he was given.

"Eight more weeks to go," Leslie confirms with a smile.

A cold silence veils the room as Elijah is greeted with the truth of the child's fate. As he dwells on the thought for a moment, Leslie's smile fades.

"That's cool," Elijah awkwardly spits out, trying to break the tension in the room.

Leslie nods and her pretty smile returns.

"What's it like?" He whispers as if the notion of growing a person inside your belly was somehow a taboo subject.

Leslie chuckles. "It's ... strange. At first, anyway, but I've started to get used to it, and now it's an incredible experience."

"Does it hurt?"

"Only when she *really* kicks," Leslie admits.

"*He*," Travis corrects, and Elijah ruffles his eyebrows in confusion.

"We don't know the gender," Leslie confesses. "He wants a boy and I want a girl, but we won't know until she's brought into this world."

"We won't know until *he* is brought into this world," Travis again inserts with a grin.

"Wanna feel a kick?" Leslie offers.

"May I?" Elijah questions as he cocks his head over towards Travis.

"Don't look at me, kid. It's growing in her belly, not mine."

"Sure," Leslie chuckles as she scoots out from behind the table.

Travis stands and begins to clear the table, and the boy scoots over towards the pregnant woman. Leslie takes the boy's hand. Her skin is soft and smooth. She then uses her free hand to pull back her shirt until her swollen belly is fully exposed. Elijah's eyes widen as he discovers just how alien and large her stomach has really become. Leslie gently plants the boy's palm against the outer surface of her womb, and then the two of them silently wait.

Elijah's raises his eyebrows as he feels the light kick against his hand. A smile forms at the edge of his mouth as another jolt follows thereafter.

"That's incredible," he admits, and Leslie agrees with a silent smirk.

Elijah withdraws his hand, and Leslie lowers her shirt back over her belly.

"Kicks like a boy, doesn't he?" Travis jokes as he re-enters the room.

The evening turns to night, and the three find themselves relaxing in the living room. After distributing warm mugs of green tea, Leslie takes the time to show Elijah her collection of old world books. The topics of the banned texts range across a variety of subjects, but all of them share a similar scent that isn't found anywhere else in the present day.

Leslie travels to another world with her nose buried within the bindings of an old book, and Travis takes this opportunity of her silence to make small talk with Elijah. He asks him things like how old he is, and how many homes he has been to. Leslie is forced to peek up over her book with saddened eyes when she hears the stories of the past homes. To Elijah, the quality of his life is normal, and the prospect of living with the young couple is an abnormal, above average exception.

In the coming weeks, the couple grows rather fond of the boy. Elijah spends his days studying while Travis and Leslie are out at work. Come nightfall, the trio gathers in the living room for tea and books. It is during these reading sessions that both Travis and Elijah converse over a broad range of topics, the likes of which the boy has never even considered to question. With Leslie off to bed at an early hour, the man and the boy are left alone with their words, sometimes until the early hours of the mornings that follow. Elijah grows comfortable with the man and, in time, musters the courage to ask Travis about something in private that has tugged at his mind since the first day of his arrival to their home.

"What will happen when she gives birth?" The boy asks on

one early autumn evening.

Elijah expects the question to shake the man, and he immediately regrets asking it for fear that it will upset him.

The man's face turns to stone as he nods in silence and then abruptly stands to his feet. Hunching down over an end table, he reaches underneath the furniture, and fiddles with an unseen switch. Following the sound of a click, the table splits into two, and a centerpiece rises from the open cavity. Nestled within the hidden compartment is a bottle of scotch and a pair of whiskey glasses. Travis removes the contraband from the clandestine alcove. He then sets the paraphernalia in the center of the coffee table and proceeds to splash a bit of the brown liquid into each of the glasses. Handing one of the drinks to the minor, Travis clinks his glass against the other and silently nods.

"Yeah?" Elijah confirms before throwing back the gift. "I've never had alcohol."

"I imagine not," Travis agrees. "Illegal everywhere except Africa, Russia, and the poles." Travis takes a sip of the scotch and closes his eyes as he embraces the fine burn. With his eyes still closed, he answers the boy's question from before. "They will come, and they will take her."

The answer arrives as Elijah is mid-gulp. He fights off the urge to exhale a breath of fire as he naively winces through the drink's hot burn.

"How do they know that she's pregnant?" Elijah forces after swallowing down a gulp of the exotic beverage.

"We're microchipped," Travis explains with his beverage raised in the air. He swirls his drink and watches the fluid spin within the glass as he speaks. "Everyone is at birth."

"Even me?" Elijah asks, confused.

"Even you," the man adds.

"Where is it?" Elijah questions, feeling uneasy about this new truth.

"Left lymph node," Travis says as he gestures to his neck with a pair of fingers.

Elijah presses the tip of his index finger into the skin under his jaw. The bulbous organ feels natural to the touch.

"You can't feel it unless you press deep," Travis points out.

"It's inside the gland," he adds as he pushes his fingers deep into his own neck.

Elijah presses deeper and then his eyes widen. "There it is!" He gasps. "I can feel it!"

Travis rolls his lips inward and nods.

"Can it be taken out?" Elijah questions softly as he is reminded that Leslie is asleep in a nearby room. Despite his hoarse whisper, his tone still reflects a sense of panic.

Travis shakes his head and says nothing as he splashes more scotch into each of the two glasses.

Despite this newfound truth, Elijah returns his thoughts to Leslie and her unborn child. "It will destroy her."

"It would," Travis agrees.

A moment of silence ensues as the two men consume their beverages.

"Did you know," Travis begins, "that beneath the city, there lies another?"

Elijah raises an eyebrow as he tries to piece together the meaning.

"Deep within the sewers are the remnants of old New York," Travis clarifies. "It's a lawless land where anarchists roam freely."

"You're saying that people live in the sewers?"

"It's underground, yes," Travis confirms, "but the network is vast and stretches for hundreds of miles in all directions." He extends his arms so that he may speak with his hands. "The microchips," he adds, gesturing back towards his neck, "they don't work underground, so it's one of the only safe places to go. Not all bad. They have shops and power and homes down there."

"You've been down there?" Elijah questions.

Travis nods. "I have an old friend who runs a greenhouse down there. He grows tomatoes the size of your head!"

"And ... you are going," Elijah phrases his question in the form of a statement.

Travis says nothing as he sips his drink and gives a nod so subtle, Elijah can't be sure if it is a gesture of agreement or not.

"What's to stop hunter drones from going down there and bringing people back?"

"People down there are pretty savvy," Travis explains. "Have to be if you want to live under the earth. Multiple hallways are rigged with EMPs, and there is a network of explosive charges in place to seal off caverns should trouble arise."

Another quiet moment arrives as the two men dwell within their own heads. Accompanied by only their liquor and thoughts, hard truths are confronted in silence.

Travis holds his glass still as he gazes into the darkened hallway behind the teenager.

"When will you go?" Elijah breaks the silence, but Travis continues to stare into the abyss.

The focus within the man's pupils returns front and center as Leslie steps out from the shadows. She doesn't take a seat, but rather stands at the edge of the couch and listens. A twinkle within the woman's eyes suggest that she has something to say, but she remains quiet, pressing her words down into her stomach where they seep into her womb and linger among the fetus of her unborn child.

"It's only right we tell him," Travis says to his wife. She nods and slides the palm of her right hand across the surface of her swollen belly. She then takes a seat beside her husband and leans into the man's shoulder. "It wouldn't be right for you to just wake up one morning and have us not be here," the man adds with an expression that could cut through steel.

Without dwelling long on the thought, Elijah blurts out his utmost desire. "What if I come with you guys?"

Leslie lifts her head and glances over to her husband, but Travis continues to stare into the eyes of the teenage boy.

"I understand the risk," Elijah adds, "and I won't be a burden."

The agreement is never verbally made, and the topic is never again discussed out loud. In the coming days, Travis brings a pair of black duffle bags into the living room and sets them behind the couch. In an unspoken expression, Elijah packs his own bag and sets it by the other two. Eye contact is made between the man and the teenager as the bag is placed among the others and a silent understanding is exchanged.

As the days press by, Leslie teeters along the edge of childbirth, and Travis continues to grow uneasy. The cheerful man has gone silent with thought as he reflects on a thousand unspoken truths.

Exiting his bedroom with a black rifle slung over his shoulder, Travis approaches Elijah and begins.

"Her water has broken, and the baby is coming."

Elijah's eyes widen as a sense of excitement collides with the thought of nervousness and unease.

"I've bought us a bit of time and given Leslie drugs that will scramble her hormones and keep the microchip from relaying her current state. We don't have long though before her levels balance out and the drones show up. I am going to deliver the baby, and then we are going." His posture is straight and his eyes are sharp. The tone of his voice is calm, yet serious. "Ever use one of these before?" He questions as he unslings the rifle from his back.

Elijah shakes his head in silence.

"Safety on. Safety off," Travis explains as he manipulates a lever on the side of the rifle. "Red means dead," he adds, gesturing to a red dot beneath the lever that can only be seen when the safety is off. He then points the firearm down the hall and pulls the trigger. There is a clicking noise, but the weapon doesn't fire. "Mag release," he adds, pressing in a button along the rifle's mag well. As he does, the weapon's magazine drops to the ground with a thud. He then kneels to the ground and withdraws a full magazine from one of the two duffle bags. He locks the fresh magazine into place with a snap and then continues. "Slide release," as he releases the weapon's slide. "That one's important," he adds as he presents the rifle and demonstrates how the slide is manipulated. He then raises the weapon and points it down the hall. "And now it's ready for bang." Travis turns to face the teen. He offers the weapon and Elijah bites into his lower lip.

"Probably won't even need it, kid" the man eases.

Elijah exhales softly and accepts the rifle. He slings the firearm over his back and then waits for what comes next.

Over the course of many hours, the teen stands in the living room and listens to the wailing cries of childbirth as Leslie brings another soul into the world. His palms are sweaty as he awaits an unknown fate.

The cries cease and Travis scurries from the couple's bedroom with a small blanket in hand. He approaches the teen with haste and gently passes the bundle to him. Elijah accepts the gift and glances down into a pair of soft blue eyes. The child tries to stare back, but its eyes shift in and out of focus as it gently begins to cry.

Rushing back into the bedroom, Travis takes a moment to dress his injured wife and escort her out into the living room. Her face is beading with sweat and her hair is a tangled mess as she gasps for air and limps towards her newborn.

"He's going to have to play carrier, honey," Travis interrupts. "You can't walk on your own."

The man slings the duffle bags over his shoulders and then retrieves a second rifle from a hidden panel in the wall. With everything needed, he double-checks the weapon's magazine and ensures that the firearm is loaded before slipping an arm underneath his wife's shoulder and helping to guide the woman to the door.

"We're going to the elevator and taking it to the ground floor," Travis explains, and Elijah follows with the infant pressed to his chest.

Once within the elevator, the group descends to the 1st floor as the infant cries within the arms of the teenage boy. The lift doors open and the trio scurries out. Travis mashes his fingers against one of the numbers on the touchscreen display before he exits the lift with his wife. He then turns back to face the elevator.

"What now?" Elijah questions.

The windows that lead out into the world reveal an active, bustling street. Despite wanting to melt into a puddle of fear, Elijah stands tall with the weapon on his back and the infant in his arms.

The elevator doors close and Travis leans his wife against the wall as he counts out loud to three. He then throws himself against the closed lift and pries the doors open. A pair of steel cables reside in the center of the dark shaft. Removing the duffle bags from his shoulders, Travis tosses the cargo into the abyss. The bags sink into darkness. A subtle thud echoes up from the open shaft. The distance that the bags have sailed before making impact with the ground below suggests that the fall is rather far, and Elijah's stomach begins to churn as butterflies flutter within.

"Alright," Travis begins. He withdraws three different pairs of heavy-duty gloves from one of the cargo pockets that are stitched into his pants. Distributing the gloves to both Elijah and his wife, he then slips his own pair over his fingers as he continues. "You've gotta hold on like your life depends on it, because it does. Climb down fast, but don't be foolish with your grip."

Standing up straight, the man then gestures for Elijah to hand him the child. The teen steps forward and hands over the baby. Travis then gestures towards the shaft and Elijah leans into the darkness and reaches for the steel cable.

"Hold it for her so that she can go first," Travis injects, and Leslie wails in pain as she grabs on to the cable. "It's just like rock climbing out west, dear," Travis eases. "This is a cakewalk compared to Rainier."

The woman squeals as she grabs the cable and begins to climb down. As she disappears into the darkness, Elijah glances back towards Travis. The man is purposefully ignoring the world beyond the open lobby windows and instead is focusing on tying the infant firmly against his chest.

"Alright, kid. Your turn."

Elijah nods and leans against the cable. It sways softly under his weight and he begins to descend. The cable wiggles further as Travis joins the climb from above. The lift doors seal shut behind them and nothing but an infant's soft cry accompanies the three in their descent into darkness.

Elijah continues to climb until his feet come into contact with something stiff below. Unsure if the ground beneath his feet is truly solid or not, he panics for a moment before letting go of the cable.

"Travis?" Leslie calls from the darkness.

"I'm almost there," the husband eases from above.

Once on the ground floor, Travis walks through the abyss and approaches one of the walls. He fiddles with something for a moment, and then the faint light of a lantern flickers to life.

Launching herself towards her husband and child, Leslie breaks into tears.

"Grab the bags, kid," Travis commands as he unties the child and passes it to the woman before helping her limp through the dimly-lit corridor.

Elijah heaves the heavy duffle bags over his shoulder. The weight of the cargo is immense, and the teen is quick to lose his breath. Ahead is a large pile of rubble and a low hanging corridor that leads further underground. The group presses through the corridor until they exit out into a standing sewer tunnel.

"How did you know that this was here?" Elijah questions in awe of the secret tunnel.

"I've been digging through for months. Only managed to finally get through to the other side a few nights ago," Travis explains. "Now step back."

Reaching up into a hidden ledge, the man withdraws a small, black cylinder with a case cover protruding from the object's tip. Flipping the cover open reveals a red switch. Travis glances back to Elijah and Leslie and then toggles the switch back and forth. A split second of nothingness ensues, but the silence is quickly butchered as the ground trembles and a muffled explosion can be heard above.

"It's a girl," Leslie exhales with a smile as she peeks under the blanket for the first time since delivering the child.

Travis turns to face his wife. For the first time in many weeks, he allows a smile to form across the surface of his face. The trio shares a giggle before embarking on their journey into the earth. They flee from the present in search of a past where rule of law doesn't take the form of a tyrannical thumb pressed firmly against the spine of its people. Their future lies in the dark sewer systems of the old world. From this moment on, they will live like rats so that they may be free.

Upon the Altar of Blood and Bone

Confined within the prison of a dark, dank sewer, I live. I have never seen the clouds of the sky, nor the stars beyond. I have never felt the warm shine of the sun upon my skin; although... I have heard stories. It sounds marvelous ... or so it was, before it died. Now it is said that the sky is always as dark as the walls of this dungeon, and because of this, escape is not worth the risk of one's life.

It all seems so hopeless.

Lying on the ground with my cheek pressed firmly against a cold stone floor, I watch as a naked man struggles to reach for his backside. His skin is inked in filth, and he is picking at a collection of scabs. Blood oozes down his spine from one of the freshly opened wounds. This man, like many of the others here, has lost himself. I do not know him, but it is sad to know that he once had a family: a wife and children. He once was a man with a purpose, but now he is a hollow shell: the empty remains of a soulless vessel.

I have lived in this cage for as long as I can remember. My sense of smell is perverted by the permanent stench of sickness that lingers in the air. I take comfort in whispering lies. I tell myself that I can recall the memory of my mother's scent. The truth is, she was taken soon after giving birth to me, and the source of her smell is likely an intricate fabrication of my own imagination. I never knew my father. He was taken soon after impregnating my mother. The elders say that I am lucky to have survived through adolescence, but I do not believe in luck, or gods, or heroes, or fairy tales. None of those folly fables are welcome here in this cage of darkness and filth.

Whilst keeping my cheek flat against the ground, my eyes drift over towards the corner of our cramped prison cell where a dozen or so people are kneeling and praying for salvation. Though religion is as dead as the sun and the sky beyond these walls, this group of helpless victims still cling to a set of ancient ideals and aspirations.

Behind the group is a woman whose face is always saddened. She is sitting on a cot that is made of skin. It is the only bed to be found in this entire stinking cage. Her sorrow is not fueled by a sense of self-pity; rather, she is a kind and gentle soul who bears the pain of her children. She never forgets a name, and she never forgets a face. She has no actual kin, but the people refer to her as Mother Magi. Some believe she is a goddess, captured by our masters and destined to share in the fate with those of us who are enslaved.

Voices echo along the stone walls that lead towards the prison. The words are unknown, but the harsh tones are deep and rhythmically in sync. There is a prolonged emphasis on their vowels that serves to raise the hairs along the basin of my neck. We have never seen their faces, and they have never spoken directly in our presence.

Their chanting and singing is done in private, but it bleeds through the walls and haunts me in my dreams. The group grows restless when they hear it begin. Their songs are always soon followed by a visit.

With my ear still pressed to the ground, I am the first to hear it. Someone is coming. A pair of bare feet can be heard slapping against the stone beyond the cell. The others fall silent as they too begin to hear the sound. The silence is brief as the group is quick to panic and frenzy. Some cling to their loved ones, while others sit alone and await the arrival of our unwanted guest. A group of religious zealots gather around Magi and shield her from view. I do not believe that there is any value in one's life over another, but protecting Magi seems to be something to believe in, and the religious among us are so desperate to believe in something that they will believe in almost anything at all.

A puddle of liquid leaks across the floor and touches my skin. The fluid is warm, and I sit upright to investigate the source. A young girl beside me has soiled herself out of fear. Her ample eyes are gawking forward.

Someone is outside of the chamber looking in. Our guest is deceitful with his identity. His head is hidden beneath the veil of a black hood, and his skin is draped in the fabrics of a matching cloak. A wide-eyed mask covers his face. He tilts his head and presses the beak of the mask through the bars of the cage. His eyes are still for a moment as he basks in this moment of power. The fiend then steps back and lifts one of his gloved hands into the air. Slowly, he sways his arm back and forth as he dwells on the decision. At last, he extends his hand forward and points a finger. The sentence has been made, and an old man has been chosen. Those around him, family and friends, begin to cry. Wise beyond his years, the old man stands to his feet and silently accepts his fate. With a peppered white beard that spans down across his bare chest, the old man has witnessed many people come and go. He has been here for as long as I can remember, but we have never spoken to one another.

The man shuffles towards the bars of our cell. A few of the children cry as they watch him go, but nobody says a word. The fiend inserts a key into the cell's lock. The door creaks as it is pulled open. The man exits and the cage is again locked. The old man is then escorted down the hall and out of sight.

People are chosen at random, it seems, so anyone could go at any time. Families, grateful to have survived another day, cling to each other and weep.

I sink back to the floor and contemplate my fate. Perhaps facing death at the hands of the cultists would be better than living like rats in a cage.

A few hours go by, and then the chanting begins. The cultists are performing a ritual, and the man they took away is about to be sacrificed. I try not to listen, but the stone walls carry the song throughout.

A few days go by and then another one of us is taken. This

time, following the abduction, Magi calls my name. I wander over towards the goddess, and her followers part so that I may approach. A man is sitting on the ground beside the praised woman. His skin is covered in dirt and grime. He is silently crying as he cups his face with his hands. The tips of his fingers are bloody and raw.

"Your turn has come, child," Magi says to me. Her eyes wash over me like the cleansing waters of a fresh stream.

"Turn?" I question. My voice is frail.

Magi nods and looks to her followers. They are shielding us from the rest of the group so that others may not see.

"Yes," the woman assures. "The children deserve to go first."

Magi rises from the skin cot and kneels on the ground beside the broken man. She welcomes his head against her chest so that he may cry in comfort. The woman's followers then lift the cot and move it to the side. Below the throne is a hole in the ground.

I glance towards Magi. Her eyes are soft, and she looks into mine for a moment before silently gesturing towards the hole.

"Follow it to the end," Magi whispers. "Once you reach the hallway, stay left."

I hunch forward towards the hole and peek down into the darkness. I want to ask a hundred questions, but I only manage one.

"How will I see?"

"Just keep crawling," Magi asures with a gentle expression.

The followers help me down into the hole. They then seal my tomb with the cot. Left in darkness, I begin to worry. I combat my emotions and remind myself of the excitement in this moment. Feeling my way forward, I crawl through the abyss. The cramped cavern twists and turns. As minutes turn to hours, I silently cry in fright as I lose track of how far I've gone, and then... a trickle of light appears in the distance.

I begin to laugh with excitement as I claw my way forward and tears stream down the front of my face. Reaching the light, I peek up from the crawlspace. Torches radiate along the walls of a cavern above. I climb up into the chamber and stand for the first time in a while. I then collapse against the cavern's wall and grip my chest. With a smile, I choke down the cavern's cool, crisp air.

Voices trickle in from down the eastern corridor, and my heart skips a beat. Reminded that I am not yet free, I climb up to my feet and cautiously make my way down the left hall. The corridor twists and turns and I quickly lose my breath as I realize I am climbing. Following the path left, I find a bright light shining into the cavern from ahead. Slowing my approach, I linger forward. An open exit leads out over an open canyon. The painted walls of the endless gorge tell a beautiful story under the light of a bright sun.

"It lives," I mumble in awe as I look out over the alluring landscape.

I press a hand forward from the shadows and reach for the sun's rays. My pale skin is brightened under the shine. The warmth is unreal, and I step forward into the light. Basking in this moment, I drop to my knees and wish to never leave.

"It is ... beautiful," I whisper with my eyes closed as the heat warms my face.

My spine begins to tingle, and then my soul is plunged into the icy waters of fear. Something has grabbed my leg, and I yelp in horror as I faceplant into the ground. I open my eyes and watch as I am dragged back inside. A trail of blood oozes from my face and leads back towards the outside world. I kick my legs and begin to scream.

"No," I deny. "No!"

Flailing on the ground, I twist my body around and catch sight of my attacker. One of the cultists is dragging me back inside. I continue to kick and scream. My sporadic movements force the attacker to reclaim his grip. I launch forward and kick him in the chest. He groans and I follow through with another blow; this time to his face as he kneels forward and tries to capture me. The abductor's mask is thrown from his face. The man staring back is old and frail. His pale skin is littered with wrinkles and liver spots. A mixture of anger and terror glimmers across the reflection of his eyes.

I scramble to my feet as I prepare to bolt for the exit. It is in this moment that I realize the truth. The cultists - these monsters who keep us like sheep for the slaughter - they are weak. We only submit to them because of the mask that they wear, but underneath the disguise is little more than a man.

Something cold sticks into my backside. I crumble forward and yelp as I smack my face against the side of a rock.

Darkness ensues.

Shadows mingle overhead and I open my eyes to find myself

in the center of a large room. A dozen torches are scattered about the room's walls. I try to sit upright, but a stinging pain pulses from my backside. I then notice that I am strapped to a platform. I cock my head to see that the structure below me is made of bone. Hundreds of human skeletons have been twisted and warped into an ancient altar. Some of the pieces even appear to be fresh. Blood and entrails ooze from the inner sanctum of the altar.

My heart begins to race as I panic, and then the singing begins. From the unlit corners of the room, the cultists are chanting their song of worship. One by one, my captors step forward. With strange, twisted daggers in hand, they approach.

I begin to sweat and plead, but my cries are drowned out by the song of sacrifice as the hooded monsters draw near. Perfectly in sync, the cultists raise their daggers above their masked heads. They hold their position as they continue to hum, and then another cultist steps out from the shadows. This one is a woman, and she is completely naked from the neck down. The only piece of clothing that she bears is a rabbit mask that drapes her face. She approaches the altar and then climbs up over top of me. Running her hands across her chest, she groans and then lies back on the platform across from me.

The singing continues and then, one by one, daggers fall. I wiggle and scream as the blades puncture my body with ease. I wince and yelp as death's cold embrace lingers. Warm blood leaks from the open wounds across my chest, and I watch in horror as the cultists take their sated weapons over to the woman. They use the daggers to smear my blood across the naked woman's skin, and then one of the cultists discards his dagger and drops his robes. He mounts the woman and begins to choke her. The remaining cultists then proceed to plunge their daggers into my chest.

The soft sexual moan of pleasure collides with my chaotic screams as I am butchered alive upon the altar of blood and bone.

Bug Out

Concealed in darkness, a storm crackles to life. It serves to wreak havoc upon the lands of the Earth. The rain sings and the lightning dances. It is an intimate love affair of expression through hate. Their cries echo through a city of glass and steel.

Amidst the sound of chaos, a set of keys can be heard faintly rattling. A handle is turned and a door slowly opens. Though mostly distorted by a sky of darkened clouds, moonlight trickles into the entrance of a home. A man wearing sunglasses steps inside and closes the door. He is dripping wet from head to toe, and his path is guided by a cane that he waves from side to side. He rests his forehead up against the door and lets out a sigh. The man then reaches to his right. Through the darkness, he flips a switch, and the room he is standing within is brightened by lights from above.

His black hair is soaking wet and adds contrast to the paleness of his skin. Beads of water run down his face and slip under the shroud of his sunglasses. He peels off his trench coat and hangs it to dry on a rack beside the door. As droplets drip from the coat and land on the floor, they mimic the sound and rhythm of a slow metronome ticking away the seconds of eternity.

The man is wearing a white button-up shirt and a pair of black slacks. A blue necktie hangs down the front of his chest, and just beside it is a plastic name tag that is pinned to his shirt. The label reads 'Steven' in big, bold letters, and below the name are the words 'Sales Associate.'

Steven walks down the hallway of his home. He doesn't turn on any of the lights other than the one by the doorway that he activated upon entering the residence. He steps into a washroom and sits on a white porcelain toilet with a stained basin. He reaches over to the tub and turns on the water. He places a stopper in the drain so that the water may rise, and then he picks up an orange prescription bottle from a hanger beside the tub. He unscrews the cap of the container and empties two large pink pills into the water. They are quick to dissolve and bubble up in the tub.

Steven slips off his dress shoes and kicks them away towards the wall. He then peels off his black socks and stands to his feet. He loosens his tie and slides it from around his neck, and then unbuttons his shirt. He drops his shirt on the floor. He undoes a navy blue belt and tosses it aside. The buckle of the belt clinks upon hitting the cream-colored tile floor. He drops his black khakis, and then his underwear.

Once fully naked, Steven places the palms of his hands down onto the granite surface of the bathroom's vanity. He leans forward and stares into the mirror. He is still wearing his sunglasses. They serve to veil the identity of the man that is gazing back in the reflection. His scruffy-looking face is a tell that he is tired. Black facial hair is coming in, and it looks as though he hasn't shaved in a few days.

The skin around Steven's shades wrinkles up. He is squeezing his eyelids shut. He gasps - appearing to be in pain. He removes his sunglasses. A lone tear slides down the front of his face. Dark rings encircle Steven's eyes. He places the tips of his fingers on the surface of his closed lids. His upper lip quivers and he fights back the urge to cry. Removing his fingers, Steven leans in closer towards the mirror and prepares to open his eyes. A moment goes by where he tries to hesitate and stall, but he then grits his teeth and raises his eyelids. His pupils grow as he looks into himself. Puffy and red, his eyes are highly irritated. As he continues to stare, something pokes through the cornea of his right eye. Steven sniffles as he watches a small, black ant climb out from the surface. Soon after, another appears, and within seconds a few dozen ants are gliding across both of Steven's eyes.

Steven sniffles again as he turns to face a full bathtub. He turns off the water and steps into the bath with both feet. Steam rises from the hot water. He sits down and then leans back until his shoulders are completely sunken into the water. Steven takes a deep breath and then plunges his face under. He opens his eyes and stares at the ceiling through the cloudy bath water. His mouth opens and air rises. The muffled sounds of his screams can be faintly heard with each air bubble that pops on the surface of the water. Steven begins to bleed ants from his eyes. What looks to be two or three quickly becomes twenty or thirty. They squirm in the water and rise to the top. Fighting to survive, they try to swim towards each other. With Steven screaming under the water, the current serves to be too strong for the ants to manage. They sporadically twitch before shriveling up and dying. The chemicals in the water seem to be the cause of their ultimate demise.

Steven lifts his head out of the water and gasps for air. As soon as his lungs are full, he drops back under and continues with his agonizing therapy. This continues on over the course of ten to fifteen minutes.

The water is mostly still, and the surface is completely dark. Hundreds of lifeless ants sway on the gentle current. It is a sea of death, and through it, a man rises. Steven opens his eyes and glances down to the water. A few seconds go by where his face churns in combat with himself. In the end, he loses to his emotions as he breaks into a cry. He grants himself this moment of self-pity before reaching into the sea of death and pulling the stopper out from the water. As the bath drains, Steven leans forward and turns on the overhead shower. He grasps his legs and rocks back and forth as the water rains down on him. It rinses away the dead insects from his skin, and he continues to cry. This goes on until the warm water goes cold.

The frigid shower is a call to exit. Steven turns off the shower and stands to his feet. His face is a tell to his hollow sense of emotion. He steps out onto the cold, marble floor and then reaches for a towel.

Steven presses the dry cloth to his face and exhales. He runs the towel through his hair, and then down the front of his chest. He checks his armpits and then his scrotum, where he spots a few of the dead ants that are lying still on the surface of his skin. Steven wipes them away and continues to dry himself off.

Once dry, Steven stands before the mirror and stares at his naked body. He is fit and thin. He dwells on his sense of loneliness and considers the desire for a companion. His moment of thought is cut short when he reaches for a vial of liquid and unscrews the top. He withdraws a glass dropper and leans his head back. After inserting two drops of the liquid into each eye, Steven looks again to himself in the mirror. The dark rings around his eyes are a tell to his sleepless nights. His prickly facial hair tells the story of someone who is on the verge of giving up. The corners of his mouth hang low, and finding comfort in his reality is a luxury that has been slain long ago.

Steven nakedly exits the bathroom and walks into a nearby bedroom. He approaches a dresser and withdraws a pair of pajamas. He sets the attire down on the surface of the dresser and then freezes in place. The lights in the room are still turned off, but through the darkness, he glances into the heart of the dresser's mirror.

Lightning ruptures through the air beyond the home and the room is temporarily illuminated. A dozen prescription bottles are scattered across the surface of the dresser.

Steven maintains his ghoulish gaze into the mirror. Something has captured his attention, and he is waiting for the intruder to again show his face.

More lightning flickers beyond the nearby window and Steven's shadow crawls up the wall beside him. Towering above, the figure watches the broken man stare at himself in the mirror.

Something within one of Steven's idle eyes interrupts the eerie tension in the room. The intruder is small and seemingly insignificant, but his appearance carries the weight of damnation.

Steven remains motionless as he watches the intruder protrude from the corner of his eye. It is an ant, and it's making way across the surface of his left iris.

The broken man remains frozen in time as a second insect pokes across the surface of his eye. Within minutes, the ants are accompanied by a third and a fourth estranged family member. The gathering continues and the colony returns to fruition; safe from the onslaught of the storm within their home inside of Steven's mind.

Christmas Kitten

White sheets ruffle atop a futon-style bed. A man exhales a breath of tremendous satisfaction and then wraps the fingers of his right hand around the edge of the cotton fabric. He pulls back the sheets to reveal his scruffy face. With jet black hair and piercing blue eyes, the man is a magnificent cousin to a forbidden fruit. A head of brown hair pops up from beneath the sheets soon after. A girl in her mid-twenties pants as she comes to the surface.

The man stares at the ceiling for a moment, trying to catch his breath. The woman shuffles closer and rests her head against his bare chest. The motion of his rib cage cradles her head like a hammock on the beaches of paradise. She closes her eyes and smiles. Her moment of bliss is cut short when the man gently tosses her to the side and climbs out of bed.

Standing before a great, curtainless window, the naked man basks in the sunlight before reaching for his briefs. To the woman, he is perfect. Both of their bodies are young and fit, but only he is chiseled from head to toe.

"What are you doing?" The girl asks.

"I've gotta go to work," the man admits as he slips his underwear on and reaches for his pants.

"On Thanksgiving?" She sits upright and wraps the soft sheets around her naked body.

"The retail world knows not of holidays," the man says. He opens a closet and pulls out a blue button-up shirt with a matching tie. He then lays the shirt onto the edge of the bed and proceeds to walk towards the bathroom. Water begins to flow as an electronic sink activates and the man can be heard brushing his teeth.

"What if we just stayed in bed all day," the girl suggests. "It's too cold out to do much of anything else." She looks out the window and watches as flakes of snow drift by. "We could bake cookies and watch the parade."

The man re-enters the bedroom. He wipes his face with a hand towel and then discards the cloth to the floor. "Cute, but I've really gotta go to work," he admits as he buttons up his shirt.

"Aren't I more important than work?" The girl plays.

"Don't get all sentimental on me, Monica. It's just sex."

The phrase stings like a slap to the face, but deep down, the girl knew that he was right. Perhaps it was the truth in the words that served to be the key ingredient of her pain.

"Yeah. I know," she replies with a forced smile. Her bright green eyes slide out of focus.

Realizing that the harshness of his comment had hurt her, the man tries to brighten the mood. "*Although...* spending the day with you *would* be better than dealing with the hordes of zombie shoppers that I'll have to face today." The man speaks the words as if he is reading from a script. He makes a ridiculous face and sways from side to side like a mindless undead corpse as he pokes fun at consumer culture.

The woman's face brightens as a genuine smile erupts.

He places a hand on the smooth skin of her face and says, "I need the money. Can't pay the rent without it."

Monica's smile fades as she contemplates the value of money against herself. She again looks to the window in the room. Outside, the city is painted white. A fresh layer of powder covers everything from street lamps to mailboxes. With a chill running up the base of her spine, Monica turns towards the man and questions, "How much will you make today?"

"I don't know," he admits, looking into the mirror at himself and wrapping his tie around the collar of his shirt. "Couple hundred if I kill it, I guess."

Monica bites into her lower lip. A mark is left as she goes to speak. "What if I pay you what you'd have made today?"

"To stay in bed all day?" The man gasps, finishing up with his tie. "I guess I'd never considered being a hooker before," he adds with a chuckle.

"You got the body for it," the girl assures with a devious smirk. She buys into the hope of him considering her offer, but he continues to get dressed.

As she accepts defeat, she pulls the sheets to her exposed flesh and uses her free hand to fish for her underwear. She slips the garments on, and then stands on the bed. Fighting to keep her balance, she reaches for a bra that is hanging from the ceiling fan above.

The man lifts his eyes towards her reflection in the mirror before him. He raises an eyebrow as her breasts sway. "Impressive shot, wasn't it?" He boasts.

She says nothing.

The girl unhooks the bra from the fan and covers her chest. With the lingerie on, she climbs down from the bed and picks up her pants from off of the floor. She gets dressed in silence while the man hums a familiar tune to himself.

The woman reaches for a pile of things on a nightstand beside the bed. A hair tie, a cellphone, a lanyard with many keys, and a silver ring. She clamps the hair tie around the back of her messy hair and then checks her phone. The battery is dead. She slides the ring onto the third finger of her left hand.

"Do you think you could give me a ride home?" She asks.

"I don't think that is such a good idea," the man says as he throws a winter pea coat over his shoulder.

"Lilah isn't home," the girl assures.

He considers it for a moment, and then just agrees in order to avoid conflict, "Yeah, sure."

Their car ride begins and a strange silence accompanies the two of them on their journey. The man kills the silence by turning on the radio, but the awkwardness remains. The girl hums the tune of a song that's playing over the air. She knows the words, but her voice is imperfect, so she refrains from singing them out loud. The two come to a stop at an intersection. A group of children cross the powdered street. They are outfitted with gloves and armed with sleds. Adventure awaits them, and the girl simply watches from her seat as the children pass by. The two continue for a bit longer before pulling up to a small Victorian-styled home and the girl speaks for the first time since their departure.

"What time will you be done?"

The man doesn't bother putting the car in park. He keeps his foot on the brake pedal and scratches his left eyebrow.

"Listen, Monica," he begins. "This isn't a thing. We were just having a little bit of fun."

The girl nods, places a hand on the door and then pauses, "Jonah," she says softly. "There is something that I need to tell you."

One of the man's eyebrows slightly twitches as he keeps his foot on the brake of the car.

"I'm pregnant," she blurts out.

With an explosion of utter displeasure, the man throws the stick of the vehicle into park and the car sways. His eyes take on an angered gloss and he grits his teeth. "Are you *fucking* kidding me?"

Monica's eyes widen as she shakes her head in denial.

"What is this?" The man flares. "Some type of fucking guilt trip? Did you stop taking birth control or something to trap me into being with you or some shit?"

His rage churns and Monica's eyes water as her entire face begins to pucker.

The man runs the fingers of his right hand through his slick hair and attempts to regain his sense of cool. He looks out his window and considers the predicament for a moment.

Tears silently run down Monica's face as she stares forward, ashamed and afraid.

"Alright," Jonah finally assures. "Alright." He leans forward against the steering wheel and digs his wallet out of his back pocket before sitting back down. He flips the leather bifold open and withdraws a pair of hundred-dollar bills. Monica watches through tearful eyes as the man hands her the money and says, "This should handle it. Get it taken care of... *today*."

Monica sniffles, nods, and accepts the money before silently exiting the car. She remains in the middle of the street and watches as the man wastes little time in driving away. The girl stands in place and watches as white snowflakes fall from the sky. Emotionlessly still, she looks like a piece of scenery to be found within a gently shaken snow globe.

***

Four weeks later, Monica finds herself sitting in a chocolate-colored rocking chair beside a fire. Her face is dimly lit by the warm glow of the burning embers, and she is watching the mellow flames consume all with ease. The gentle glimmer is comforting to watch. Hanging from the mantle of the fireplace is a pair of stockings. One has the name *Monica* etched across its surface in vibrant green text, and the other reads *Lilah* in a matching style of cursive lettering.

A heavy wooden door can be heard opening, and a cold draft lingers through the darkened corridors of the unlit home. Monica maintains her stare into the heart of the flames as the door closes and, a moment later, she is greeted with a gentle kiss atop her head. She forces a smile and glances up towards the intruder with an expression that is very different than the one she wore just minutes ago.

"Hey," Monica says softly.

"Hey, you!" The feminine guest returns as she removes a pair of cotton gloves from her hands. "It's like traveling through Antarctica out there," she adds, running her now-ungloved fingers through her head of thick, red hair. Bits of snow rain from the elegant curtain of curls. Melting into droplets of water before colliding with the floor, the flakes of snow wither under the strain of the fluctuation in temperature. "So ..."

"So?" Monica questions softly.

A devious sort of smile manifests along the rim of the red-headed woman's mouth. "So, I know that Christmas is *technically* tomorrow, but you've gotta open one of your gifts tonight," the woman instructs, fighting back the urge to let her smirk erupt into a full-fledged smile.

Monica continues with her facade. Beneath her false expression of interest lies a hollow wasteland of torment.

"I couldn't wrap it because," the woman adds as she withdraws a cardboard box from the shadows and gently hands Monica the package, "well, you will see!"

"Oh, okay," Monica tries a little harder to force an expression of gratitude as she accepts the gift. The sound of something scratching within the package forces her to lift a brow of inquisition. She lifts one of the box's tabs to find a silver-haired kitten within. "Lilah," she gasps in awe.

"Do you like her?" Lilah grins from ear to ear.

Monica's smile grows authentic as she wraps her fingers around the kitten and lifts it from the box. The young cat cries as it grows paranoid.

"Wait, she is a her, right?" Lilah questions. "Ryan said she was, but God knows he's never actually seen a vagina before," she giggles.

Monica says nothing as she cuddles with the soft kitten. The cat chirps as its eyes bolt across the room and it analyzes its newfound surroundings.

"She can keep you company while I'm away," Lilah inserts.

"Yeah," the word disperses into a thousand secret emotions.

"Ryan says that I should be done with the travel meetings by May, then I can transfer back into a desk job here in town," Lilah explains.

Monica says nothing as she continues to stroke the cat.

"You know I wish I could be around more," Lilah's words fade as her eyes begin to water and she struggles with a difficult truth.

"It's fine," Monica lies.

"She was abandoned," Lilah deflects in an attempt to change the subject. "The litter that she was born into was left in a dumpster behind work," she confesses with heavy eyes. "Ryan heard her crying, and when he found her, she was the only one left alive."

Monica remains silent. She pets the kitten as the words manifest into speechless thought. The story fills her with pity for the cat and disgust for the person cold enough to abandon the litter.

"But don't worry, I walked her over to Stacy's. You know she owns a salon next door to the shop now, right? Well, anyway, she cleaned her up. Gave her a good scrub and a shine."

Monica glances into the eyes of her wife. A twinkle glimmers as a silent connection is made. "You always find the best in things."

Lilah's skin glows as she basks in the warm comment. "So," she chokes up. "What are you going to name her?"

Glancing back down to the kitten, Monica strokes the feline's neck, and the cat begins to purr. "What about Nala?"

"I love it," Lilah exclaims as she plants a gentle kiss against the lips of her sweetheart. "I'm going to take a shower," she then adds as she turns to walk away. "Flight back from Detroit was a nightmare."

Monica says nothing as her wife takes leave from the room. She cradles the kitten like a child, but the cat begins to squirm as it gets restless in the arms of the foreign woman.

"How about some milk?" Monica offers. "Maybe you are hungry?"

She sets the cat down on the chair and then scurries into the kitchen where she pours some milk into a glass bowl and microwaves the liquid for ten seconds. She then returns to the living room to find that the cat is no longer on the seat where she had left it. A moment of panic arises as she glances around the room.

"Nala?" She calls, setting the warm bowl of milk down on the floor.

Monica drops her head to the carpet and peeks under the chair. She then sits upright against her knees as she glances around the room. A gagging sound redirects her attention towards the fire, where she spots the kitten.

The cat has its back arched, and it's making strange noises.

"Nala?" Monica repeats softly.

The feline is struggling to breathe as it gags on the floor. Its muffled cries are both chaotic and distressed. Monica dives towards the kitten. The presence of fear lingers through the fog of a present danger. The cat finishes heaving up something foreign, and then darts away as the woman draws near. Monica tries to snatch the kitten up, but the feline weaves in between her hands and disappears into the shadows of the empty home.

The sound of shifting liquid redirects Monica's attention towards the floor. Something is moving within a puddle of fresh vomit, and Monica's stomach drops.

"What..." Monica's thoughts drift away amidst a sea of

demanding resolve.

The heap of organic innards shifts as something struggles within. Monica's pupils dilate and her gut wrenches. Sweat begins to bead from her face and her breathing intensifies as she watches the creature wiggle and worm. Its body is that of a small fetus - an undeveloped child - and it squirms in the vomit as it tries to create sound. Its eyes are pinched shut within their depressed sockets.

Monica's upper lip begins to quiver as she continues to watch the thing worm within its liquid tomb. Tears roll down the front of her face as a severed connection is once again made. In a sudden burst of both panic and fright, she scoops up the fetus and tosses it into the flames of the fire. A high pitched squeal ensues and Monica presses the palms of her hands against both sides of her head as she breaks out into a silent cry.

"Monica?" Lilah questions as she drifts further into the room.

This moment of chaos ceases and a stagnant white noise is left behind.

Monica jerks around in panic. Her hair is wet and her face is dripping with sweat. "You alright?" She presses with concern lingering in her elevated tone.

Monica tries to remain calm as her chest rises and falls. She looks into the eyes of her forgotten lover and smothers her secret behind the veil of a false expression. Her upper lip twitches as she bears the weight of this discomfort, and the lie bleeds through her skin like smoke from a fire.

"Yeah," Monica squeals, her voice cracking under the strain of this soul-saturating torment. "I'm fine," she lies.

The Greys

"Leave it to the FBI to get suckered into this one," a potbellied cop snickers as he escorts a woman up an old, wooden staircase.

The woman ignores the comment. She climbs the staircase with ease. The exotic scent of a fine Panama roast wafts from the mouth of a coffee cup that she is holding, and she basks in the aroma before indulging in a warm sip. A soothing comfort washes over her stone face.

The cop reaches the top of the stairs. Huffing and puffing, the swine struggles for air as the woman slips past him. Dressed in a black suit and tie, she approaches a younger cop who is standing guard before a closed door.

"I've got it from here," the woman informs, flashing a Federal Bureau crest in the air.

The young officer nods and walks towards his girthy superior, the piglet snorting by the staircase.

"What a fuckin' bitch," the fat cop mumbles under his wheezing breath. "DC sends their lapdogs down here at the drop of a dime," he complains as the two begin to descend the stairs. "Might as well just hand my paycheck directly over to the cunt. Would save the IRS a whole lotta time."

The woman wraps the fingers of her left hand around the door's handle and waits for the men to get out of earshot. She taps the knuckles of her right hand against the entrance, but she doesn't wait for a response. Instead, she turns the handle and gently presses the door forward.

The entrance leads directly into a kitchen where the sink is filled with dirty plates and the countertops are littered with trash.

"Cassandra?" The woman calls as she enters. The soles of her black dress shoes stick to the vinyl tiles below her feet.

As the woman turns the corner, she discovers a girl sitting at a small plastic table. Once white, the surface of the table is now mostly brown. The girl's skin is pale, and her face expresses no emotion as the detective draws near. The girl's hands are crossed over her privates as she remains in the chair and stares off into the abyss with bloodshot eyes. She is dressed in an ivory-colored sweater and designer blue jeans. Her greasy hair is a long mess of tangled golden knots.

"Cassandra Kalai?" The woman presses as she slowly approaches.

The girl doesn't flinch. Her face remains perfectly still.

"Cassandra, I'm a detective with the FBI," the woman begins as she takes a stand directly opposite the girl. "Mind if I have a seat?" With a shift in tone, the woman sets her coffee cup down and switches tactics. Her eyes secretly observe the messy room beyond the kitchen as she pulls a plastic chair out from the table. "Heard you've been through a lot," she emotionally presses as she slides into the chair and glances into the eyes of the girl across from her.

The depressed sockets of the girl's eyes are blackened, but she isn't wearing any makeup. Her expression remains hollow as she slowly cocks her head to face the detective.

The woman slips her left hand into her black blazer and withdraws a grey ballpoint pen. She maintains a cold gaze into the girl's lifeless eyes as she begins to twirl the instrument between her fingers. The words *to see without blindfold* are etched across the surface of the pen in a vibrant golden cursive. She abruptly stops twirling the pen and then clicks in the tool's plunger with her thumb.

She releases the button and then repeats the process a second time. The clicking noise cuts through the air like an index finger snapping against the palm of a hand.

The girl's pupils swell and her eyes return to focus as her mind is forced to the present. She glances at the detective with an expression that says that she is both curious and confused.

"You alright?" The detective questions with a soft tone.

"I…I…" the girl tries to speak. Her voice cracks and she fails to produce any words of substantial meaning.

"You were just about to tell me about last weekend," the detective pushes. She tucks her grey pen back into one of the hidden pockets within her blazer. "Take me back, Cassandra, back to Sunday night."

The girl arches one of her eyebrows. She drops her gaze down towards the surface of the unclean table below, and her eyes wander towards the coffee cup. "They think this is some kind of joke," she forces with a dry tongue as she stares at the inanimate cup.

"I don't think that this is a joke," the woman eases.

The girl's eyes go in and out of focus as she continues to stare at the cup. "Like I'm looking for attention or something…"

"I don't think that, either," the detective reassures.

The words don't seem to register as the girl continues, "but *how* would've I done *this* to myself?"

This time, the woman says nothing and instead watches as the girl lifts a hand from her lap and tugs at one of her sleeves. The pale white arm is covered with circular burn marks that run deep into her flesh. The tender scars range in size between a quarter-inch and a half-foot in diameter. The rims of the craters across her skin are near perfect in their spherical impression.

"They said that they were burn marks from a cigar or piece of wood or something," the girl drones, "but burn marks are a pain I could bear."

The detective's head remains perfectly still as her cold, green eyes examine the scars under the umbrella of heavy brows.

The girl drops her hand back down to her crotch, and her face winces as she begins to silently cry.

"Have you showed this to a doctor?"

"I don't have insurance," the girl chokes out.

"Anyone other than the local police?"

"They all laughed at me," the girl forces with tears streaming down the front of her face. Her stare remains locked onto the still coffee cup on the table.

"Forget about them," the woman cuts. "It's you and me now."

"There is no pain-" her thoughts are conveyed through words that begin to trail off. "-no pain like the torment that *they* bring."

The woman sighs as she grows bored with the games. "I'll be honest with you, Cassandra. I'm not interested in what you've already told the police. I've read through all of that. What I want to know is what you *haven't* told them."

These tactics catch the girl off guard, and she stutters as she lifts her eyes to meet the detective. "I-I don't understand."

"Yes, well. I wouldn't be down here if this was just a rape case, Cassandra," she pauses for a moment as her eyes darken. "You and I both know what this really is."

The girl's mouth widens as she stares forward in horror.

"Take me back," the detective guides. Her words seep into the girl's skull and saturate her mind like ink to fresh, white linens. "You weren't raped by men four days ago, so let's get on with the truth."

"How..." the girl stutters. "How do you...?"

The detective stands and examines the messy apartment. A purple hat lies on the ground. A tiger logo has been sewn into the visor. The hat is sitting on top of a stack of papers. Incorrect calculus equations are scribbled across the white lines of loose leaf.

The woman approaches one of the walls and taps her knuckles against the white plaster. "The walls of your apartment are not very thick. Did you scream or shout for help?"

The girl follows the conversation's lead like a dog obeying commands. "I tried," she admits. Her watery eyes twinkle as they follow the woman to the far side of the open studio apartment. "But they stop you from screaming."

"They gagged you?" The woman offers as she wanders over towards an open window.

"I screamed," Cassandra admits as she struggles to regain control of her composure.

There is broken glass on the floor below the window and a silky curtain dances under the presence of a warm wind. The woman can see out into the street. People shuffle about their daily lives as they mindlessly travel along a sidewalk four stories below.

"Why could nobody hear you, Cassandra?"

"You're not *listening*," the girl moans as she becomes angry. Her mind is unchecked as it pings across a spectrum of emotion.

"I'm just trying to understand, Cassandra," the detective hisses as she turns back to face the girl. "How do they keep you quiet?"

"They can control sound," the girl admits. Her voice is now hollow as she obeys the commands and answers swiftly.

"How?" The woman presses further.

"I don't know how, but when they are around, everything is silent."

The only source of light in the room is coming from the open window. With the woman standing in place, most of the light is blocked out by her dark silhouette. Her figure seems abstract as the shadows mingle along the white walls of the apartment.

"There *is* a noise though," the girl admits, adding to her previous statement. "But it's this piercing white sound." Her lips are dry as she speaks. She is a hollow shell with a mind that has been shattered. "It's kind of like a ringing noise: a single note that never ends. It plays in your head and drowns out all of the other sounds."

"So other people can't hear this noise," the detective assumes out loud from where she continues to stand across the room.

"The note drowns out all of the other sounds," the girl repeats like a broken record.

"Did they take you, or did you stay?" The woman questions from the open window. Her words linger through the shadows of the room as the sun's shine is barred from entering the messy studio.

"We stayed," the girl answers in a monotone.

The detective approaches the table. As she leaves the window, the sun's shine is disencumbered, and the room is again brightened by the warm rays.

"Did you try to fight them?"

"I was paralyzed," the girl says as she forcefully pinches her eyelids shut. A hint of humanity returns to her expression and tone as she slowly shakes her head. Her breathing succumbs to the influence of an incoming cry. "You can't move when they are near."

The woman returns to the table, but she does not sit.

"What do they look like?" She questions from above the girl. Her towering figure demands authority, and something sinister radiates from the agent like the exerted will of a slaver to a slave. The girl's eyes remain closed as she basks in the unholy presence.

"They are without gender and completely hairless from head to toe," her upper lip quivers as she clings to the words like a sheep to shepherd. "Their skin is grey and their eyes..."

The detective retrieves her coffee cup from the table. The brew is now room temperature. She raises the cup to her lips and consumes her drink as she listens to the sniveling girl fight with the words in her mouth.

"Eyes of darkness that wash over you like freezing cold water," the girl sniffles as she opens her eyes and the floodgates open. Tears stream down the front of her pretty face.

Eye contact is made between the woman and the girl.

The girl's tears dry as her face locks up, and her eyes begin to panic before they too stiffen under the strain of internal torment. A one-way conversation is silently spoken through the woman's sharp, green stare. The irises of her eyes melt away, and reptilian pupils are left in the wake of the fiery burn. There are no verbal words exchanged, but the detective continues to gawk at the girl for minutes that feel like a lifetime.

The woman's eyes return to their normal deep green. She polishes her drink and raises her upper lip. She leaves the girl with a distasteful smirk as she heads for the exit. She doesn't bother to close the door behind herself as she takes her leave. A heavy gust of wind from the open window slams the entrance shut as the detective descends down the old wooden stairwell. She exits the building.

The sound of a power drill can be heard, and the woman turns to face a dark-skinned man with snow white hair. His face is covered with liver spots and wrinkles. A grease-stained shirt rests beneath a pair of well-worn overalls. A dirty rag hangs from one of his pockets, and a tool belt is strapped to his waist. The man is standing on a ladder while he screws a wooden sign into place against the surface of the building's exterior. The words on the sign read *For Rent*.

"You do maintenance on the building?" The detective questions as she disposes of her empty coffee cup into a nearby trash can.

"Yes, ma'am," the dark skinned man calls from above.

"Mind if we chat?"

"Why, sho' thin'." The man clips the drill to his waist and climbs down from the ladder. Wiping sweat from his brow, he catches his breath and approaches the woman. "Name's Sully, Ma'am. Can I do fo' ya'?"

"Were you around last Sunday, Sully?"

"Yessum. I live down in one of 'ha studios in 'ha basement." He raises a calloused hand and wicks more sweat from his head. "Wew, me. Month's been gettin' hotta'.

"Have you lived here for a while?"

"Yessum, Ma'am." The man plucks his rag from his pocket and uses it to dab at his forehead. "Been takin' care o' 'ese parts since Mr. Styles passed. Lor' rest his soul. Ya' see, him wife too old to do the work 'erself, so I handle 'ha 'ings around here like washin' 'ha windows and collectin' 'ha rent. Not all bad work 'hough I can stand to make-"

The woman lifts her hand in an attempt to silence the man. He continues to drool words as she speaks over him. "I'm not-... No, Sully. I don't care."

The man raises his cheeks and lowers his brows. "Well then. What is ya' 'ere fo' 'hen?"

"What do you know about the girl in Four-C?"

The man's nostrils flare and his tone becomes irate. "Now I ah-ready tol' 'em 'ere cracka' jacks everythin' I seen."

"I'm not them cracker jacks," the woman mocks. Her piercing, green-eyed stare cuts through the man like the fangs of a deadly viper.

"Dozen times now, I been callin' the law and dozen times now they been out this here way. Comin' roun' here do laugh like it's some kin'a joke or sumfin, but now ad'a white woman seen harm, they gonna go an' listen."

"Multiple calls?" The woman's interest is peaked. "What about?"

"Strange things been happenin' righ' roun' here," the old man pauses to sigh, "an' 'hey been happenin' that way fo' a *while*."

"Strange things?" The detective presses.

The man nods his head. "Well, fo' one. People disappearin' all 'ha damned time."

"Skipping out on rent?" The detective assumes.

"Sho, that happens, but a lot of 'ha time, they just up an' vanish. Leave all of 'er belongings behind!"

"Okay," the woman shrugs. "People leave. What else?"

"Animals be turnin' up dead, too, when they go."

The detective nods as her eyes lower towards the ground. She thinks on the comment for a second and then lifts her head up towards an open window on the fourth floor. A cream-colored curtain flaps from out of the open frame.

The man puckers his lips and follows her gaze.

Cassandra is standing in the window. She pokes her head out of the open frame and glances up towards the sky for a moment. She then returns her gaze forward. Her facial expression is completely devoid of all emotion and life. In silence, the girl leans forward and exits from out of the window.

The detective remains perfectly still as her eyes follow the body in its descent towards the ground. The girl doesn't fight against her fall, and she doesn't scream as she makes impact with the cement. The sound of splattering meat and cracking bones echoes through the quiet street. Sully winces and screams in distress as he watches the event unfold.

An eerie silence lingers as the old man stands in total shock with his mouth open wide. He slowly turns to face the detective with an expression of utter horror, but the woman is gone, and the man is left standing alone on the empty sidewalk.

Cellar Door

Heavy rains pelt against the window of a car as it drives through the darkness of an apocalyptic storm. A well-dressed couple, husband and wife, sit in the backseat of the SUV as their driver navigates up a twisted, muddy road. The woman has her hands folded on her lap. She remains silent as she watches her husband. As she thinks of him, he thinks of the world beyond the car's glass windows.

Lightning tears through the heavens and a mansion made of stone at the end of the road is briefly painted bright by the strobe. The husband focuses on a row of stone gargoyles along the walls of the castle. Water pours forth from the mouths of the statues at a steady rate. The man's eyes play tricks on him as the statues seem to move. He squints as he fixates on the stone objects above.

"Are you alright?" The woman says, placing a hand against her husband's inner thigh, but the man pays her no mind. "Nicolás," she presses.

The leather of Nicolás' seat crunches as he jolts around to look towards his wife. With dark circles around his eyes, his head is heavy and he is tired.

"I take that as a no," his wife says.

Nicolás takes a deep breath and then clears his throat. "I just haven't been here since I was a kid. Feels a little odd to be back, is all."

"I bet. How long has it been?"

More lightning strikes in the distance and Nicolás returns to looking out the window towards the castle.

"I left when I was seven," he admits. "Right after my brother disappeared."

As the car pulls up to the gates of the mansion, the driver unrolls his window. The weight of the rain can be heard thumping against the ground. The driver reaches out of his window and presses the button of an intercom.

A moment passes, and then a frail voice responds through the speaker. "Yes?"

"I have Mr. and Mrs.Jodorowsky here to attend to the estate," the driver informs.

Instantaneously, the metal gate opens, and the driver takes the two into the courtyard of the mansion.

Great oak trees tower over the vehicle as they pull up to the end of the driveway. As they come to a stop, a man with an umbrella approaches the vehicle. The husband opens his door and exits the SUV. As he steps out into the rain, the man with the umbrella tries to shield him, but the husband declines and gestures to his wife, who is still sitting in the car. The man with the umbrella briskly walks to the other side of the car and opens the door for the woman. He then extends the umbrella so that she may be dry while he becomes wet. The three of them ascend a stone staircase. Once they reach the entrance of the mansion, the escort lowers his umbrella and folds it closed before placing a hand on the iron handle of a great wooden door. He engages the lever and presses the heavy door open. The three then silently step inside.

With his black hair and charcoal-colored trench coat dripping water onto the marble floor, Nicolás rolls his eyes up to examine the inside of the mansion. He gazes upon shadows that mingle in the darkness. The escort flips on a switch, and a glass chandelier brightens the room. The shadows are quick to die at the hand of a light.

"Lo siento," the escort says. "Debería haber traído dos sombrillas."

"Está bien," Nicolás reassures, "Pero ingles por favor."

"Ah, of course," the escort agrees. His Spanish accent bleeds heavily into his broken English. "My name is Señor Fernández, and it is a pleasure to finally meet the two of you in person," he speaks as he plucks off his wet, pleather gloves and reaches out for a handshake.

"Likewise," Nicolás halfheartedly complies as he shakes the hand of the escort. His attention is still captured by the endless detail within the mansion.

Along the walls, seventeenth-century paintings are covered with a thick layer of dust. One in particular depicts a line of men being decapitated at the hands of a horned creature. Nicolás squints his eyes as he continues to examine the creature in the painting. Although the monster is covered from head to toe in feathers, the creature has the body of a man and the hooves of a horse. Its face has a beak, and horns stick out from the center of its head. Concealed within the darker shades of paint are the eyes of many watchers.

"Shall we?" Mr. Fernández inquires. His voice pulls Nicolás back into reality.

"Yes," Nicolás agrees, reclaiming his attention from the painting's unnatural draw. "Señor Fernández, this is my wife, Olivia. She is also a lawyer and will be working with you to finalize things here."

"Yes. We spoke over the phone," the butler recalls as he nods to the wife. "Shall we?" He adds, extending a hand towards a room beyond the entrance as he bows his head.

Olivia nods and begins to follow the man into a dining hall. She pauses for a moment and then leans in towards her husband. "Are you sure about this?"

Nicolás nods. "We don't need this place, nor would we ever want it." His expression lacks emotion.

"Okay," Olivia accepts with a smile before following the butler into the next room, where three cream-colored envelopes reside at the center of a long wooden table.

Nicolás turns to face a marble stairwell at the other end of the room. In his head, he can hear the whispers of his youth. He indulges

Kevin Laymon

himself in reflecting on the innocent memories of the past. He watches as his younger self slides down the stairwell banister. A second boy, slim and frail, tries to mimic the slick maneuver but fails. Tumbling down the stairwell, the little boy lands with a thud. Filled with vigor, the child rises and forces a toothless smile.

The vision into the past fades, and Nicolás returns to inspecting the mansion. He runs his fingers along the dust-covered walls and travels down an open hallway. He freezes when he comes upon a closed door. He wraps the palm of his right hand around the door's handle and gives the nob a twist. The door, unlocked, freely opens under the strain of a loud creak. The room beyond is dark, but the light of the hallway trickles in. Nicolás reaches a hand into the room and flips a switch. A chandelier in the center of the room flickers to life. One of the bulbs pops and dies, but Nicolás is unmoved. His eyes scan the room. A black piano resides in the corner, and an ancient brazier is directly to the right of the open door. Nicolás steps inside and turns to face the brazier. Resting above is a collection of strange-looking masks. Nicolás glances towards one of the masks. The dark-colored veil has long feathers running along its uneven edges that seem strangely familiar. With hundreds of sharp, jagged teeth protruding from the oval center and a pair of twisted horns sticking out from the top, the mask is the visual embodiment of total chaos.

Nicolás can hear the sharp whispers of a diluted tongue as words are spoken directly into his mind. A distinct pain begins to tear at the inner walls of his stomach. Fear manifests and bleeds from his belly like a pulsing ulcer. Nicolás wants to run, but he is frozen in place, staring at the mask. He can't make out the dialect of harsh sounds being spoken to him, but somehow he understands. They are commands, and not the kind to be ignored. He wants to wrap his fingers around the mask and lift it off of the wall, but his train of thought is broken as someone calls his name. His heart skips a beat as he spins around to see his wife standing in the open doorway.

"You okay?" She asks.

"Yeah ... I just - what's up?"

"The documents are the same as what was faxed over, so everything seems to be in order," she explains. "Mr. Fernández is filing the paperwork now, and we should be good to go pending the bank's acceptance letter."

Nicolás silently nods as he tries to acknowledge his wife, all the while deciphering the voices he had heard just moments ago.

"I can't believe that you actually lived here," Olivia says, shifting her tone as she leans up against the open door frame and looks out into the hallway.

"Pretty wild, isn't it?"

"It's like something from another time," she adds as she turns back towards her husband.

"Yeah. Took it all for granted as a kid."

Olivia scrunches her face as she notices the strange collection of masks along the wall. "What is this room?"

Nicolás returns his gaze into the hollow eyes of the feathered mask. "I don't know," he admits. "We were never allowed in here, and the door was always locked." Nicolás glances at the piano in the corner of the room and then continues. "My father would practically bar himself in here for nights on end. At first, I thought that he was mourning the loss of my mother, but in time, things became clear; the man was simply insane."

"Did he teach you how to play?" Olivia questions, trying to brighten the mood.

"No," the word drifts softly from his lips. "I remember hearing him strike the keys from time to time, but I don't think he even knew how to actually play it," Nicolás explains as he wanders over towards the instrument and lifts the wooden lid. "The piano was originally a gift to my mother. She was quite good apparently."

"Do you remember your mother?"

Nicolás lowers his eyebrows and entertains the thought.

"I can see her face, but I can't hear her voice. She died when I was very young, and I never knew her when she was healthy."

Olivia reacts to the sound of something vibrating in her pocket. She withdraws her cellphone and reads the display. "I've gotta take this," she explains, glancing back up towards her husband.

Nicolás curls his lips inwards and nods.

"We should be finished in about an hour or two," Olivia adds as she raises the phone to her ear and turns to leave.

Left to himself once more, Nicolás slowly lifts his eyes towards the far end of the small room. His gaze cuts through the air like a hot knife as he makes silent contact with the mask, and the feeling of total dread returns.

Biting his lip, Nicolás squirms in place. In a mindless effort to quell his pain, he drifts his fingers across the ivory keys before him. He subconsciously recites his father's tune from memory. The tune that he plays is surprisingly complex. Upon striking the final key of the nostalgic melody, a loud click can be heard. The chaotic sounds cease and Nicolás breaks eye contact with the dormant mask. He slowly turns towards the sound of the click, where he finds that the wall has split open behind him like a fresh wound.

Nicolás' stomach drops as a cold draft blows into the room from the open entrance. His eyes linger towards the unearthed corridor, where the subtle echo of insanity lingers like damned souls marching through the lands of purgatory.

In a sudden burst of panic, Nicolás scurries over towards the room's main entrance. He sticks his head out into the hallway and listens for his wife. The sound is distant, but he can hear her chatting with the caretaker. He recedes back into the room and closes the door. Locking himself within, he then returns to the open tear in the wall.

Indistinguishable cries linger from the wound, and the man's curiosity is greeted with fear as he pokes his head into the darkened corridor. The passage leads deep into the walls of the home. Stepping within, Nicolás finds a pair of lanterns suspended from a cobweb-infested ceiling. He reaches up and unties one of the metal lamps. A shower of dust rains down from above. The lantern squeaks and squeals as Nicolás twists a nob and the inner wick rises. He digs into his back pocket and withdraws a lighter. The words 'to my beloved' are etched into the Zippo's casing. He sparks a flame and lights the lamp. The wall recedes back into place behind him. He spins around and nervously lunges towards the closed wall, but it doesn't budge. Slipping the tips of his fingers into the cracks along the wall, he manages to pry the sealed tomb open.

"Okay. I'm not trapped," he eases with a sigh of relief.

Letting go of the wall, he watches as the entrance again seals shut.

The soft glow of the lantern illuminates the stuffy corridor, and Nicolás shuffles forward as his curiosity tugs him towards darkness.

As Nicolás ventures through the passage, he considers for a moment that perhaps this hidden corridor is merely a service entrance used for repairs across the mansion. The ambient cries say differently, and the man presses on.

The storm beyond the outer walls can be heard as rain pelts against the surface of the opposing side. Nicolás presses the palm of his free hand against the wall. Minute vibrations can be felt as the droplets of water pound against the other side.

A soft moan lingers from ahead, and Nicolás retrieves his hand as the hairs stand up on the backside of his neck. His heart skips a beat, and as the noise quells, he continues forward. Stone steps, older than the home that hides them from the world, descend underground, and the corridor's dusty, wooden walls turn to stone as Nicolás sinks into the earth. The temperature drops and a stinging silence pleads with the man's conscious to turn around and go back, but he ignores sanity's call and continues underground.

Nicolás stops as he makes it to the bottom of the long, ancient staircase. Ahead, a strange light demands attention and a lump forms in the center of the man's throat. He forces a painful swallow and then lingers forward as he goes to discover the source of this vibrant, underground light.

Nicolás slows his movement and cautiously peeks his head around the corner. Another series of cries cut through the air as he does and he panics, pulling back towards the safety of darkness. He blinks his eyes and squishes his brows together as he tries to understand what it is he has seen. In disbelief and shock, he forces himself to turn the corner and face what his eyes have seen.

In the center of a great room lies a pentagram. Painted into the stone with a crimson smear, the distinct symbol is brightened by many lit candles. Glued into the rock via a heap of melted wax, the black candles radiate with a supernatural glow.

Nicolás begins to tremble, but he disregards his instincts and instead shuffles forward into the room. Hanging from the cavern walls is an assortment of strange tools. The items, mostly metallic, vary from sexual to surgical.

Another moan cuts through the air and Nicolás, startled by the sound, drops his lamp as he jerks back and lifts his eyes. The cavern's caller is hanging from above.

"Oh my god!" Nicolás gasps under the sound of shattering glass.

The woman shrieks. Her cry cuts through the air like lightning and Nicolás' heart skips a beat.

A woman hangs from the ceiling. Nicolás fails to get a good look at her before losing his brightest source of light. His heart races as his eyes adjust to low-light vision. The candles near the pentagram are still lit, but Nicolás can only make out the silhouette of the woman suspended from a canopy of shadows.

His eyes catch movement along the far end of the room. A collection of dusty ropes rest anchored across the stone walls. The web of hemp subtly twitches as the woman above trembles and moans. Intricately intertwined, the pulleys lead up towards the figure. A wooden lever protrudes from the grid of cable.

"I will get you down!" Nicolás'assures as he lunges towards the lever in the wall.

A white static noise hisses between the man's ears. He contemplates for a split second as to what exactly he is doing here. Before he has time to reason with himself, he thrusts his weight against the lever, and it drops to an alignment that is perpendicular to the stone wall. Dust billows from the contraption as the ropes across the room tighten and pull.

With his heart racing faster and faster, Nicolás watches as the device lowers the woman from above. The black candles continue to flicker light across the cavern and Nicolás trembles in place as he watches through the shadows.

Nicolás is frozen in astonishment as he looks on. The girl is something more than human. With blond hair and tan skin, her beauty shines as her essence continues to glow. It's almost as if the woman is basking directly under the sun's rays on an early summer's day. She is more beautiful than anything he has ever before seen. A pair of white, feathered wings hang from her sides.

The prisoner continues to scream, her call awakens a strange lust between the man's thighs. He finds himself drooling from the mouth as the contraption ceases movement and the girl is left hanging just above the floor. Her sight is blinded by a tattered white bandage. A black ink drips from the fabric like tears as she continues to cry.

"What *are* you?" Nicolás groans. The word leaves his crusty lips like a fawn seeking shelter from a storm.

Despite her blindness, the woman twitches her neck and glares directly towards Nicolás. She stares through the blindfold and flares her teeth as she begins to hiss and shriek. Her celestial cry serves to raise the hairs on the man's neck. His upper lip quivers as he stands under the towering presence of the bound creature. She continues to struggle, and as she does, feathers are torn from her wings. The quills sputter towards the ground.

"An angel," Nicolás incoherently mumbles out loud as he looks to the elegant wings on this girl's back.

The first feather touches the ground. It ignites into flames, and the celestial being screeches in pain. Nicolás flinches as he glances down at the pentagram on the floor. One by one, the feathers are colliding with the stone, and as they do, they burst into a hellish fire.

The scent of sulfur fills the bitter cavern air.

"No! Don't!" Nicolás cries. His voice cracks under the strain of conflicted thoughts as he rushes over towards the angelic figure.

A metal contraption is connected to the woman's back. Infused with her spine, the device has eight legs like a spider. A cable runs from each of the chrome ligaments and converges across the center of her belly. A series of cogs activate through the darkness and the device along her back twitches. The girl shrieks in pain as the chromatic legs peel the belly of her skin back. Her entrails fall to the ground like the lace garments of a sexual gown. She twitches and groans in agony as her life is taken.

Nicolás is showered with a rain of blood, gore, and organs. The entrails are warm and divine. The properties of the inner liquid is embedded with a mystic property and Nicolás's mind is transported into a plane of pure bliss. The warm blood has triggered his senses into succumbing to something more.

The pentagram below his feet ignites in flames and the world around him instantly melts like wax. The man is plucked from his plane of existence and thrown into a lower dimension. An endless sea of fire rages and the sky above is filled with soot and ash. His eyes bulge from their sockets as he tries to understand. A trio of skeletons are cemented into the earth before him. Muscle and meat hangs from them, and they are stuck in a position that reflects their dying moment. With their arms raised to the burning heavens, they cover their face. Their jaws are twisted and mangled.

Nicolás' feet begin to sink into liquid stone. He tries to flee, but he is embedded into the earth. Nicolás panics and wails. Before he has time to reason with this madness, a horn sounds in the sky. The fiery silhouette of an angelic figure descends from the sky. She is an enormous creature whose wings span across continents. Her divine presence vaporizes the world around her.

Nicolás is suspended within a jelly of conflicting emotions. He trembles in fear and succumbs to total agony, but through this moment, he also finds pleasure.

This moment, despite its eternal agony and pain, is also attractive. His existence is gorgeous - so physically alluring, that Nicolás groans softly as he uncontrollably ejaculates. He closes his eyes as he basks in this surreal moment of euphoria. He is suspended within the grasp of pure ecstasy, and from this moment, his mind will *never* leave.

Mage Hunter

Atop the highest peak of a foreign mountain range lies a city whose stonework is built upon the foundation of many secrets. From the misty streets below to the skyline of buildings, with pinnacles reaching high up into the heavens above, the fingerprint of an ancient magic lingers. Its greasy smudge has left a residue over the city's abandoned urbanity.

The metropolis has been worn by the ages of time. Devoid of all societal life, the city's buildings and windows are caked over with thick layers of dust and debris. A strange looking clock tower resides at the head of a courtyard in the forgotten city. Heavy orbs lie still along a three-dimensional track that encases the clock. Though alien, they seem to be the intricate hands of the deceased timepiece.

Plant life has taken over much of the courtyard. The cobblestone road throughout the city is mostly faded and nonexistent. The ruins of an ancient fountain can be seen in the center of the city's courtyard. The air crackles in the heart of the fountain with a sudden burst of energy, and nearby plants begin to sway in a fabricated breeze. At first, the gust is gentle. Nothing more than a push, it could easily be mistaken for something natural. The air then quickly becomes violent as static flares continue to crackle. Everything falls eerily silent, and a moment of peace comes to know the present. A high-pitched scream cuts through the air and then spacetime ruptures. A perfectly still wound is torn wide open. A burst of energy erupts from the sliver of insanity and then everything again falls silent. Time itself is fractured for a moment and the speed of sound is lost. The chaotic energies of the wound stabilize, and a wormhole is formed.

The edge of a makeshift spear slices through the portal. Its edge is a piece of steel shrapnel that is tied to the end of a metal shaft. Just as soon as the weapon appears, it recedes back into the wormhole.

A steel-tipped nose pokes through the portal. It is followed by the face of a mechanical hound, whose features are cut from thick slabs of sheet metal. Its eyes look like flashlights from a familiar time, but this creature is not of the past or present. As the hound continues to walk through the wormhole, electricity sparks across a collection of spikes that run across the backside of the dog's spine. Twisting and turning, the spine is made up of a dozen or so steel cylinders that rotate with improper balance. Above its rear legs is a drivetrain that is attached to the cylindrical shaft of its spine. A tarnished-looking exoskeleton of steel does little in concealing a network of crowded cogs and sloppy wiring within the mechanical canine's frame.

The hound exits the portal and moves to the side. It then sits upright amidst a bank of thick grass. It looks to the wormhole and waits.

A moment passes, and then a girl steps through the rift. She is wearing a pair of dust-covered goggles, and a shemagh scarf is wrapped around her neck. Peppered with dirt and sand, the girl's short and choppy golden hair looks naturally brown in color. She appears to have come to this place from the heart of a sandstorm. A makeshift spear is strapped to her back, and a collection of strange gadgets hang from her leather belt. She lifts her goggles and rests them against her forehead. Her bright, green eyes scan over the town in a way that suggests that she is familiar with the urban layout. With the gentle breeze of the wind washing over her, she inhales a breath of the fresh air and basks in this moment.

As the winds carry on over the horizon, the girl is brought back to the present. She unholsters a strange-looking firearm and points it back towards the portal. As she squeezes the trigger of the weapon, the wormhole screams. It bleeds its power into a thin string of glimmering chaos, and the gadget then devours the line. Once fed, the weapon glows blue as its inner charge is restored. She holsters the device and glances over to the pup, who is still sitting and staring at her. She gives it a nod forward and the two of them set off towards the clock tower.

Remnants of an ancient beast lie strewn across the city. Bits and pieces of the colossal skeleton are embedded into the debris of fallen buildings. The skeletal remains of a tail lead towards the clock tower like a trail of breadcrumbs to be followed by a hungry rodent.

The pair of drifters pass by a collection of abandoned homes and shops. A foreign magic lingers within decayed runes that are etched on the stone of the buildings. Some of the symbols still glow as if their hearts are still trying to beat in the hour past their own demise.

A sheet of paper blows by the girl's feet. She picks it up, but she cannot decipher the words of a deceased tongue. Scribed in a faded ink are the characters of a language that is long forgotten. The girl reaches for one of the gadgets on her waist. She unties an electrical doodad that looks like a diamond-encrusted clarinet. She points the thin end of the device to the sheet of paper and clicks in one of the instrument's buttons. The gems begin to glow as they wake up and shimmer the light of the sun across the paper. One of the red jewels on the surface of the instrument shines brighter than the rest of the other stones. The gem begins to scream like an irate child. The girl jumps and mashes in a button on the device, and a slider switch erupts from the side of the instrument. She uses the slider to tune the gem to a pleasant frequency.

"Bibdasob was arrested by authorities for his negligence in selling astral potions to children. If convicted, the young alchemist faces exile, and the fate of his family's shop looms overhead as an unknown."

The girl smiles as she silently mouths the words, "it works," and listens to the rest of the instrument's translation.

"His family's shop is one of the oldest in Parabor...Bibdasob was arrested by authorities for his negligence in selling astral potions-" the instrument repeats before being shut off by the girl. She snaps the gadget back onto her belt and lets go of the leaflet. The piece of paper sails away with the wind.

There is no magic to be had in the girl and her hound. Both of them are relics in their own right, but they come from a world that is distant from this one: one where the native sun is hostile and violent, machines are the way, and wonder is lost adrift an endless ocean of sand. The pair is awkwardly out of place, but comfortable and determined to be here.

They arrive at the entrance of the clock tower. The girl stops and pulls her scarf down and away from her mouth. She looks up to the pinnacle of the tower with eyes full of wonder while her mechanical companion takes a seat by her side and waits for what comes next. The girl reaches for a door handle and gives it a twist. Unlocked, the door swings open, but gets caught on some freshly fallen debris. The girl squeezes her thin frame through the cracked door and then turns to face the canine. The hound pushes the door further open with tremendous strength as he follows her in, and the girl greets him with a silent smile.

The clock tower is the only mechanical object in the entire city. Although that much is familiar, the way in which it works is strangely foreign. Fallen bits of debris litter the ground. Empty jars sit abandoned on a bookshelf. The girl crosses the base of the tower. With the exception of familiar footprints leading forward, everything within the tower is encased in dust. The girl and her hound follow the path up a wooden staircase. The tracks in the dust belong to their feet and serve to be markings of a recent visit they paid to this place. As the two ascend to the top of the tower, they squeeze under fallen planks and avoid broken bits of wood.

The staircase creaks under the weight of the girl and screams under the bulk of the hound. The girl becomes winded as the two of them reach the top of the tower. She takes a brief moment to catch her breath as she glances at the room on the top floor. Metal shafts are woven together like nerves, and glass deposits encase the golden beams like the tissue of an intricate brain. The alcove is the mind of the clock, and light trickles in from the shattered face at the far end of the room.

The girl shuffles forward and dust particles, highlighted by the sun's rays, wash over her like bits of pollen on a warm spring day. The girl kneels down to a wooden chest and plucks it open. Within is a stack of notebooks. She withdraws one and then reaches for the gem-coated gadget on her waist. She flips the notebook open and activates the instrument. As the gems struggle to translate the words, one deciphers the code and the rest of the stones fall silent.

"The book of Chronos," a blue gem reads to the girl, "and the magic of timekeeping."

The girl's radiating smile is fueled by an unearthed curiosity as she listens to the translation. The book includes the details of how the clock functions. Embedded with a magic that is especially resistant to the decaying torment of time, the clock has been constructed with a series of failsafes so that it may be easily repaired should it ever fail.

The girl follows the instructions and spends the afternoon repairing the clock. She takes the glass jars from the ground floor, fills them with dirt, and then carries them up the steps. Placing the jars along one of the golden tracks serves to restore a delicate balance. After double-checking her work, the girl tries to wind one of the clock's tracks, but the hunk of metal is stuck at an awkward angle. Part of the track is digging into the ground, so it doesn't budge far.

Winded by the laborious work, the girl catches her breath and then withdraws her spear. She kicks the sharp end into the wood under the track and pries the metal up. Droplets of sweat bead from her forehead as she struggles to return the track to its rightful position and, as if on cue, the canine approaches from behind.

The mechanical dog bites down on the spear and helps the girl lift the track. The metal falls into place with a click, and the girl drops her spear. Winded, she uses her left hand to brace herself against her left thigh. She uses her free hand to ruffle a cluster of wires atop the hound's head. With the spear still in its mouth, the canine offers the tool, and the girl accepts with a smile. She returns the weapon to her back and then proceeds towards the golden track. She winds the clock's track back a few hours and, before releasing her grip, she looks to the hound and crosses the fingers of her left hand.

The hound watches the girl release the clock's hand, but nothing else happens. The girl's expression of joy dissipates, and she wicks sweat from her face. She reaches for the notebook and flips through the pages. All are intact, and with nothing missing, she is left feeling lost in her quest. She activates the translator and then uses it to decipher a few miscellaneous pages. Midway through her read, one of the gems bursts into fine bits of glass. The girl frowns and clips the broken translation device to her waist. She spends a moment staring at the inner face of the clock. Annoyed, she discards the book and heads towards the staircase to take leave from this world.

The hound turns to follow her and clumsily bumps into one of the golden beams. The metal shaft tilts and the jars of dirt slide to the far end of the track. Spooked by the sound, the hound jumps. It spins around and knocks into another section of the clock's inner workings. The girl pays no mind as she heads for the stairs. A high-pitched ping rattles through the air as one of the golden beams is struck like a bell. More of the glass canisters slide around and, as they do, one of the balanced tracks begins to sway at a steady rhythm. The girl stops on the stairwell and glances back into the room.

The clock's beams seem to be magnetically charged. They begin to tilt weightlessly from left to right. Every time one falls to a single side, half of the metal shafts within the room sing a high-pitched song. The girl watches in astonishment as one of the orbs beyond the face of the clock begins to glow. It rolls along the outer track and enters into the mind of the clock. Powered by the vibrations of sound, the shimmering globe picks up speed and travels along its path until it sings with a song of its own. Another orb is activated and as it begins to travel along its track, a third sphere activates and ensues.

The girl watches with widened eyes as she stands on the staircase and listens to the symphony of sound. The orbs continue to ring and then one of the clock's many hands begins to move. The hound looks to the girl, and then back at the chaos in the room. Together, the two bask in the moment of their untimely success.

The image of a green-skinned man is projected in the corner of the room. His ears are pointed, and a jagged mouth of teeth poke out from around his lips. Covered in a shimmering residue, the man is slouched over and appears to be disoriented as he watches one of the clock's orbs sing.

The girl's eyes focus in as she glances towards the hound and then back to the man. She slowly rises from the stairwell, and as she does, the transparent image of a small, two-legged creature waddles up the stairs behind her. With greasy brown fur and a bald tail, the beast looks like the intelligent cousin of a sewer rat. The image pays her no mind as it walks through her occupied space and mutters something in a foreign tongue to the man.

The girl quickly reaches for the translator and fiddles with the dials. With one of the gems gone, the instrument's efficiency is crippled. The girl races to tune into the correct frequency as the rat continues to speak in an unknown tongue. The gems fall silent, and then a purple one projects a voice over the images as they speak.

"Jester!" The rat cries as it shakes the man.

The girl holds the instrument perfectly still as she looks towards the projections with eyes of astonishment.

"You've gotta speak to the clock," the drugged man mumbles. A string of drool bridges the edge of his mouth with the shoulder of his frame. "It is all-seeing."

The rat-like creature looks at the clock and then back to the drugged man. "C'mon, Jester," he shouts as he runs a hand through his head of fur. "We have to get out of here!"

"Relax," the intoxicated man hisses. He closes his eyes as his motor functions stumble under the weight of his own confusion. "The Loresi can handle it."

"No, they can't," the rat screeches. "The beast is feeding on their magic!"

The green man opens his eyes and looks to the rat with a strange stare before stumbling to his feet and limping towards an opening on the face of the clock. He freezes for a moment as he stares out towards the city.

The girl sets the translator down on a shelf along the wall. She then begins to climb up into the rafters, where a small hole in the ceiling grants sight to the world beyond the clock.

A transparent veil layers the city. A story is unfolding over reality, and for a moment, the city is rewound to an earlier time. Projected across the entire metropolis, visions of the past play forth like a time-lost film.

A shimmering dome encases the city, and what lingers beyond the magical perimeter is something the girl has never seen before. A colossal creature, towering over the highest of buildings, has its face pressed up against the city's barrier. The insides of its mouth consist of many different suckers, each lined with vicious-looking teeth.

The hairs raise along the back of the girl's neck, and her eyes reflect both confusion and unease as she continues to examine the creature from afar.

The beast is standing on two legs. A pair of clawed arms scrape at the barrier as its wretched mouth continues to feast on the magical ward. The monster's skin is brown with the texture of a reptile. Its spine is covered in thousands of hardened scutes. The creature appears to be a distant, colossal relative of a prehistoric dinosaur, but its face and mouth come from a place of chaos. As if forged in the fires of hell, the tremendous brute is single-handedly besieging the city.

People scurry in the streets below. A blue-skinned woman drops a stack of books as she collides into a father who is running with a child on his back. The man doesn't stop to help the woman as she falls to the ground. A stampede of frightened people tramples over the woman as she tries to collect her books.

The girl looks back to the dog, whose mechanical facial features seem to reflect an emotion of unease. She then notices that the green-skinned man and the rat are gone.

She climbs down from the rafters and then gestures to the hound to follow her as she races down the stairs. Amidst her speed, the girl forgets about the translator, which is still sitting idle on a nearby shelf.

Arriving downstairs, the girl steps out into the street and then delays her hurry. The city is alive, or so the projection reflects. A time long since forgotten is being played out for as far as her eyes can see. Strange beings, humanoids, and monsters alike run and flee as the colossal monstrosity feeds on the outer shell of the city's magical barrier.

Mechanical sounds echo from behind as the hound crashes into a pile of lumber and debris. The noise is lost on the girl. Her attention is fully submerged in the moment.

A dozen robed men shuffle past the girl and she takes off after them. Weaving through panicked crowds and refugees of chaos, the men are rushing towards the beast on the far end of the city.

The hound runs behind the girl. It tries to avoid colliding into the projections, so its movement is awkwardly angled and sporadic. A few of the projections phase through the metal housing of the dog's physical body. They do not notice him, as he does not exist within their plane of space and time.

After a distant run, the robed men arrive at their destination. The magical barrier screams under the torment of the colossal beast as the monster's jaw hangs open and scrapes against the shell of the living dome. It gnaws at the shield with jagged teeth that slice through the magic with relative ease.

The girl watches with eyes that reflect a mixture of horror and curiosity. The mechanical pup stays close, his chassis planted firmly between the girl and the colossal creature above.

A sharp cry cuts through the air as the barrier is breached. A projection of dust billows from the shell's wound, and the men begin to shout commands in a foreign tongue. They plant their feet and endure the storm as the creature's face drifts through the hole in the shield. Its mighty presence spreads fear across the faces of all who observe.

One of the men steps forward through the cloud of unease. Robed in blue silks with silver bits of embroidery throughout, the wizard approaches the barrier and withdraws a wand. The strength of this man is masked by a long, pepper-colored beard and shoulder-length hair to match. He extends his wand to the sky and unleashes a bolt of lightning that arcs up towards the hole in the barrier. Crackling and burning, the bolt pelts the creature in the face. The static runs across the surface of its skin, yet the monster simply continues to feast on the barrier.

The wizard fires a volley of lightning bolts. Each of the attacks lands, but the colossal foe remains unscathed. The old man looks back to his comrades and nods. The men exert their magical might and conjure a storm of fire above the wound in the barrier. Smoldering balls of fire reign down across the monster's face, but still the beast remains unharmed.

A mechanical bark can be heard as the hound lowers its chest to the ground and warns the images of the danger at hand. One of the wizards glances back as if he can hear the sound, and the girl raises a brow in confusion as she ponders the unlikelihood.

The lead mage uses a sandaled foot to draw a pentagram in

the dirt. Once it is complete, the wizards take position on the points of the false star. The lead mage positions himself in the center of the circle and the men begin to chant an eerie hymn. They raise their wands and point them towards the center. Electricity sparks through the air, and the mage standing in the center of the star begins to levitate in the air. His eyes burn with a mystic blue energy, and his essence shimmers with a gifted power. The hymn turns violent as the men continue to channel their energy into the lead mage. In a violent burst, the archmage shrieks a heart-piercing cry and his physical form implodes. He disintegrates into a shimmering pile of stardust and, erupting from the bits of cosmic powder, a glittering dragon rises.

A series of etched runes line the skin of the dragon. The conjured creation is a magical manifestation of raw energy and power. It leaps into the air and sails towards the wound in the barrier. The great beast merely watches as it continues to feed. The dragon drifts towards the beast like the arrow of a skilled marksman. On impact, the magical creation slices through the face of the beast. As it does, the illusion implodes in an explosion of glittering dust.

The siege monster squeals as its face is torn from its head. Colossal bits of meat and flesh rain down, leveling a building to the ground as they fall. As the shimmering stardust clears, the beast can be seen still standing. In place of where its face used to be is an open wound. A stub lined with teeth leads into its neck. Sizzling droplets of blood spew from the open wound and rain down. They burn into the ground as they fall into the dirt.

Despite tremendous injury, the faceless monster becomes enraged and ignores the agony of the assault. It stumbles forward and thrusts its tremendous weight against the wounded barrier. The exhilarating sound of chaos ensues as the barrier is split from the hole in the sky down to the dirt and the ground. From this severed breach, the barrier begins to retract and wither away. The creature plows through the besieged line and tramples the wizards below.

Homes crumble to dust as the creature wanders deeper into the ancient city, and the girl backpedals as her hound growls with a false sense of heroism.

Soldiers and mages alike rally towards the breach and begin attacking the monster from all sides. Many men are slain as the city continues to fall under the might of the colossal siege weapon.

With the wings of a moth, an angelic creature flies towards the beast. Wielding a shimmering sword and rune-inscribed shield, this fighter sails through the sky with elegance and grace towards a foe of unimaginable strength. She dodges and weaves as the creature lunges and snips at her. She then plunges her blade into the beast and a burst of acidic blood ruptures from the fresh wound. The winged fighter screams as she is burned by the liquid. Her wings wither away, and she plummets to the ground.

The beast begins to sway as the soldiers and wizards press their attack. The winged fighter makes impact with the ground. Her body fragments into pieces as she slams into the dirt. Unaware that the winged fighter is already dead, the beast swings its tail through the air in an attempt to swat down the menace. The tail slams into the clock tower, and the side of the structure crumbles. Beneath the veil of the projection, the gaping hole along the structure's current form can be seen.

The image of the clock tower flickers, and the projection over the city blinks. The feed shows a series of quick fragments in time. The siege monster can be seen destroying a line of buildings with relative ease. A group of refugees flee. Mages and civilians alike get devoured by the great beast. Summoned illusions sail through the sky as the battle ensues. With each flickering image, the city crumbles further to dust. The tone then shifts as the beast can be seen on the ground. With the monster slain, the look of relief washes over the faces of the people within the fallen city. Their moment of triumph quickly turns to despair as a creature of chaos follows the path carved out by the siege monster. This new, smaller monster wanders into the heart of the besieged city.

The traveler is no taller than a man, but with gooey-looking skin and a mouth that extends around the side of its face, the intruder is of demonic origin. Only a thin patch of skin shields the conduit of muscle and bone that connects the upper portion of its head to the rest of its body. The lanky creature bursts towards a nearby mage, its movement sporadic and unreasonable.

The wizard grits his teeth and raises his hands forward. As if playing the keys of an ancient piano, the magi flickers his fingers, and sparks of fire manifest before him. He charges up a wave of fire and then unleashes the inferno with a sudden burst.

The attacking creature is embalmed by fire, but it continues to sprint forward. The monster's body appears to be unaffected by the flames as the fires wither and die.

"Actombre vala nas!" The mage shouts and his two remaining allies spring forward. Together, the three of them inscribe the air with a neon-colored magic. They then retreat as the monster dashes directly through the trap. Etched runes ignite into symbols of solid energy. Thick like the steel bars of a prison, but glowing blue with an ancient magic that is alien to the girl who still watches, the energy burns through the monster with a distinct, sizzling hiss.

The monster continues its awkward sprint forward. Massive lesions stretch across the demon's face, but the wounds seal shut, and the creature grows in size as it absorbs the lingering traces of magic. The demon then comes to a sudden stop and raises its horrific mouth into the air. It screams with the sound of a thousand tormented souls and then something unexpected occurs. The mages and soldiers alike fall to the ground as the laws of gravity are taken away like candy from an ill-behaved child. With muffled screams of agony and sorrow, the living are drawn towards the demon by an invisible force. The image continues to flicker as the clock tower returns to a state of decay, and the girl watches as the beast devours the city's population within a matter of minutes.

The projection falls and the city returns to its lifeless, abandoned state. The images wither away as time erodes the illusion, but - still standing firmly in place - is the demon. Its form has shifted away from projection and now exists entirely in the present.

The girl's eyes widen and she looks to her hound, who is locked into an angered stare with the creature of chaos. Frozen in horror, the girl watches as the demon awkwardly shuffles towards the pair of drifters. The hound growls but doesn't turn back to face the girl. Instead, it lunges forward and snaps at the wretched monstrosity. As the hound dives, the hellish creature screams. The echo of its cry travels far, and the hound is pulled apart like unwoven cloth. The automated beast continues to put up a fight until he is nothing more than mechanical bits and pieces strewn out across the ground.

As the final piece of metal falls to the ground, the girl's heart skips a beat. Her stomach turns like a chalice overrunneth, and a swirl of emotions collide within her. A sliver of time grants her instincts a moment to trigger as the demon draws near. The girl reaches to her holster and withdraws her firearm. She points the pistol forward, and with a squeeze of the trigger, lightning bursts towards the creature of chaos. A fissure in space and time ruptures through the air, and a portal is torn open. The girl dashes forward and the demon shrieks. She can feel her soul being torn from her body at the hands of the creature's call as she dives into the portal. Her essence bleeds into another dimension, and she crashes into the hard pavement of a foreign city street.

Standing to her feet, the girl glances back at the wormhole to see that the fiend is stepping through. Fueled by adrenaline, the frightened girl flips a switch on the weapon and the open portal bleeds back into the firearm. Her reaction, while swift, comes too late as the demon has followed her into this strange, new plane. The girl tears open a second wormhole and then dives into the next pocket dimension. As she goes, she takes notice of the world that she is leaving. Mechanical vehicles come to a screeching halt in the street and people observe the chaos from a nearby sidewalk. A skyline of metal towers casts shadows under a cool, yellow sun.

Leaping through the rift, the girl lands in the dirt and spins around with great speed. This time she is fast enough to seal the demon into the dimension behind. The portal implodes and the screams of a foreign people can be heard as the hellish monster is left behind with a new civilization of prey.

The girl drops her arms and stares up to a cloudy, blue sky. A moment of eerie silence ensues as she remains on the ground until a cool, relieving wind washes over her. She reclaims control of her sporadic breathing and then stands to her feet. She is back in the ancient city, and the mechanical debris of her hound is nearby.

The girl glances back to where the portal was. She then sighs and holsters her weapon. She approaches the bits of metal as a heavy storm of glittering pollen rolls in over the fallen city's skyline. Raising her scarf to her face, she secures the cloth before dropping to the ground and retrieving the pieces of her fallen friend.

Outpost 2187

Trapped within reach of a large, red planet's gravitational pull, I float. Although I'm fit and thin, my body feels sluggish and heavy. I'm not wearing a spacesuit, and so I cannot breathe, but somehow I'm still alive. I continue to slowly drift. The gravity of the large, red planet is tugging at my chest. My insides feel as though they may erupt through my stomach. I'm screaming as I enter the red planet's atmosphere, but nobody is around to hear my cries. I'm completely alone. As I begin to fall faster, I can see the inner-workings of a city below. Still, I scream out in terror as my inevitable fate of destruction draws near. I pick up speed and slice through a collection of darkened clouds. I then notice that my body is covered in a thick, black soot. My spine tingles and an unbearable warmth manifests from within. The screams of my vocal cords are drowned out by the sound of my soul as it ignites into flames. Now on fire, I'm falling faster towards the city. I can see millions of still corpses, and as I draw near, I begin to smell their rot. My skin melts away, and the insides of my body begins to stink like the city of the dead below. My stomach flutters like a butterfly, and my heart ruptures out from my chest. At the very last second before I make impact with the ground, I close my eyes.

I pitch forward screaming. The sliver of time between dreaming and waking is maddening. Although it is merely a fraction of a second, the level of agony and hatred that I feel in this moment exceeds my current level of understanding.

I'm drenched in sweat. The pattern of my breathing is sporadic, and for a moment, I'm unsure as to if I'm dead or alive. Perhaps I'm still dreaming, or maybe this is something more. At times, my mind is not my own.

"You are okay, Abigail. Just breathe," says the robotic voice of a drone who is hovering above me. Her LED lights blink softly as she wirelessly analyzes my vitals.

I run my fingers across the chassis of the bot. The metal that the drone is constructed with is thick and cold to the touch. She is dinged up with scratches and scuffs. These are scars that tell a story of a life that she once lived long ago. There is one cut in particular that runs deep across the surface of her chassis. A handful of wires with frayed ends embody the crevice like coagulated blood to the scab of a human wound. Though artificial, Aries has personality. At times, she seems more human and alive than I.

I'm in my bedroom, which is nothing more than a steel cage with white walls and an uncomfortable cot in the corner to sleep on. Like with most nights, Aries is close by and watching over me as I sleep. I'm often plagued by nightmares. Sometimes they make sense, but usually they do not. They are slowly eating away at my sanity, and my body is beginning to physically suffer as a result. I have always been skinny, but now, Aries is having trouble keeping me fit. She tinkers with my diet every day, but it is proving to be a difficult math problem that even an advanced supercomputer such as herself cannot solve.

The drone is equipped with weapons that it no longer needs. A railgun hangs from one of the bot's sides, and an outdated pair of lasers are planted on the adjacent edge of her chassis. I've never seen the weapons in action, and I doubt that they even work. Aries seems self-conscious about them, so I've learned to refrain from asking. Broken weapons of war do nothing in helping to conquer the task of raising me alone in a space station.

I look over to a black panel on the wall. A string of bold, red letters read *05:22*. It's a little early, but my heart is racing, and I know that I will not fall back asleep. I sit up on the cot and lower my feet to the ground. The tiled floor is cold, but I'm used to it. I place a hand on my head and ask Aries for a glass of water.

"Certainly," the drone responds as she drifts towards the entrance of the room.

A hydraulic door opens, granting the bot leave, and she turns the corner out of sight. I walk over to one of the room's four empty walls and press the palm of my right hand against a panel. The wall reacts. The panel recedes, and those around it follow suit. They retract into themselves until the opening is large enough for a rod to slowly poke out from the wall. A series of clicks can be heard, and then a thin hanger slides down to the end of the rod. On it is a clear, airtight package. I unhook the package and glide the rod back into the wall. The opening closes, and I return to my cot. I open the package and withdraw a fresh pair of clothing and then proceed to take off my shirt and pants.

The hydraulic door opens, and Aries glides back into the room. Levitating in the air before her is a clear polymer cup that is filled with water. The drone freezes in place and spins her broken body so that she is facing away towards the hall. I do not know where a robot learns of courtesy and manners, but somewhere along the lines, this one has.

I finish getting dressed and then tell Aries that she may come in. She spins around. Her LEDs are slowly blinking as she hands me the cup of water. I wrap my fingers around the cup, and for a moment, I can feel her hold over it. She is so strong. I often wonder what her limits are in terms of levitation. She releases the cup, and I proceed to drink the water. It is beyond refreshing.

My stomach growls and Aries glances down. She listens to the organ as if they were living souls speaking out loud in the presence of our company.

"We have another twelve days, sixteen hours, forty-seven minutes, and thirteen seconds until we can harvest the lettuce," Aries says as she hovers in place. A port on her disc-like chassis opens and a needle ejects. She grabs ahold of it remotely and levitates it down towards my shoulder.

Aries has everything mapped out and calculated down to the

thread count of my shirts. Normally we eat on the first day of the month, but last month I depleted too much energy in training and convinced Aries to let me eat a little more than I should have. As satisfying as it was, we now have no food for this month's meal. So in the meantime, it will be another two weeks of stimpacks until I get to have a regular meal once again.

"I'm sorry, Abigail," Aries apologizes.

"It's okay. It is not your fault," I admit as I turn my head and wait for the injection.

I wince as the needle pricks through the surface of my skin. It is sharp and cold. I should be used to these injections by now, but the thought of the needle still makes me queasy. The energy boost works quickly to empower my senses. I close my eyes and take a deep breath. It is as though my body has been fully nourished, and the thought of hunger vanishes like a forgotten memory into the past.

I turn my head back towards the drone as she places the needle back into one of her storage ports. Despite all that she has seen, all that she has done, all of the death and the war and the killing and the blood ... she still carries out the daily task of raising me like an adoptive daughter, and for that, I'm eternally thankful.

"Clouds are clearing," Aries informs.

I force a smile and stand up to leave the room. The hydraulic door opens, and Aries follows me out into the hallway. The white walls of the station are cold and bare. I walk down the hall, and Aries silently glides behind me. I approach a small nook with a round glass window. Through the darkness of space, a planetary body is within view. I take a seat on a ledge below the window and press my face against the frigid glass.

Billions of stars lie beyond the transparent enclosure. Their shine serves to illuminate the darkness of space, and with their existence, a false sense of warmth manifests in the pit of my stomach. Below the horizon is a large, green planet. Its surface is often shrouded by toxic green storms, but today the clouds are lifting.

I run my fingers across the transparent glass, and a heads-up display zooms in on a section of the planet that is visibly free of obscurity. I enhance the image a few times until I can make out the planet's surface. A mountain range of lush, green plant life towers above a valley of rapidly running water. I zoom in further to see a forest of trees that sway at the hand of a gentle breeze. My curiosity is silenced before it can go any further. The veil of green gas clouds drift over the area that I'm viewing and again cloaks the surface of the planet.

Aries once said that there are animals that call the green planet home, but I have never seen them. She says that no man has ever set foot on the planet due its toxic environment, but many organisms have evolved and adapted to live within the complex ecosystem of poison and gas.

Usually once per day, there is a brief break in a random section of the planet's toxic storms. This allows for a chance to glimpse into the details of the mysterious heavenly body, but it never lasts very long. Today's viewing is painfully short. I bite into the skin of my lower lip as I combat a mixture of frustration and disappointment.

All I've ever known is life aboard this station.

All I've ever wanted is to know what lies beyond these white walls.

"Shall we begin today's lesson?" Aries offers.

Every day, the drone teaches me something new. She says that my education is important, and I have never questioned her reasoning. New knowledge is both a blessing and a curse. It serves as a distraction to occupy my wandering mind, but also raises two questions for every new fact that is discovered.

I shift my body around in the nook so that I can face the drone. She then goes on to tell me stories of a man by the name of Sir Isaac Newton. She teaches me about his theories and laws. She shows me how his math changed the course of human history, and before long, the hours of the day slip away. She concludes the lesson and suggests I run for an hour.

I climb down from the cubby and stretch my sleeping legs before making way for the gym. Beyond a pair of doors down the hall lies a small, empty room with a clear glass wall. I step inside of the room and press the palm of my hand against one of the three white walls. The wall materializes, retracts, and reveals a collection of unmarked options in the form of many buttons. I press one, and the floor of the room shifts. A treadmill is constructed from mechanical matter that is hidden within the floor. I step onto the machine and begin to steadily walk. The glass wall before me reveals a section of space that is magnificent to behold. I pick up the pace as my walk breaks into a light jog. The stars beyond the glass twinkle as they roar with all their might. My eyes gaze towards the heavens as my mind is enslaved by lingering thoughts of today's lesson.

Aries tells me that most spacecrafts today are self-sufficient and equipped with warp drives that power everything aboard the craft. My outpost, being one of the furthest away from any known civilization, is one of the first of its kind. Outpost twenty-one-eighty-seven gently rocks back and forth between two planets of equal size. Both of the celestial bodies share the same gravitational pull. The pull is so minute that I wouldn't even know that it was there, hadn't Aries informed me that it were so.

Both of the planets that we float in between are inhospitable to man and have been for some time. One is covered in methane ice with temperatures that are so frigid, not even Aries could survive them. The other planet is a lush rainforest. It sounds promising at first, but acid rains fall from the atmosphere at all hours of the day, and toxic clouds disguise the inner portions of the planet. The secrets of the green planet's surface are mysteriously distorted. Both of these planets share the same orbit around the star of their system. It will take many years, but Aries says that these two planets will inevitably collide. I forget what her exact calculation of this happening is, but it won't happen until well after the point in which I myself cease to exist, so I guess it doesn't matter much. Aries says that when the two worlds collide, they will become one, and particles of dust and debris should spew out into space, which will then create a moon to the single, deformed planet. When the planets collide, their blend of elements may very well create a body that is hospitable and worthy of human life. In a couple hundred billion years, the single planet may have oceans, animals, and even various forms of intelligent life.

Many of my days are spent sleeping. If I'm not sleeping, I'm reading manuals on how to fix things. These information indexes are mostly outdated, though. Given that Aries controls and maintains everything aboard this station, I guess the extent to which I understand the inner workings of it all is mostly irrelevant.

Aries stays pretty busy for the most part. Aside from single-handedly managing everything aboard our outpost, she still finds time to teach me stuff. I guess this is because she doesn't sleep. In a way, Aries is both my teacher and my mother. I have never known anyone or anything other than her. My earliest memories are that of her teaching me how to speak, read, and write. Everything that I know, I know because of her, and for that I am grateful, but part of me does wish that I could communicate with another human being.

I once asked Aries why we are alone on this outpost, and she simply said that it was complicated. She informed me that when I was a little older, she could perhaps try to explain everything, but as of right now she felt as though the answer would be too much to process. The question keeps me awake at night sometimes, but I trust the drone's judgment. The only time I have ever seen her become uneasy is when I asked her that question. Maybe the answer is a burden that she carries. Perhaps it is heavy to bear, even for a drone.

History is my favorite subject of study. Aries once said that the history books of the old world were written by those in power: the victors of war and the political leaders in control. An artificial intelligence drone, however, can decipher the past and present knowledge in a truly unbiased way. This makes learning about the past all the more fascinating.

As I grow older, I find myself also becoming more cynical by nature. The optimism and eccentric personality of my youth has become a stagnant memory of my past.

There isn't much life aboard the station. Aries manages a small green room where she grows food, but I don't actually eat any of it. In fact, it is rare for me to consume a real meal. Aries extracts vitamins and minerals from the vegetables and uses them to make stimpacks that she then injects me with. These injections keep me alive and healthy.

After spending an hour running, I step down from the treadmill. My shirt is stuck to my chest, and my dirty blonde hair is sopping wet. Sweat drips from my forehead, and I feel like disgusting, yet satisfied, for the work that I've achieved. I run a finger across one of the buttons along the wall, and the treadmill crumbles to ash. The matter then seeps back into the floor, and the room returns to its empty, abandoned state.

I exit the room and make way for the showers. Though recycled, the warm water feels incredible on my skin. The blast rinse only lasts a minute. I've always wished for more time under the water, but Aries is a stickler about not wasting a single drop.

After my shower, I redress in a fresh pair of clothes and wander down the silent halls of our outpost.

I climb back up to a viewing window to peer out into the darkness. Stars twinkle across the landscape of endless space, and I simply observe in silence as I stare out into oblivion.

Aries appears from one of the station's rooms.

"I have something for you, Abigail," the drone says softly as she glides towards me.

Levitating beside the drone is a small pastry. A wire, lit aflame and flickering, rests in the center of the makeshift treat.

I climb down from the viewing window and approach the drone.

"Happy birthday, Abigail."

My eyes begin to water and I force a smile. Memories surface as my mind races to recall the savory taste of real food.

"Thank you," I choke out.

"Be sure to make a wish," Aries instructs as I lean in to blow out the burning wire.

I smile and then pause for a moment before snuffing the flame.

"Do you know how old you are today?" The bot inquires.

Aries has tried to explain the concept of time to me, but it makes no sense. At its core, time seems simple; there are sixty seconds in a minute and sixty minutes in an hour. Beyond that, things become far more complex. The hours in a day are based on the time that it takes for a planet to rotate along its axis. Years are then based on the time it takes for said planet to revolve around its home star. It is said that humans come from a planet where a day consists of twenty-four hours and a year is composed of three-hundred-and-sixty-five of those days. For a while, humans clung to this ideal as the standard for which they judged time. As a courtesy to me, Aries has established that we will follow the laws of time as if we were on Earth. I think that she may be under the impression that keeping time as my ancestors once did will somehow bring me comfort. It never really meant anything until a few weeks ago when Aries taught me about birthdays. Aries informed me during the lesson that by Earth's definition, I would be sixteen years old, but the earth on which my ancestors once walked is simply no more. I have never seen it, and I never will.

"Sixteen in Earth years," I answer.

"You were," Aries corrects, "but now you are seventeen."

"Oh, right."

I consider the notion of wishing for something to be true for a moment, and then I gently blow on the flaming wire. The fire withers, and in its place, a thin smoke rises.

"Can I eat it?" I question softly, referring to the pastry.

"You can," the drone says as she remotely plucks the burnt coil from the treat.

The drone releases her wireless grip on the pasty, and the gift gently falls into my hands. A smile appears on my face as I observe the rare pastry. The sweet treat smells like an exotic fruit that I can't quite place. With watery eyes, I glance up towards the drone and thank her. She says nothing as she watches me bite into the gift, and I'm overcome with a pure sense of divine satisfaction.

"It's incredible," I mumble with a mouthful of pasty, and the drone says nothing.

I finish the snack and then hug the drone. Her chassis is freezing cold, but that doesn't matter. I'm filled with warmth for her kind offering and this bot is, without question, my best and only friend.

A few days go by, and then I awake to something out of the ordinary. Aries is nearby, watching me sleep as she always does, but purple lights are flashing along the corridors of our station. The lights tick between purple and red at the steady pace of a metronome, and I glance up, both confused and bedazzled by the blinking array of colors that manifest from above.

Aries glides towards the door and I follow.

"What is it?" I question.

The drone ignores me as she sails towards a collection of windows. She peers out of them for a moment and then continues down the hall.

"Aries?" I call.

The drone enters the station's docking bay, where large windows allow for a wide viewing angle into space.

"Aries?" I say softly as I enter the large room behind her.

The drone is hovering near a window and watching out into space, where a lone spaceship slowly drifts.

"Maybe it's abandoned," I suggest as I observe the construct from afar. It wouldn't be the first time that an abandoned vessel has drifted within view of our station.

Aries continues to watch the ship as it sails through the empty landscape of space. Her sensors and lenses are far superior to my eyes, so I can only assume that she is thoroughly examining the ship.

After a moment of staring at the spacecraft with aspirations of curiosity and wonder, my train of thought is interrupted and lost as the space station's speakers crackle to life. I flinch, startled by the sound.

"Outpost twenty-one-eighty-seven, do you read?" The voice of a man says through some static. "Outpost twenty-one-eighty-seven, this is Spacecraft Mahogany; requesting permission to dock so that we may utilize repair bay."

I launch myself towards the nearest intercom. Practically throwing my frame against the com's buttons. "Hello? Mahogany?"

I feel the tug of Aries as I levitate up off the ground. Against my will, she has picked me up and forcefully removed me from the intercom.

"Aries! What the hell?" I yell out as I float over to the other end of the corridor.

Whilst maintaining her control over me, the drone floats forward and intercepts communication with the approaching spacecraft.

"Spacecraft Mahogany, this is Watcher Eight Seven. Permission to dock has been denied."

"Let me go, Aries!" I yelp as I fight against her gravitational restrain.

"Outpost, we are a neutral party. This is a mining vessel that is in dire need of repairs. Please reconsider."

"Be advised, Mahogany," Aries warns. "You are unauthorized to access this military outpost. We order you to change course immediately."

Her technical response is met with silence.

I try to spin myself around, but Aries' grip leaves me with little wiggle room.

"You gonna turn us away?" A second man says over the intercom. This one sounds less professional than the last. "First livin' folks we come across in years and you guys shut us down."

"Mahogany, you have been advised to change course. This is your final warning. Failure to comply will result in forceful action."

"No. Stop it, Aries!" I screech helplessly in the air.

The drone begins to process a heavy amount of data. Her LED lights flash and the intercom display begins to blink with the words *escape pod activated.*

"I don't know about that, *Watcher*" the man injects. "My systems admin here says that your outpost isn't built for combat. You lack external weapons, so how exactly do you plan on using forceful action?"

The display panel before Aries reads *coordinates accepted. Initializing launch.*

"Aries! Let me go!" I scream like a child throwing a tantrum.

I can see through the window as the escape pod detaches from the station's bay and sails towards the approaching ship. Impact is made and a small explosion ruptures from the traveling vessel.

"Aries!" I scream.

As if on cue, the drone releases her grip, and I fall back to the ground. I'm quick to stand up and throw myself against the intercom. "Hello? Mahogany? Do you guys copy?"

Silence.

"Why would you do that?" I flare, turning back to face the drone.

"I'm sorry, Abigail, but we do not know them."

I open my mouth and shake my head in disgust. There are a million and one things that I want to say. Overwhelmed by emotion, I spit out the first thing that comes to mind.

"That was murder."

"I was protecting you."

"And who told you to do that?" I squeal.

I storm off towards one of the transparent windows and sit before the glass. I watch as fire bleeds from the open wound across the traveling ship's surface. I lean my head against the glass and my eyes begin to water. I cry myself to sleep as I watch the ship sail off into the abyss.

Time fades as my consciousness lingers on the edge of dreaming. A gentle push into the warm waters of slumber, and the fabrics of reality dissolve. The waters, however, turn frigid, and I pitch forward, gasping for air.

The static hiss of a nearby intercom has pulled me from a trance-like sleep. A voice then speaks over the static. "That wasn't very nice of you."

My eyes widen as I glance around the bay for Aries, but she is nowhere to be found. I then peer out the window to see that the Mahogany is still within view. Lunging for a nearby control panel, I respond to the mysterious voice. "Hello?"

"Hey," the man answers, his voice raspy amidst the static.

"I'm sorry! That wasn't me who attacked you!" I cry into the telecom. "I wanted to let you guys dock! I have an AI drone and she-"

"Relax, kid," the man eases. "The impact severed one of our storage bays, but we contained the damage. Everyone here is fine."

I sigh, and relief washes over my face. "I'm glad to hear that."

"AI drones can have a mind of their own sometimes, can't they?"

"Yeah," I chuckle nervously.

A moment of awkward silence ensues and I worry that the short conversation is over.

"Do you have AI aboard your ship?" I choke out.

"Nope. Our ship's computer is old school."

"Old school?" I confirm, confused by the term.

"Yeah. Our system lacks free will."

Aries drifts into the far end of the room. I arch my back and scowl like a feral beast protecting a sacred meal.

"What's your name?" The man questions.

"Abigail," I answer, watching the drone hover in place. The steady rhythm of her LEDs confirms that she is listening. She has wireless access to everything aboard the station.

"That's a pretty name," the man compliments, and I blush. "You can call me Rickon."

I count the seconds as they pass by, and I remain awkwardly silent, unsure of what to say.

"So, how many people are aboard your station?"

"It is just me," I admit.

"You're all by yourself?"

"Yeah. It's just me and my drone, Aries."

Aries silently glides closer. Her LED lights flicker as she burns through processing power; essentially, she is deep in thought.

"You shouldn't have said that," the drone states softly.

I look back out the window and ignore the drone. The Mahogany remains still.

"Well, listen, kid," the man states. "I know we aren't welcome, but we could really use your station for some repairs, especially after that... *accident* on your drone's part."

"I know, I'm so sorry."

"It's alright," the man assures. Just let us dock for an afternoon so we can run some proper repairs, and we will be on our way."

"Yeah, that's fine," I agree, ignoring eye contact with Aries.

"You aren't gonna fire anything at us this time, are ya?"

"No. We only had a single escape pod, so that was our only trick," I admit.

"Excellent. See ya' soon, kid."

I fight back a smile as an odd mixture of excitement and concern churn within my belly. I have never seen another person face to face, so the moment at hand is rare beyond belief.

I spend the next hour glued to the window as I watch the guest ship approach. In that time, Aries hovers near, but I purposely avoid eye contact with her.

The ship docks in the bay and I wander over towards a door. I can hear the oxygen being pumped into the airlock. A yellow light above the door turns green, which serves as a signal that it is now safe for the guests to open their hatch and continue into the station.

This moment lasts forever as I nervously bite into my lower lip and wait for the arrival of my guests.

The door recedes into the wall, and the sound of excess oxygen hisses as it billows past the open entrance. The Mahogany's blast door opens, and a pair of men exit the craft. They step into the station. One is blinded by the bright lights, while the other looks directly at me and grins. Both of the men are dressed in torn rags. Their skin is filthy and their hair greasy. Behind them is a third man, whose height is oddly non-existent. The short man waddles as he walks. If it weren't for the scars on his face, I'd almost think he were a child.

The men say nothing as they continue their approach. All three of them examine the innards of our station with observant eyes.

"Abigail," the lead man says with a grin, and I return a gleeful smile.

The three get within arms' reach of Aries and I.

"Such a beautiful girl," one of the men observes out loud.

The lead man leans in towards me and reaches for my hair. His dirty hand is bandaged in an old, filthy-looking rag. Confused as to why he would touch me, I pull back. He then smirks and glances around the interior of the station.

"Out here all alone," he says in a condescending tone. His breath stinks of rot, and his teeth are mostly black.

I catch a glimpse of the short man out of the corner of my eye. He throws back his cloak and slings a rifle around. He points it at Aries and squeezes the trigger. I shout, but my words are lost under the weight of chaos as electric bolts spark from the weapon. Aries is encased within a ball of lightning, and the drone loses power before dropping to the ground like a heavy rock in the ocean.

I scream and run towards the bot. The flooring around her is caved in under her tremendous weight. Sparks of electricity flicker from her motionless chassis.

The short man approaches with his rifle aimed down towards the bot. He kicks the drone with a booted foot and then chuckles. Looking to his comrades, he smiles and gives a nod. His mouth is full of rotting teeth.

"Why!" I scream, my eyes watering and my voice choking as I fight back tears with anger.

"Because she's a fucking cunt, kid," the lead man spits. His twisted smile curls around the edge of his cheeks and his tone of voice leads me to believe that he is Rickon.

I run a sleeve across my face and wick tears away. Inner rage boils over hot water, and I dive towards the short man. Rickon intercepts me and spins me around. Dropping to the floor, he throws his weight down onto me and cackles. "She is a pretty little thing, isn't she?"

My nostrils flare as I stare up into his hateful eyes. I then spit in his face, and he flinches.

"Looks like she's a spitter," the short man observes from afar.

"We'll see about that," Rickon sneers as he runs a hand down to his belt and fiddles with the buckle. "Give me twenty, boys. I can't remember when the last time was that I got to taste a young one."

My anger withers as fear takes hold of my mind and I begin to tremble.

"Built-in vibrator," Rickon gasps, amused at my horror. "Why don't you guys take a look around and see if there is any food around here."

The two men head towards a nearby door as Rickon lifts his hands from me so that he can unbutton his shirt. As he does, I lean forward, but the man is quick to palm my face and slam me back to the floor.

I squeal as the man's greasy fingers slide across my forehead. I can hear him using his free hand to fiddle with his pants. As a pair of fingers slide closer to my lips, I widen my mouth and snip at the limbs. Biting down as hard as I can, I sever the man's index and middle fingers. He pulls back his hand. Blood can be seen gushing from his knuckles.

"You fucking cunt!" The man bellows as he grits his teeth. With his free hand, he reaches for a boot and withdraws a rusty-looking dagger. He brings it to my face, and I squirm under his weight to pry the blade from him. The sound of skin slicing forces me to wince as the cold steel tears through my hands with ease. I scream but continue to fight for the dagger. The man kicks my leg. I hear the distinct sound of bones cracking from within. I immediately begin to feel sick as the pain sets in. I glance down at my leg to see that it hangs at an awkward angle. My hands are gushing with blood and deep cuts liter the surface of my skin.

I continue to scream as I search for the strength to overcome my attacker, but the man plants the palm of his stubbed hand against the side of my face. He then lifts my head and slams me into the floor again and again. My neck cracks and I begin to choke as I find it impossible to breathe.

Rickon then freezes in place, and his body begins to levitate up off the ground. Aries is floating in the air behind him. I hear the other two men enter the room and, while maintaining her grip on Rickon, Aries spins towards the entrance. The electric sound of her weapons charging hums throughout the bay and then the drone releases a sudden burst of energy from her railgun. The screams of the men ensue as the drone lets loose a volley of lasers.

Pinned to the ground by paralysis, I continue to wheeze and stare as Rickon is crumpled in on himself from where he floats. The drone is compressing the man into a heap of skin and muscle. The man's screams are like nothing I've ever heard. The pitch in his tone fluctuates as his bones crumple in and I succumb to a veil of darkness.

***

I open my eyes, but it is too dark to see. I can feel, but I cannot move. I can reflect, but I cannot breathe. Overcome with fright, I panic and tremble at the thought of this unknown existence within a realm that I do not fully understand. There is no material. There is no matter. There is no pain, warmth, or reason. There is only darkness.

At last, a light punctures through the silence. It beams an array of warm vibrations that wash away my fear. In this moment, I'm saturated with the emotion of love.

The beam widens. Heat and sound radiate from its core. It begins to draw me in. I exist without body, and my existence feels like a vibration that is traveling along an unknown linear path.

I consider for a moment the possibility of being asleep, but this dimension is far beyond anything my consciousness could ever conceive. Gravity and logic are not welcome here. Only light and love exist to vibrate through a never-ending sea of total darkness. Once I reach the outer edge of the beam, I continue to float alongside it. I would never choose to leave it, and in this moment, my only desire is for it to never leave me. We dance together through the twilight of eternity until, at last, our vibrations become one.

Chaos ensues as the truths of existence and reality are bestowed upon me. It is merely a flicker in time. I embrace the light and my soul ignites. I awaken.

I am every thing, every being, every emotion, every event, every situation. I am unity. I am infinity. I am love/light, light/love. I am.

**

I gasp for air as my eyes open to face blinding lights.

Aries is nearby. Her LEDs are blinking faster than I have ever before seen. She is processing power on a scale that is nearly unimaginable.

"Aries?" I say softly. "Are you ..." My voice is lost, and I find it hard to speak.

Was I dead?

I'm dressed in a blue medical gown and lying on a cold metal table in the middle of a room that I do not recognize. There is an empty glass tank in the corner of the room that is filled with water and hoses. I look at my hands and find that my skin is soft and unbroken. There are no wounds: no scabs to suggest that I've been injured and no scars to say that I've been healed. I'm left questioning the truth of my reality.

The muscles in my face feel stiff. I dwell on the possibility of my memories being false, and as time blurs by, I snap out of my moment of wonder. Aries' lights are still flashing brightly.

Something is wrong.

"Aries?" I say with a crack in my voice.

She does not respond. It is almost as if she is having a robotic seizure.

"Aries!" I say again, this time with panic.

I can hear the hum of her power core. The electronic circuitry that is shielded within her chassis is overloading.

I spring from the table, but my legs give out and I crumble quickly to the ground. The muscles in my body feel like gelatin, and I smack my face against the cold, hard floor as I land. Feeling weak and dizzy, I struggle to lift my head back up. Specks of blood drip from my nose at the steady rhythm of a metronome. A loud ring pings through my ears and ricochets within my skull. I raise my eyes to see that Aries is trembling in the air. Despite my ringing deafness, I can still hear the hum of her power core. I reach up like a lost infant who is grasping for its mother.

In this moment of desperation, something strange captures

my attention from across the hall. Time slows down and I can feel my own heartbeat as it pulses through my throat. Sitting on the table in the room across from us is a white tarp that's soaked red. Sticking out from the tarp is a pair of bare feet. They are pale and smeared red with blood. One is broken at a ninety-degree angle.

I lose focus on Aries as I thrust my weight against my elbows. I use my forearms to drag myself forward like a child who is learning to crawl. Maintaining an unbreakable fixation on the unknown contents of the table, I reach the hallway and press on. Long, blonde hair hangs from the far end of the cloaked table.

Once inside the room, I throw myself against a nearby med cart. Fueled by confusion and fear, I pull myself up to my feet. The cart tips over, spilling its contents out across the floor. With my crutch gone, I'm left standing on my own. I feel woozy and begin to sway, but I press the thought from my head as I focus on using the muscles in my legs. I stumble towards the body under the tarp. Once within reach, I fall forward and plant the palms of my hands on the table.

The ringing in my ears is sharp and painful. My breathing is sporadic and lost to the frenzy of fear. I run my fingers through the tarp and then tighten my grip.

My breathing slows as I prepare myself. Then, without thought, I pull back the veil.

Lying on the table before me is the naked and broken body of a girl who is all too familiar. Her skin is pale and without life. Her neck is twisted, and her head sits at an unnatural angle. I slowly run my eyes down her body. Deep wounds run across the palms of her hands. The body is mine, but I am no longer within it.

"I died ... in this vessel," I whisper as I run my fingers across the cold skin of my former self.

I then focus my gaze into the reflection of my current face within the metallic table. I'm identical, in every way, to the body that lies motionlessly on the table.

Lost in a sea of thoughts, I'm pulled into the present as I notice the gravity within the room is failing. Small objects are being flung towards the hall. I spin around to see that Aries is still trembling in the other room. Her weapons systems come online and she begins to exert energy through them. She obliterates the tank before her.

I flinch and try to make sense of it all.

The drone pulses a flash of blinding lights. It forces me to look away to where I see the clock on the wall. Instead of displaying a numerical time, the clock is flashing red with the word *run*.

"Aries?" I whisper.

The drone erupts with another burst of energy, and with it, another layer of gravity withers away. Heavier objects begin to slide across the ground. The smaller ones from before are being torn through the wall as they try to propel towards the drone.

The heels of my feet begin sliding across the tiled floor. I'm slowly being pulled back towards Aries.

I try to think, but it's near impossible with the skull-splitting hum of the drone. It is obvious that she is overloading.

I stumble backward, staring blankly at the drone across the hall. She has tapped into something that is beyond herself. She has achieved something that I struggle to fully understand.

The drone is radiating with a glow of blinding light. Another pulse bursts from her core. With it, the station falls silent.

I call out to her again, but my voice is lost in the vacuum silence.

All sound is dead.

Lights begin to flash along the walls of the corridor beyond the room. They capture my attention as I realize that Aries is silently telling me to leave.

It is difficult to abandon her, but the heat that radiates from her fiery core washes over me, and the human instinct for survival kicks in. I try to form words with my mouth as I turn to leave the drone behind, but nothing comes out. I step out into the hallway and look up to the lights that pulse down the corridor. I follow them as I break into a weak run. As I turn towards another corridor, I notice that the way in which I came is shining brightly. Aries is burning with the potency of a thousand suns, and her shine is bleeding into the hallway behind.

The corridor ahead flashes from red to green, and I continue to follow the light's guidance. It feels as though the drone is holding my hand as I stumble forward with no single destination in mind.

The station's lights go out and the corridor succumbs to total darkness. The station's backup power restores dimly-lit emergency lights along the walls. The LEDs take on the form of blinking arrows. Aries is still in control. I put my faith in the bot and stumble forward through the darkness. I continue to twist and turn down a series of corridors until I reach the station's bay. The large, glass windows allow for natural light to the brighten the massive room.

Stuffed into a wall near the bay's entrance is one of the men from before. His insides hang from a scorched hole. I can only assume that his deformities are the byproduct of direct railgun blast to the chest. The lifeless expression on the man's face is one of agony. His lifeless hands cup his open stomach. The last moments of his life were spent trying to stuff his organs back inside his belly.

Bits and pieces of the dwarf can be found scattered around the doorway near his friend. Scorched laser burns litter the white walls of the open bay room.

Crumpled up like a discarded plastic cup, Rickon's body lies in the center of the room. His mass has been crushed inwards, and it's hard to make out any of his features. His arms and legs have been twisted and compressed around his body's core, and his head has been stuffed in between his shoulders.

A puddle of blood marks the area of the room where I likely died. A trail of red leads from that pool back towards the darkened door from which I came.

I lose control of my breathing and begin to cry as my stomach churns with sickness. I'm filled with a mixture of emotions as I look upon the horrific scene. My face is brightened by the radiating shine of emergency lights blinking above. The lights plead for my attention, and I glance around to see where they want me to go. The station's only escape pod is no more, so I shuffle towards the bay door where the Mahogany is docked.

I try to access the airlock's wireless control panel, but the software locks up and crashes. A yellow light above confirms that the door is still locked.

"Aries!" I panic and scream as my tomb is sealed.

The input sound of the door's access codes can be heard as the yellow light above turns green. Aries has overridden the system and unlocked the door. The hydraulics are gone, so I throw my hands against the exit and push with all my might. The door gives way and recedes into the wall. The airlock is directly ahead; the entrance to the Mahogany is open with its lips sealed against the station's dock. I leap through the door and enter the foreign ship. Everything within the aircraft is filthy, and it's easy to understand that this vessel belongs to the past. With no time to waste, I press forward towards the bridge of the ship.

I pass by a series of netting and cargo holds. Weapons and contraband line the ship's rusted walls. Reaching the cockpit, I dive into a seat and spin around towards a dashboard of controls. The sea of levers and buttons is overwhelmingly complex. Aries has run me through flight simulations before, but the layout of this cockpit is mostly foreign.

"Incoming transmission," a loudspeaker sounds, causing me to flinch in my seat.

I glance over at a glowing display where the words *receive* and *deny* flash across the screen.

"Receive," I command out loud, but nothing happens.

I run my fingers across the screen, and a series of code begins to process before my eyes. Red letters report errors in the code, and I'm left feeling confused.

"Disable the firewall," Aries instructs through the crackling hiss of the incoming transmission. The bot's voice is full of static, and her tone fluctuates under the pitch of torment.

"Aries?" I cry.

No other words are said.

A series of panels within the cockpit begin to flash with the words *disable the firewall.* I spot a console display with a familiar-looking operating system. I drag my fingers across the screen and open a digital command prompt. The input caret blinks as my mind races to remember the correct computer code.

I type out the phrase */firewall.disable* and hit enter. The code is accepted, and the red error text on the nearby display rises to the top of the screen as new characters automatically fill the space below. The text is moving too fast for me to decipher, but I catch a few of the phrases and translate them out loud.

"Disabling-receiving-downloading-packet data-extracting-installing."

The text runs up the screen faster and faster with every passing second and then the Mahogany's computer speaks over the loudspeaker, "Manual controls disabled. Autopilot engaged. Engine one online."

The metal cockpit begins to rattle as the ship's engines start up and my eyes widen.

"Aries?" I call softly.

"Engine two online," the ship informs. "Undocking in 3... 2... 1..."

A blast shakes the ship, and I'm thrown forward into the controls. As I lift my head, a trail of warm blood leaks from my eyebrow. Reaching for the buckles in my seat, I frantically strap myself in and watch as the ship undocks from the outpost.

"Coordinates received," the ship's computer confirms.

I watch through the cockpit's glass as one of the space station's outer walls bursts into flames. A plume of fire silently ruptures from the wound and then a second explosion ensues. I wince as hard truths set in. Everything I've ever known is gone in the blink of an eye.

The Mahogany spins itself around, and the remnants of the imploding outpost slide out of view. Warning lights flash from above, and the chaotic cry of the engine's roar drowns out the computer's call from the loudspeaker. I glance at a nearby display that reads *warp drives online... preparing to jump.*

Aries spent her final moments hacking into the Mahogany. I don't know the extent of her data breach into this system, but I can only assume that she has enabled the ship's autopilot and that the coordinates were defined in the hack.

The input code continues to blink on the screen for a moment, then a final line of text is rendered across the display.

Warping to Flare in 3... 2... 1...